VALAQUEZ BRIDE

Grenada ☝ **T5-BCD-065** ~~golden~~ light of the setting sun, and Raul Valaquez still kindled unpleasant memories from Juliet McKay's past. Even though he hated her, he couldn't stay away. An unexplored hunger raged between them, and Raul blatently offered Juliet the intimacy he knew she craved. A year ago she would have welcomed his touch. But now she wanted his love.

VALAQUEZ BRIDE

Valaquez Bride

by
Donna Vitek

MAGNA PRINT BOOKS
Long Preston, North Yorkshire,
England.

British Library Cataloguing in Publication Data

Vitek, Donna
    Valaquez bride.—Large print ed
    I. Title
    817' .54(F)   PS3543.I/

    ISBN 0-86009-650-5

Published in Large Print 1984 by arrangement with Hodder & Stoughton Ltd, London and Simon & Schuster Inc., New York.

Photoset in Great Britain by
Dermar Phototypesetting Co., Long Preston, North Yorkshire.

Printed and bound in Great Britain by
Redwood Burn Limited, Trowbridge.

CHAPTER 1

The tortuously winding road led down Spain's Sierra Nevada mountains. Below, nestled in a valley fringed with forests of austere pines and chestnut trees, the city of Granada shimmered in the golden light of a setting sun. On a high plateau of solid rock stood the Alhambra, ancient Moorish castle, which sparkled like a topaz gemstone, encircled by emerald cypresses and pines.

As the ramshackle and rusting orange Volkswagen van followed the twisting road, Juliet McKay gazed pensively out the window. Twirling a silken strand of sunstreaked auburn hair around and around her finger, she breathed a silent sigh. Despite the beauty of the scene below, she wasn't looking forward to returning to Granada.

'I still can't believe it,' Benny Talmadge interrupted her reverie though keeping his eyes on the winding road.

'After we finish our two nights in Jaen, we're actually booked for a whole week in Seville. And in the same coffee house! The smartest move I ever made was to make friends with you last year, Juliet. You're a regular miracle worker. That's the only explanation for it. I'll never understand how you persuaded the manager to book us for the entire week.'

'Trade secret,' Juliet quipped, smiling fondly at him. 'If I told you my methods, you might not think you needed me anymore.'

'Fat chance,' Benny answered with a grin. 'As a business manager, I'm a dismal failure.'

Juliet dismissed his words with an exaggerated sweep of her hand. 'But you are an *artiste*,' she said teasingly. 'You don't have to be practical, just talented.'

Frowning as her accompanying smile seemed unusually forced, Benny turned his troubled gaze back to the road again. 'You can still back out you know,' he announced abruptly. 'It isn't too late. Just say the word and we'll drive right through Granada without stopping and head straight for Jaen.'

10

'No.' Shaking her head, she tossed her small determined chin up slightly. 'No, we'll stop. I've come this far now so I may as well go all the way.'

'Why?' Benny snorted, brushing back the reddish brown shock of hair that habitually grazed his forehead. 'Are you sure you know what you're doing?'

'Sure, I'm sure. I at least owe Uncle Will a visit.'

'You don't owe him a damn thing,' Benny growled. 'After the way he tried to manipulate you, I'm surprised you'd even consider speaking to him again. He was so anxious to become part of Spain's aristocracy that he was trying to coerce you into marrying Pablo Valaquez. I hope you haven't forgotten that.'

As Juliet shrugged, Holly, Benny's wife, who sat between the other two, turned on him with an exasperated sigh. 'Of course she hasn't forgotten that, you big nitwit,' she chided. 'So try not to be so tactless.'

'I'm not being tactless, just truthful,' Benny defended himself impatiently, colour rising in his cheeks. 'I just don't see how she can...'

'And I don't see how I can just ignore what I read in the newspaper this morning in Malaga,' Juliet interrupted firmly. 'For heaven's sake, Uncle Will's been in a car accident. I have to go see him. After all, he didn't desert me nine years ago when I needed him. After my parents were killed in that plane crash, he took me in without a moment's hesitation and it couldn't have been easy for him. Fifty-six year old bachelors just aren't accustomed to dealing with twelve year old girls. But he was very good to me; he cared about me and provided security when I was feeling very much alone in a suddenly crazy world. *You* seem to be forgetting he didn't have to do any of that for me. He could have let me become a ward of the state but he didn't.'

'I know but still, he had no right to try to force you into marrying that spoiled little rich boy, Pablo Valaquez, now did he?' Benny argued vehemently. 'Answer me that. Did he? Of course he didn't and you know it. That's why you left Granada eleven months ago, isn't it? So you wouldn't have to argue with him?'

'Yes, but...' Shrugging again, Juliet turned to gaze out the window once more, her expression musing. 'I'll never understand it, I guess. Uncle Will always seemed like the last person in the world who would believe in arranged marriages. He's always been such a romantic. After all, he sold a prosperous art gallery in California and risked immigrating to Granada to open one, simply because he was so infatuated with Spain's old world atmosphere. That certainly makes him a romantic, don't you think?'

'I think it makes him as bad a business manager as I am,' Benny retorted bluntly. 'Obviously, things weren't going too well in the gallery here if he had to sell half-interest in it to the high and mighty Raul Valaquez, who's already so influential he can make any artist famous just by showing his work. He needed another art gallery in Spain like he needed another hole in his head. He owns one in just about every town, doesn't he? I'm surprised he didn't already own one in Granada before he bought your uncle's.'

'Oh, but he did,' Juliet announced. 'Now he owns two there.'

Benny jerked his head around to stare at her, his eyes glittering with suspicion. 'Why does he want two galleries in the same town? It doesn't make sense unless —unless your marrying that immature little brother of his was part of the deal. Maybe he agreed to save your uncle's gallery if you'd marry Pablo.'

'Now that's just ridiculous!' Juliet countered, laughing softly as she shook her head. 'You make Pablo sound like some kind of booby prize who has to be foisted off on some unsuspecting female. Maybe *I* didn't want to marry him but I assure you there are young senoritas all over Spain who'd love to wear his ring on their fingers. He's rich, handsome and boyishly charming most of the time. So, I don't think it's likely that Raul was desperate to find a bride for his little brother.'

'But he didn't object to the arranged marriage,' Benny argued. 'Did he?'

As Juliet's smile faded, Holly eyed her perceptively, then interceded again. 'Don't let Benny upset you. You know

14

what a vivid imagination he has. Raul made no deal with your uncle, I'm sure of it and you are too. Aren't you?'

'Yes. Of course I'm sure,' Juliet murmured, her delicate facial features losing some of their usual animation. She spread her hands in a resigned gesture. 'But Benny's right about one thing. Raul didn't object to the idea of my marrying Pablo. In fact, Pablo said Raul thought it was an excellent idea. So I just hope I don't see him while I'm in Granada. I don't think he'll give me a very warm reception. And let me tell you, he can be a very intimidating man, when he wants to be.'

'So? Why should that bother you?' Benny scoffed, then frowned again and threw her a speculative suspicious glance. 'Or was I right last year when I thought maybe you were a lot more interested in Raul than his little brother? Is that the real reason you don't want to see him while you're here?'

Wishing Benny would keep his embarrassing theories to himself, Juliet felt a blush rise warmly in her cheeks. She turned hastily to look out the window again, refusing to answer, then half smiling in gratitude when Holly came to the rescue.

'Really, Benny, you have the biggest mouth,' his wife said bluntly. 'Don't be such a busybody.'

With those fighting words, the marital spat of the day commenced. While the couple engaged in their exaggerated bickering, Juliet tuned them out, chiding herself mentally for still thinking about Raul after all these months. Yet, he had fascinated her since the first time they met and as time had passed, he had seemed to become genuinely fond of her. They had spent many companionable hours together, simply talking about anything and everything, but while her feelings for him had swiftly taken a romantic turn, he had treated her with tender indulgence, as if he saw her as a very young child. *Except that one time...* She and her uncle, Raul and Pablo had gone out to dinner one evening and when Raul had graciously asked her to dance, she had been delighted. It had been intoxicating to be held by him for the first time, in his firm, oddly protective, embrace. Her heart had beat with fluttering irregularity as he had enfolded her in strong arms and the soft contours of her slight body had yielded to the hard lean line of his. His warmth emanated outward, enveloping her in a distinctly masculine lime scent and she had detected a hint of latent power in him, that had both excited and frightened her. When the dance ended, she tilted her head back automatically to smile up at him and some indefinable emotion in his mesmerising green eyes captured her bemused gaze. For a breathtaking moment, as he lowered his dark head slightly, she felt sure he was going to kiss her but he hadn't, and thereafter, he had never again given any indication that he thought of her as anything other than a rather amusing child. Yet; she had still felt betrayed somehow when she had learned Raul agreed that Pablo should marry her. 'Simpleton,' she called herself now. A sophisticate like Raul could never have been romantically interested in an ingenue like her anyway. Still, even that realisation didn't prevent her heart from beating erratically as she thought about him and stared morosely out her window. At last, she managed to convince herself that she was only in the throes of a rather schoolgirlish infatuation and if she had good sense, she would forget about him. For an unworldly girl like her, a man like Raul was as unattainable as the pot of gold at the end of the rainbow.

She turned to her friends again and an amused smile danced in her amber eyes when she found Holly brushing a lingering kiss against Benny's cheek. Obviously their quarrel was ending as abruptly as it had begun, as did all their daily spats. Often Juliet suspected they only engaged in these half-hearted arguments simply to have the opportunity to make up again. In actuality they were wild about each other and for that, Juliet was grateful. Though she had fled Granada eleven months ago with Benny, she hadn't been able to return the romantic feelings he had felt for her. So, it had been a relief when, two weeks later, they had made Holly's acquaintance in Madrid and Benny had truly fallen in love with the tiny raven-haired girl. They had married a week later and were now less than two months away from becoming parents, a fact that Benny proudly proclaimed to anyone willing to listen.

Even now, he was smiling mystically as he pressed his hand against Holly's burgeoning abdomen. 'Wow, that kid's got some powerful kick,' he announced in awed tones as he snatched his hand away. He smiled at his wife. 'Did you feel that one, honey?'

'If *I* didn't feel it, I'd like to know who did,' Holly retorted, stroking Benny's cheek and laughing merrily as he realised how foolish his question had been.

Juliet laughed with them but during the next fifteen minutes her heartbeat became increasingly erratic until she began to feel slightly nauseated with its irregular thudding. When the van travelled through increasingly lush countryside, silver-threaded with irrigation channels, she paid little attention to the fertile hillsides beribboned by neat green vineyards. When the road led into the suburbs of Granada, however, with their inevitable blocks of new apartments, she sat up straight in her seat, her spine stiffening. Granada proper rose on the edge of the fertile Vega plain, the snowy peaks of a Sierra Nevada range providing a magnificent backdrop for the city's pristine beauty. Narrow slate-grey streets were flanked by white stucco houses with tiled roofs that gleamed like burnished copper in the golden sunset. Flower bedecked balconies with intricately shaped wrought iron railings set in heavy balustrades added a decorative touch to the simplistic lines of gleaming white structures.

Benny knew the exact route to Will McKay's house. Before Juliet could fully compose herself, he stopped the van before a narrow white house with slated shutters on the windows. Three stories high, it was located on a cypress lined street with some of the most prestigious older homes of Granada.

Swallowing with difficulty, Juliet stared at the gleaming mahogany front door. It fleetingly crossed her mind that she could tell Benny to start up the van again and take her far away from here but she dismissed that thought with a

20

resolute tightening of her lips. She refused to be such a coward. She could stand to spend a couple of nights in this house and pay a few visits to Uncle Will in the hospital. She would simply refuse to allow him to renew their argument about Pablo.

'Well, here we are,' Holly prompted unnecessarily, giving Juliet a compassionate smile. 'Are you sure you don't want us to go in with you?'

Though Juliet shook her head, she chewed her lower lip and continued staring at the house. 'No. Thanks anyway but I know you two want to reach Jaen as soon as possible tonight. And I think you should. You especially, Holly, need a good night's rest before you open in the coffee house tomorrow evening. We don't want you getting too tired.'

The expectant mother grinned. 'I'm going to miss having you to fuss over me for the next couple of days,' she said wryly. 'Between you and Benny, you make me feel like a precious pampered princess. Besides, Benny and I will probably go broke without you to manage our finances for us. So don't stay here too long or we might end up begging on street corners.'

'Yeah, don't you dare decide to stay here or we'll be destitute within a week,' Benny agreed gruffly. Then to mask his rather over-protective affection for Juliet he winked at his wife and added teasingly, 'Of course it's a good thing she can handle money. She certainly couldn't make it as a singer. Talk about awful! This girl couldn't carry a tune in a bucket.'

'That's not true, Benny,' Holly protested earnestly. 'I've heard Juliet singing in the bathtub. She has a nice voice.'

'Sounds like a scalded cat,' he persisted mischievously. 'The first time I heard her sing, I was in another room. I went running to her. Thought she must have hurt herself somehow and was in terrible pain.'

Juliet wrinkled her nose at him but her slight smile didn't quite reach her luminous amber eyes. Though she knew Benny was merely trying to take her mind off her problems, she was too apprehensive to be cheered. Foremost in her mind was her uncle's condition. The item she had read in the paper hadn't given the details of his injuries; it had only said he had been admitted to the hospital for treatment. All she could do was pray his injuries weren't extensive, yet, even if he were well enough to talk to her when she saw him, she had no idea what they could have to say to each other now.

That was something she would fret about when the time came, she decided, and with a resolute squaring of her shoulders, she gathered up her purse, then gave Holly's hand a quick squeeze. 'Well, this is it, I guess. You two drive carefully to Jaen and I'll see you there day after tomorrow.'

Holly frowned. 'You're sure you don't want us to come back and get you? I hate for you to have to ride the bus.'

'It isn't far so I don't mind. Besides, you don't need to be riding around any more than you have to, in your condition.' After brushing a kiss across Holly's cheek, Juliet gave Benny a slight nod. 'Would you open the back of the van for me so I can get my suitcase?'

'I still don't see why you think you have to say here long,' he renewed his argument. 'After trying to arrange a marriage for you with someone you didn't love, he shouldn't expect you to come here for a grand reunion.' His expression was adamant but a warning glare from his wife silenced him and with a resigned shrug, he got out of the van.

Juliet joined him on the street, smiling her thanks when he opened the van's back doors and removed her leather-trimmed canvas suitcase. Suddenly, she felt as if she were preparing to walk into a battleground. She didn't want to upset her uncle, especially now that he was injured but if he started hassling her again about marrying Pablo, she would have to protest vehemently. An arranged marriage would never be acceptable to her. She wanted love and if she never found it, then she would simply live her life single. Eyeing the house warily, she sighed and as she did, Benny reached out and drew her clumsily into his arms, patting her back. After stretching up on tiptoe to give him a light kiss on the cheek, she pulled away, her expression resigned. 'Well, I might as well go in,' she murmured softly. 'Hadn't I?'

Benny nodded but lifted his eyes heavenward. 'I guess so, since you're hell-bent to do this. Just don't let your uncle browbeat you or play on your emotions because he's been injured. And if you happen to run into Pablo or Raul Valaquez, be sure and ask them what century they think this is. I thought arranged marriages went out with the Stone Age.'

Juliet smiled wryly. 'I would tell Pablo that but Raul's a different matter. He'd probably throw me in his dungeon if I expressed disrespect for such an aristocratic custom.' When Benny frowned, she patted his arm. 'I was only kidding. He doesn't have a dungeon. I guess. Besides, I probably won't even see him while I'm here anyway. So just drive on to Jaen and don't worry about me. I'll be just fine here. I'm a big girl. I can take care of myself.' As Benny nodded reluctantly, she picked up her suitcase, then turned toward the fine old house. 'See you day after tomorrow,' she murmured, walking away before he could say anything else.

Like most other prestigious older

dwellings in the city, Uncle Will's house had no front yard. An ornate statue rose from a stone pedestal in the centre of a small flagstone terrace and a cultivated elm tree grew on one side, providing welcome shade. There were ornamental evergreen shrubs along the front walls of the house and trailing bougainvillaea vines festooned the wrought iron railings of the second floor balcony. Juliet paused at the gleaming black door, memories overwhelming her as she caught the sweet fragrance of orange and the more citric scent of lemon. Those trees grew in the walled courtyard behind the house, a courtyard where she had spent many pleasant hours. Nostalgia overswept her and she felt a real regret that she had been compelled to leave here the way she had, but it was useless to think about that now. As the van's engine sputtered to life behind her, she turned, waved good-bye to her friends, then reached out toward the heavy brass knocker adorning the front door.

Before she could lift the hammer, however, the door was flung open from inside and Rosita, Uncle Will's housekeeper and cook, gestured excitedly for her to come in. Though she was a tiny woman, she was wiry and strong and she embraced Juliet with enthusiasm, all the while chattering away in rapid-fire Spanish. Juliet understood only a little of what she was saying because she was speaking so quickly and Juliet's Spanish had gotten very rusty during the eleven months she had spent travelling through Europe with Benny and Holly. Finally, as Rosita chattered on, Juliet laughed and caught the housekeeper's wildly gesticulating hands.

'Whoa. Speak English, please. Remember, I don't speak Spanish like a native.'

As Rosita's brown eyes swept over Juliet, they lost some of their excited sparkle. Her broad smile began to slowly fade, accentuating the network of wrinkles that lined her brown face. She abruptly extracted one of the hands the girl held and waggled a bony finger disapprovingly. 'You did a bad thing,' she accused very seriously. 'You make everybody sad when you run away. And with a silly little boy. *Nina!* Why you do such a crazy thing? Senor McKay, he...'

'How is Uncle Will?' Juliet interrupted hastily. 'I read about his accident this morning. Is—is he badly injured?'

'You care?' Rosita countered mockingly. 'You run away and send him only some letters in the past year and now...'

'Just tell me how he is,' Juliet pleaded. 'You can lecture me later. Okay?'

Rosita shrugged, ceasing her sermon with obvious reluctance. 'Senor McKay is not too bad. He break a leg and...' She tapped her head, 'He has a—what is it you call it? A percussion?'

'A concussion?' Juliet exclaimed softly, amber eyes mirroring her dismay. 'How bad a concussion? Is he still unconscious?'

'No, he wake this morning. Asks for you,' Rosita added reproachfully, waggling her finger again. 'Are you not ashamed, *nina?* The senor wanted to see you but you were not here. He is a good man and he has smiled little since you run away. Why you want to leave with that—that *tuno,* that rock singer?'

As Rosita gave a disdainful sniff and gyrated her scrawny hips in a comical

28

parody of a rock musician, Juliet had to smile. 'Benny is not a rock singer. He sings ballads and folk songs.'

'Is the same thing,' Rosita proclaimed with a disparaging toss of her hand. Her sharp brown eyes bore into Juliet's. 'Why you want a boy like him when you could marry into the *grande* Valaquez family? Or is it perhaps it was the wrong brother who wanted to marry you? Would you run away if Don Raul wanted you as his wife? Hmm, *nina?*'

As embarrassing pink colour tinged Juliet's cheeks, she half turned to stare at the white plastered walls of the entrance hall. 'I don't want to discuss Senor Valaquez,' she said stiffly. 'I just want to change out of these jeans into a dress and go visit Uncle Will at the hospital.'

'Too early,' Rosita declared but her tone gentled and she reached out to pat Juliet's arm. 'You cannot visit the hospital until eight o'clock. When you come back, you will have dinner with me. Si? It is *cocido*. You always like that. At the market today, I find beautiful fresh chick peas, big and yellow. And I put in only the nicest bits of bacon, beef and chicken. Will be *muy delicioso*. Si?'

Juliet nodded automatically but without much real enthusiasm. Though she had always enjoyed sharing *cocido* with Rosita at the small wooden table in the vast airy kitchen, right now the idea of any kind of food just didn't appeal to her. She smiled apologetically at the housekeeper. 'It does sound delicious but I may not be very hungry, even after I get back from the hospital.'

'Yes. You will be,' Rosita announced, pinching Juliet's forearm appraisingly. Then she shook her head. 'Too skinny.'

'You've always said I'm too skinny,' Juliet protested, though she smiled affectionately. 'If you had your way, you'd feed me until I popped out of all my clothes. But really, I'm no thinner now than I was before I—than I ever have been. So don't fuss over me.' Bending down, she lifted her suitcase from the floor. 'I think I'll go have a long bath.'

'Have strong coffee first,' Rosita commanded, pointing toward the closed double doors of the *sala*. 'Go sit in there; I bring it.'

'But I don't want any coffee. Really. I

just want to...'

'Go sit,' Rosita repeated sternly.

And because it was easier than arguing, Juliet went into the *sala* and sat. It was a mistake. Her uncle's favourite room evoked too many memories. Shifting restlessly on the sofa upholstered in dark blue brocade, she gazed pensively at the brass lamp on the round mahogany table beside her. It provided the only illumination in the large white-walled room and the far corners were shadowed. She smiled wistfully, remembering all the quiet summer evenings she and Uncle Will had shared in here, sometimes playing backgammon or games of poker that were supposedly lessons but which usually disintegrated into hilarious defeats for her. Her logical feminine mind had refused to accept the fact that four of a kind beat a full house.

Those companionable times had ended last year, however. When the Valaquez men had entered their lives, she had been interested in the wrong one while Uncle Will had suddenly decided to climb society's ladder by marrying her off to Pablo. While she had tried to explain to him that she couldn't marry Pablo, he had insisted she was being unduly apprehensive about such a marriage. And considering his advancing years and the debt she owed him, Juliet had been unwilling to allow their disagreement to deteriorate into a bitter battle of wills. Fearing they might lose all the closeness they had shared if they continued to argue, she had decided retreat was in order. So she had left Granada with Benny, as much for her uncle's sake as her own.

The sound of the *sala* doors opening roused Juliet from her disturbing memories. She sat up straighter on the sofa but as she turned, the smile she had meant for Rosita faded abruptly from her lips. Heat suffused her cheeks. Her hands began to tremble. Her amber eyes widened with surprise as her heart seemed to lurch against her breastbone, then plunge down to her stomach. She couldn't quite catch her breath. It wasn't Rosita who was walking into the *sala*. It was Raul Valaquez and the expression on his angular face made Juliet realise that if he had owned a dungeon, he would have gladly tossed her in it.

CHAPTER 2

Every muscle in Juliet's body seemed paralysed. Raul walked into the circle of lamplight, stopping only a few feet from the sofa where she sat, unable to move.

'Well, Juliet,' he murmured tonelessly. 'This is something of a surprise.'

She could only stare at him. In her thoughts during the past months, he had become a nebulous being, almost unreal. Now that he was within touching distance and she had heard the deep timbre of his voice again, she was disconcerted by the conflicting emotions rising in her. She had nearly forgotten exactly how tall and muscularly lean he was and how overwhelmingly masculine. Her body traitorously responded to the reality of him, her senses reawakening to the vital aura of male magnetism that had always intrigued her. Though she berated herself for being so aware of him, she couldn't help noticing how his dark vested suit subtly defined broad powerful shoulders, tapered waist and lean hips. The muscular lineation of his long legs was accentuated as he widened his stance, flicked back the sides of his unbuttoned coat, and placed lean brown hands on his hips, his long fingers slipping inside his trouser pockets, as he assumed a posture that was at the very least intimidating, if not downright threatening.

Subjected to his relentless stare, Juliet felt rather like a germ under a microscope and swallowed convulsively. He looked the same, yet different somehow. The chiselled features of his dark aristocratic face were unchanged, except perhaps for a tauter set of his strong jaw. Yet, as Juliet stared silently at him, she began to recognise an unfamiliar iciness in his green eyes, eyes that had never failed to fascinate her. Dark jade, they commanded attention because they were set in such a bronzed, obviously Spanish face and should have been black or at least brown. But Pablo had once explained Raul owed their unusual colour to the bride of Rafael Valaquez, the family's eighteenth century black sheep, supposedly a pirate who kidnapped a green-eyed Englishwoman, with whom he subsequently fell in love and married. Juliet had suspected this story was more family fiction than fact but now, impaled by Raul's piercingly cold green eyes, she could believe one of his ancestors had been a ruthless pirate. His merciless appraisal of her conveyed no hint of the tenderly amused indulgence she had become accustomed to last year.

Looking up at him, she could scarcely breathe. Then, when two long strides brought him to the sofa and he stood towering over her, it took all her courage not to shrink back against the cushion. Why was he here? And why did he look so furious? Though she had expected him to be displeased with her, she hadn't imagined he would be this angry because she hadn't wanted to marry Pablo. After all, his grandmother had never been thrilled with having an American girl as a prospective grand-daughter-in-law. So why was Raul looking at her as if she had committed an unpardonable sin?

Rose colour bloomed in her cheeks as he continued to stare down at her, those magnificent eyes icy, yet conveying a vague resentment. At last, she could withstand his intense scrutiny no longer. Jumping to her feet, she walked jerkily across the room but Raul followed, stopping so close behind her that his warm breath stirred a tendril of her hair as he spoke, 'Well, what do you have to say for yourself?'

Juliet spun around, stilling her trembling hands by clenching them into fists at her sides. Her heart was beginning to thud quite violently as she took a step backward, intimidated by his very size and far too aware of the fresh familiar lime scent of after shave that emanated faintly from him. To avoid looking directly at him, she instead riveted her gaze on the strong smooth column of his neck, noticing how the crisp while collar of his shirt accentuated his mahogany skin. She felt rather stupid, just standing there staring at the pulse beating strongly in his throat but she was totally unable to answer his question, having no idea what it even meant.

After what seemed an eternity of dreadful silence, Raul reached out as if he meant to touch her but he let his hand drop to his side again. 'Juliet,' he muttered brusquely, 'I want an explanation.'

She gestured nervously. 'Explanation of what?'

'Everything,' he retorted obliquely. 'You might start by explaining why you've come home now, after all this time.'

The tip of her tongue came out to moisten her dry lips and because she forced herself to look directly at him, her voice was embarrassingly shaky when she answered at last. 'I've come t—to see Uncle Will, of course. I read about his accident.'

A sardonic smile curved Raul's lips and added a ruthlessness to his finely chiselled features. 'Since you've shown so little concern for Will in the past eleven months, I'm surprised even his accident brought you back here. But that's not the only explanation I want—I want to know why you ran away in the first place. You obviously decided you didn't want to marry Pablo, but wouldn't it have been more mature of you to tell him that, instead of sneaking away without a word to him and with only a brief note to Will? That was a childish way to solve your problem, Juliet. I know you were only twenty but I'd always assumed you had some regard for other people's feelings. I certainly was wrong. You were so eager to run off with your third-rate rock singer you didn't even have the decency to talk to Pablo. What a disappointment you turned out to be.'

Unprepared for this unjustified attack, Juliet took a sharp breath, her cheeks paling, then flaming scarlet as angry resentment erupted. He really had some nerve! How dare he stand there and act as if this situation had been her fault. She hadn't owed Pablo any explanation for leaving. She had never been romantically interested in him nor wanted to even consider marrying him and she had told him so as gently as possible countless times. But Pablo had insistently pursued her and elicited the support of both her uncle and Raul and now she was being blamed for the whole foolish mess! Her amber eyes glittered as she glared at

Raul, wanting badly to tell him his family's ideas about marriage were archaic and ridiculous. But the expression on his face kept her silent. She was indignant, not suicidal, and besides, knowing how extremly close-knit Spanish families were, she didn't imagine Raul would listen if she tried to tell him Pablo had simply pushed her too far.

Tilting her small chin up, she gave him what she hoped seemed a cool unconcerned smile instead. 'I'm sorry you're disappointed in me. But maybe you're right. I guess I was too young last year to think of marriage.'

'I guess you were,' he responded tautly, a muscle ticking with fascinating regularity in his clenched jaw. 'But immature or not, you should have had the decency to tell Pablo you didn't want to marry him. He thought you were very serious about him. Even our grandmother assumed you were because you went out with him without a *duenna.*'

'A *duenna!* Good grief, I thought chaperones were passé these days, even in Spain,' Juliet answered flatly. 'Besides, I'm sure your grandmother wasn't heartbroken when I left. She would never have approved of Pablo marrying me.'

'She told you that?' Raul questioned, a deep frown marring his brow. 'She actually said she didn't approve of you?'

Juliet shrugged. 'Well, she didn't actually come right out and say that but I got the message. It was obvious from all the disapproving glances and all the little hints that she dropped that she would much rather see Pablo marry a little senorita from another fine old Spanish family. You know, she wanted him to marry an aristocrat, not a little commoner like me.'

For an instant, a strange light appeared in Raul's narrowed eyes but the coldness returned almost immediately. 'If my grandmother made you feel unwanted, I apologise. But her behaviour certainly doesn't excuse your own. If you cared about no one else, you should have cared about Will. He was very upset and worried about you when he got up that morning and found you gone. And it's been embarrassing for him to have all his friends know you ran away. In Spain, young women show a great deal more respect to the elder men in their families.'

'Well, well, now I begin to see why you're so angry,' she rejoined, smiling up at him much more tauntingly than she meant to. 'You think a mere female like me shouldn't have dared defy a male, even if he was trying to control my life, don't you? I guess that's why you're looking at me as if you could kill me—I actually had the nerve to show disrespect for a man. Me! A mere female! Really, I thought all those years you lived in England might have rid you of the old-fashioned sexist notion that men must be lords and masters and women must be their willing obedient slaves. Obviously, I was mistaken. You're still Spanish through and through. Well, I guess I should go down on my knees and beg forgiveness for bruising your precious male ego but maybe an apology will suffice. If I upset your antiquated ideals, then I *am* so terribly sorry.'

Juliet's defensive mockery elicited swift and ungentle retaliation. Raul's hand shot out, hard lean fingers clasping around her wrist. He muttered something in Spanish that needed no translation because his tone indicated quite clearly that his words were far from complimentary. 'You really are a silly little girl, aren't you, Juliet?' His icy green eyes raked over her, conveying anger and obvious disdain. '*I* won't tolerate your disrespect so watch what you say to me. I've often thought during the past year that you needed a good spanking and if you persist in this little outburst of defiance, I might be very tempted to turn you over my knee.'

'You wouldn't dare hit me!' she gasped softly, dismayed that his mere threat made her legs weaken beneath her. 'Y—you're bluffing.'

'Am I, Juliet?' he countered with a devilish smile. 'Why don't you try me and see.'

Detecting the menacing glint in his eyes, Juliet had to wonder if he would carry out this threat if she pushed him too far. Impotent fury built in her and she tried to twist free of his iron-hard grip. As his lean fingers simply tightened, pressing down to the delicate bones of her wrist, she winced. Regret flickered in his dark face, then vanished almost before she recognised it, but his hold on her did ease. His fingers became caressing, brushing with evocative lightness over the frantically beating pulse. Now, his touch was electric, evoking a wicked warmth that spread through Juliet's limbs. To mask her reaction, she stiffened, only her wide eyes darting up to meet the enigmatic glimmer in his. 'Let me go,' she insisted. 'You're hurting me.'

As he surveyed her delicate features intently, he allowed his gaze to drift down and linger on her soft, slightly parted lips. He shook his head, whispering, 'No. I'm not hurting you and I don't want to let you go. Yet.'

He began to pull her slowly toward him and Juliet's free hand came up to press against his hard chest, an involuntary attempt to protect herself. 'Raul, please,' she whispered breathlessly. 'Let me go.'

As the iciness returned to his eyes and he lifted his broad shoulders in a bored shrug and released her wrist, Juliet swiftly stepped away from him, her own gaze unwittingly reproachful. 'Why are you here?' she asked impulsively. 'I mean, since Uncle Will's not here, why did you come?'

'Rosita called me at the gallery to tell me you'd come home.' Raul's expression hardened though he gave Juliet a mocking smile. 'She knew I was going to visit Will at the hospital and suggested I take you with me since you meant to go tonight too.'

Damn Rosita and her foolish interference, Juliet fumed silently, clenching and unclenching her hands at her sides. Though she knew the housekeeper had meant well, she wished she had minded her own business. This confrontation with Raul was the last thing Juliet had needed. As usual, simply seeing Raul was enough to upset her equilibrium. She was certain she would never be able to maintain even a semblance of composure if she went with him to the hospital. Bending her head, veiling her eyes with the thick fringe of her long, brown lashes, she murmured, 'I'd rather see Uncle Will alone and since it's already seven-thirty, why don't you go visit him now? I'll drive over later.'

'No. I'll take you with me,' Raul replied, his sensuously carved lips thinning into a grim line of warning when she started to protest. Then those cold green eyes raked mercilessly over her. 'Go change into some decent clothes, preferably a dress. Your free spirited singer might not mind if you look like a derelict but I do, and so will Will. And I don't think it will inconvenience you too much to look presentable when you see him for the first time in nearly a year.'

Bristling at his demanding manner and supercilious tone, Juliet thrust out her small chin defiantly and tugged her light blue T-shirt down over her slim jean clad hips, inadvertently emphasising the round fullness of her breasts. When Raul deliberately allowed his narrowing eyes to drift downward and linger, she released her shirt-tail immediately but, though she blushed, she succeeded in meeting his now amused gaze without flinching. 'I'll have you know I'd planned to change clothes but now that you've made such a big deal of it, I think I'll just go to the hospital in my jeans.'

Raul cursed softly. One long stride

brought him so close to Juliet that she was forced to press against the cool white wall behind her to avoid his body brushing against her own. His large brown hands gripped her upper arms. 'Didn't I just tell you not to try my patience?' he asked, his voice deceptively soft. 'Your adolescent behaviour has caused your uncle and my family enough trouble, Juliet. I promise you I won't tolerate your juvenile tricks now or ever again. So, you'd better go upstairs and change to a dress right now or I'll carry you up and change your clothes for you. Understood?'

The light that flared in his jade green eyes both frightened her and incited her to violence at the same moment. She wrenched free of him; her hand swung out, her palm open as if she meant to deliver a stinging slap to his face, but before she could make contact with his cheek, he moved swiftly to catch her wrist. He smiled tauntingly as she called him a none-too-complimentary name. Then his muscular arm glided around her slender waist, tightened and hauled her close against his long, lean body. His hand pressed hers against his chest. 'You're playing with fire,' he muttered ominously. 'I don't think you realise what I'd like to do to you right now.'

Juliet could guess, though his intense reaction to her attempted slap astonished her. Beneath her trembling fingers his heart was beating strongly, rapidly, and she knew its fast pace was not a result of the little effort it had taken for him to subdue her. His response to her foolish show of bravado was wholly masculine and suddenly she was scared. She had never seen him like this before, with a relentless glittering in his eyes. The hard inflexible contours of his body conveyed the same relentless message and when he lowered his dark head, her breath caught. 'All right, all right,' she whispered haltingly, straining back against the muscular arm around her slender waist. 'I'll go put on a dress. Just let me go. Now, please.'

A grim yet triumphant smile tugged at the corners of his sensuously carved mouth as he released her, saying mockingly, 'A very wise decision, Juliet.'

She couldn't even think of a retort to

utter. Unable to bear being close to him a second longer, she turned and walked out of the *sala* with as much dignity as she could muster. As she trudged up the stairs a moment later, she massaged her throbbing temples with shaky fingers. Tears of sheer frustration burned threateningly behind her eyes. She was shocked at the depth of Raul's resentment. Why should he care that she hadn't wanted to marry Pablo? Keen as he was about arranged marriages, he should have logically planned a more suitable marriage for his brother, a marriage to some aristocratic girl instead of a mere commoner like her.

Thoroughly confused, Juliet walked into her old bedroom without even noticing the gleaming hardwood floors, the simple, yet elegant, mahogany furniture or the cool aquamarine draperies and bed coverlet that provided bright accents to the room's decor. Chewing her lower lip, she stared blindly out one wide window, gaining no pleasure from the panoramic vista of the snow-tipped Sierra Nevadas rising majestically in the distance. A soft sigh escaped

48

her. This confrontation with Raul had been the worst possible way to begin this visit. Maybe he saw her lack of interest in Pablo as an affront to the precious Valaquez family honour. And if he did, he would undoubtedly make her stay in Granada as unpleasant as possible.

Grimacing, she shed her jeans and T-shirt to slip into a sleeveless linen dress of periwinkle blue that enhanced her fair complexion and the fiery highlights of her auburn hair. But after stepping into cream-coloured espadrilles and going to stand before the cheval glass, she hardly noticed her reflection. Her mind was occupied with matters far more important than mere appearance.

She had never realised Raul could be the way he had been tonight—mocking and deliberately hurtful. Last year, he had actually seemed very fond of her and her only complaint had been that he didn't see her as a desirable young woman rather than a child. It was difficult to believe that same man was now so mercilessly taunting. And he had actually tried to lay the blame for last year's marriage fiasco at her feet! She had once foolishly assumed he was a fair-minded man but now it was apparent that she hadn't known the real Raul Valaquez very well at all. She couldn't have known him because the man awaiting her downstairs seemed a total stranger, a dangerous stranger she knew intuitively she would be extremely foolhardly to antagonise any more than she already had.

Dread dragged at her stomach and with a muttered imprecation, she went to the vanity across the room. Sitting down before the oval mirror, she brushed her thick russet hair with long thorough strokes, postponing going downstairs again as long as she possibly could. But with the sudden realisation that Raul might tire of waiting and come up to get her, she hastily put down her brush and hurried out her door.

The ride to the hospital in Raul's elegant cream BMW was silent and excruciatingly tense. Juliet sat as close as possible to the far edge of the brown leather passenger seat and clutched her straw purse in her lap. Staring out her window at the black velvet, star-studded sky, she tried not to think about the man beside her but failed miserably. The lean brown hand that was casually gripping the steering wheel evoked the unbidden memory of how she had felt that evening they had danced together and that same hand had curved almost possessively into the insweep of her slim waist. Why did he have to be so damned attractive and magnetic? And why was she such a sap? Considering his insulting treatment of her tonight, she knew she shouldn't see anything at all attractive about him. It simply wasn't logical for her to even be aware of his male magnetism, yet she realised rather bleakly that logic had little to do with her responses sometimes. And this was one of those times. With an inward sigh of resignation, she closed her eyes.

After a moment, she reopened them, actually noticing the plush interior of the car for the first time. Judging by this expensive vehicle and by Raul's tailor-made suit, the Valaquez family fortunes obviously hadn't suffered any losses in the past year, not that she had really thought they might have. Raul was well-known as one of Spain's most successful young entrepreneurs and now she could imagine why he was so successful. If he was as ruthless in his business dealings as he had been with her tonight, he couldn't fail to succeed.

Her wry smile faded abruptly when she suddenly sensed Raul was watching her but when she looked at him, he turned his attention back to the narrow winding streets of the city without a word. A slight confused frown knitted her smooth brow as she realised they were approaching Alhambra, rather than driving away from it, which they should have been.

'This isn't the way to the hospital,' she spoke up, her voice quavering as all sorts of crazy suspicions popped into her head. 'Why are you going this way? Where are you taking me?'

'To see Will,' Raul answered, his low-timbred voice conveying more than a little impatience. 'I had him transferred to a private clinic in the suburbs where he'll receive more personalised care.'

Juliet subsided into silence, feeling very much the fool. She really had to regain control of her emotions. Raul might be more ruthless than she'd ever imagined but he wouldn't resort to kid-napping, just for the sake of revenge. Still, despite the logic of that thought, she didn't really feel particularly safe until Raul turned off the road onto a winding paved drive that led across the lush grounds of what appeared to be an estate. It *was* the clinic, however, evidenced by the long low white building with its typically Spanish flat roof and arched arcade, gracing the front. Baskets hanging from the arches spilled over with the nodding blossoms of scarlet fuchsia. Well-tended palms were planted before each arch column and there was the clean fresh scent of orange and lemon in the cool night air. All in all, the clinic looked like one of those exclusive spas where the affluent go to escape the pressures of their lives and Juliet wondered how Uncle Will would be able to pay the bill for his stay here. He was by no means destitute but he wasn't a millionaire either and to stay in a place like this, it would certainly help to have a small fortune stashed away somewhere.

After Raul opened Juliet's door and she got out of the car, he cupped her elbow in one large hand as they walked inside the clinic. Once in the spacious reception area, however, he allowed his hand to drop and moved away from her. Illogically, she almost regretted the distance he deliberately put between them, especially when the pretty young woman seated at the reception desk gave him a blatantly flirtatious smile and he returned it, then began to converse with her in Spanish. As they talked and laughed together, Juliet stood back feeling left out and berating herself for feeling that way. After all, she knew Raul disliked her immensely and also knew if she had good sense, she'd dislike him too. He had certainly given her no reason to nominate him for Spain's Mr Congeniality award.

Wandering away from the chatting couple, she went to stand before a painting displayed on a whitewashed wall. Seemingly endless rows of olive trees gleamed golden in an exquisite sunset and glancing down at the corner of the canvas, Juliet recognised the artist's name. The painter was one who frequently brought his work to Uncle Will's gallery but she couldn't recall her uncle mentioning that he had sold any paintings to a clinic. Perhaps he had made the sale within the past eleven months or perhaps Raul had sold it. Coming from such a prominent Granada family, she imagined he had connections with almost everybody who was somebody.

Despite her firm resolution to completely ignore Raul and the flirtatious receptionist, Juliet couldn't prevent herself from glancing over her shoulder. Her cheeks warmed with colour as she found Raul walking toward her, the parting smile he had given the receptionist fading from his lips and the warmth leaving his eyes as his gaze flicked over Juliet.

'You wait here,' he commanded brusquely. 'I want to tell Will you've come. It might be too much of a shock to him if you just walk into his room. Sit down somewhere and I'll come for you in a few minutes.'

'Wait,' Juliet said swiftly as he started to walk away. Before she thought, she reached out to lay her hand on his forearm, then quickly pulled it away when she felt his muscles tense beneath her fingers. She gestured uncertainly. 'Is—why do you think my coming might shock him too much? Is he that badly injured? Rosita said he only had a broken leg and a concussion.'

'A fairly severe concussion,' Raul responded tersely. 'Will isn't a young man and when you see him, I think you'll realise he's changed since you left last June.'

On that ominous note, Raul walked away and Juliet felt a sinking sensation in her stomach. Too nervous to sit on one of the rattan chairs behind her, she stared up at the painting again but without really seeing it.

Though she was still disappointed in her uncle for what he had done last year, she didn't want to think about that right now. She owed him so much. No one had expected him to take her in when she had become an orphan at age twelve and it would have been far simpler for him to allow her to become a ward of the state. But he hadn't and because he now needed her, Juliet couldn't really regret coming back to Granada, even if she did have to endure Raul's animosity.

For the next long five minutes, Juliet paced the floor of the deserted waiting room, beginning to wonder if Raul was ever coming back. At last he did, but he neither smiled nor spoke a word as he led her out of the reception area, down a long corridor. Two nurses in white starched uniforms glided past them almost noiselessly, their feet making no sound on the cork-tiled floor. Only their skirts rustled softly as they hurried by. Raul stopped by the next-to-the-last door at the end of the hallway but before Juliet could take a step to precede him into the room, he caught her arm.

'He's still weak and a little groggy so you can only stay five minutes.' Hard green eyes bored into the amber depths of hers. 'And whatever he says to you, you agree with him. Is that understood? I won't have you upsetting him.'

Juliet yanked her arm free, righteous indignation making her cheeks bloom with crimson colour. 'I can't imagine why you'd think I'd upset him!' she whispered furiously. 'For God's sake, Raul, he's my uncle; I'd never do anything to hurt him! And I don't need you telling me how to act around sick people. Who do you think you are? The wise and powerful reincarnation of El Cid or something? Well, don't expect me to jump to your every command! I don't want you telling me what to do and how to act. You have no right to treat me like I'm a rather stupid child!'

'Don't I, Juliet?' he countered with infuriating calm. 'Considering how stupidly childish you acted last June, I think I have every right. As long as you act immature, I'll treat you accordingly.'

She glowered up at him, her fingers itching again to make stinging contact with his cheek. She ached to wipe that mocking, sardonic expression right off his face. Yet, she didn't dare slap him. This was a hospital after all, not exactly the place to start a fist fight. Besides, she suspected that if she ever struck Raul, retaliation would come swiftly and with such vengeance that she shuddered now with the very thought of what he might do to her. Oh, but she longed to hit him though, to flail at his chest with her fists for his mocking and supercilious attitude. And apparently her desire to do him some bodily harm revealed itself in her eyes.

'Don't do anything you'll regret,' he warned, his voice a low growl from deep in his throat, his eyes like glittering green ice. 'Now, try acting your age for once and go in there and make Will feel like he's a little bit important to you.'

Vehement protest trembled on Juliet's lips but she had no time to voice her indignation. As Raul pushed open the door and his hand pressed against the small of her back, impelling her forward, she had no choice except to move into the room. She glanced back over her shoulder, her expression reproachful yet uncertain too. 'Aren't you coming in with me?'

Raul shook his head. 'You can only stay five minutes and Will wants to see you alone. I'll wait out here for you but just remember what I said. Don't do anything to upset him.'

'I got your message the first time, lord and master,' Juliet whispered recklessly. 'You don't have to repeat yourself.' And with a rebellious uptilting of her chin, she left him in the doorway.

Will McKay's private room was as

quietly elegant as the reception area had been. Apricot draperies of silk covered a wide window and complemented the cream-coloured walls and the furniture which was upholstered in natural earth tones. Juliet tiptoed into the room, approaching the bed with a concerned smile trembling on her lips and when her uncle turned his head on his pillow to return her smile, tears filled her eyes. Raul was right. Uncle Will had changed. There seemed to be more grey streaks in his thinning light brown hair and the lines on his face had deepened. To Juliet, he looked ten years older than he had last June and there was a fragility about him that nearly caused her to burst into tears. Yet, knowing she would upset him terribly by crying, she controlled her emotions and immediately took the thin blue-veined hand he extended to her.

'You've lost weight,' was his first comment.

'Only a few pounds,' she answered, relieved to see that his blue eyes were alert and appraising as they swept over her. 'Besides, you're thinner too so don't fuss at me when you've obviously lost more weight than I have.'

Her teasing tone elicited a grin. 'I can afford to lose weight. I'm an old man.'

'What nonsense. You're only as old as you feel and you always told me you felt like a teenager.'

'So I did,' Will McKay replied, his grin beginning to fade. His thin fingers plucked at the crisp white sheet that covered him. 'But lately my age has been catching up with me. I don't feel so young anymore. But I think maybe I've just been missing you.'

With a muffled sob, Juliet bent down to kiss his lined cheek. 'Oh, Uncle Will, I've missed you too.'

As she straightened again, Will caught one small hand between both his and patted it gently. 'Why did you run away with that unkempt singer, child? I just don't understand why you did it.'

'Oh, let's not talk about that now,' she murmured hastily. This was definitely not the time or place to argue with him about their lack of agreement regarding arranged marriages, so she lifted her shoulders in a slight shrug instead. 'I just needed to get away, that's all.'

Will grimaced as he shifted his position as much as was possible with his right leg suspended in traction. Then his eyes met hers again and he indicated with a sweep of his hand that she should sit down on the chair by his bed. 'Well, tell me, are you and—that young man still—er, together?'

'Right now I'm with you,' Juliet answered with forced cheeriness, giving him a weak smile. As she pleated the cotton blend fabric of her skirt, she stared down at her lap. 'Well, how are you feeling? Is your leg giving you much pain? And how about your head? Raul said you had a concussion.'

'I'm a tough old bird; I'll be okay,' he murmured but his voice quavered slightly.

Juliet jerked up her head, then jumped to her feet when she saw that his face had suddenly gone very pale. 'Are you all right?' she exclaimed softly, leaning over him. 'Uncle Will, do you hear me?'

He had closed his eyes, but now they fluttered open. 'I have to get out of this place,' he muttered, a disoriented look in his eyes. 'I'm late for an appointment at the gallery.' Then his eyelids drooped shut again.

Tears blurred Juliet's vision as she clenched and unclenched her hands around the metal bed railing. The narrow white bandage across Will's forehead took on a more ominous significance now. Obviously his concussion had been much more severe than she realised. She glanced toward the door, needing Raul to come in and help her cope with this situation, yet reluctant to ask anything of him. When she had almost decided to go get him anyway, however, her uncle awakened again.

'You're still here, child. Good,' he murmured, reaching out one hand to her. 'I seem to doze off every few minutes. Guess the medication I'm getting is making me groggy.'

Breathing a silent sigh of relief, Juliet smiled down at him, squeezing his thin fingers gently. After releasing his hand, she carefully straightened the sheet that covered him. 'Since you're sleepy, I'm going now. I wasn't supposed to stay long anyway.'

'But you'll be back?' Will questioned

urgently. 'Won't you? Promise me you'll stay in Granada until I'm back on my feet again. I know I'm asking a lot but...' His words trailed off on a hopeful note.

He *was* asking a lot but Juliet knew she couldn't refuse him. It had been wrong of him to try to manipulate her into marrying Pablo but, intuitively, she realised he had probably thought he was doing what was best for her. She had to forgive him, especially now when he needed her. Finally she nodded. 'I'll stay until you're well again, I promise.' And when Will smiled as he drifted off to sleep again, she breathed a sigh. She had made the commitment; she couldn't back out now, but as she walked out of the room to join Raul in the corridor, she really felt a great need to run away again.

The drive back from the clinic was as uncomfortable as the drive there had been. Raul didn't speak until they were nearly at Will's house and then his tone was cold and unfriendly. 'Will wants you to stay here.'

'I know that,' Juliet responded stiffly to the abrupt statement. 'He asked me to stay until he's well.'

'I hope you told him you would because you will,' Raul announced, turning his head to give her a level stare. 'He's a sick man and I won't have you upsetting him by leaving again. So you'll be staying in Granada for a while whether you want to or not.'

'For your information, I already told him I'd stay,' Juliet said indignantly. Half-turning in her seat, she glared at him. 'And even if I hadn't already promised him, you can bet nothing *you* could say would make me change my mind. You seem to think you have some right to boss me around. Well, you don't!'

'Don't I, Juliet?' Raul drawled, more than a hint of mockery in his deep melodious voice. 'I think I have the right. Will asked me to take care of you until he's better. And I intend to do it.'

'Take care of me! Hah! I don't need anyone to take care of me. I'm twenty-one years old, not ten, and since you're only eleven years older than me, I don't think you qualify for the role of surrogate father.'

'You don't arouse my tender paternal

instincts anyway, I assure you. To deal with a brat like you, all a man needs is the strength to turn her over his knee. And if you push me too far, I'll do that to you.'

'You and who else?' she challenged recklessly as he parked the BMW in front of Will McKay's house. 'If you ever try to lay a hand on me, you'd better have help.'

Raul simply laughed. 'I'm beginning to see Pablo didn't handle you right last year. And obviously your singer doesn't either. You need to be taught that men are a great deal stronger than women, physically at least. And if you give me any trouble whatsoever, I'll be delighted to teach you that unavoidable truth,' Raul said calmly, getting out of the car and coming around to her side to shut her door as she got out. He laughed again, more softly, the sound coming from deep in his throat as he gazed down at her from his considerable height. Then, incredibly, he reached out and trailed one fingertip along the enticingly curved outline of her lips. As she hastily drew back, trembling, he smiled almost triumphantly, lowered his head and whispered softly into her ear, 'You might even discover you enjoy the lessons.'

'Very amusing,' Juliet drawled, managing somehow to sound composed and cool. But as her cheeks warmed tinglingly, she was grateful the darkness masked the revealing blush. She was so anxious to end this dreadful evening that when Raul impelled her none-too-gently to the front door of the house, she lost no time fumbling in her purse for her key. 'You don't have to go in with me. You've already been too, too kind to me tonight by driving me to the clinic,' she said sarcastically. 'So you needn't escort me into the house.'

'I'm not escorting you; I'm coming in for the night,' Raul countered matter-of-factly, then took her key and unlocked the door. As he handed it back to her his fingers deliberately brushed across her sensitive palm. 'I've decided to stay here since I have to go to the gallery every day. No use driving back and forth from Casa Valaquez. Besides, Will asked me to stay with you. He doesn't want you to be alone in the house.'

'But I'm not alone! Rosita's here,'

Juliet protested swiftly, peering up at him, wishing she could see his expression. But his face was shadowed; he was a broad silhouette in the shaft of moonlight that shone behind him and she felt suddenly overpowered by his dark form looming before her. 'You can't stay here,' she continued weakly. 'I...'

'I'm staying. So just accept that fact graciously and get inside,' he commanded imperiously, nearly pushing her into the brightly lit entrance hall, then shutting the massive door firmly behind them.

The sudden silence that filled the hall was unnerving; Juliet swallowed uneasily, tilting her head back to look into Raul's lean face. Though she was of average height, the top of her head didn't quite reach his shoulder and a very real awareness of his superior physical strength struck her with near breathtaking force. That awareness coupled with the strange unrecognisable light in his eyes caused her to move backward, away from him. Then the phone rang and the sudden unexpected jangle nearly made her jump out of her skin. Although she was illogically reluctant to turn her back on Raul, she did so and hurried to the round mahogany table that graced the centre of the hall.

It was Holly calling. 'How's it going? How's your uncle?' she asked quickly. 'I bet seeing him wasn't as bad as you thought it would be. Right?'

'He's still in the hospital, of course,' Juliet answered evasively, feeling Raul's intense gaze burning into her back. 'He seems very weak and—and he wants me to stay until he's well again, so I guess I won't be seeing you in two days after all. I hope you understand.'

'Of course I do. I never thought you'd be able to leave him that soon anyway,' Holly answered compassionately. 'I just hope you get lucky and don't run into Pablo and Raul Valaquez.'

'I'm afraid my luck's already run out. With the latter.'

Holly got the rueful hint. 'You mean you've seen Raul? Oh, what rotten luck. Well, how did his royal majesty act?'

Juliet shuffled her feet uncomfortably and twirled a strand of auburn hair around and around on her finger. She felt as if Raul were so close behind her that she'd soon feel his breath against her neck. Lowering her voice slightly, she answered Holly. 'Look, I can't really talk right now. Why don't you call me tomorrow morning?'

Holly was a perceptive girl. 'Oh, dear, he's right there with you now, isn't he? That's why you can't talk? Well, all right, I'll call you tomorrow. Just keep your chin up and remember that Benny and I love you.'

'I'm glad somebody does,' Juliet answered softly and after saying good-bye, she replaced the receiver. She took a deep shuddering breath that became a soft startled cry as, suddenly, hard hands descended on her shoulders and she was spun around to face Raul. Her breath caught in her throat as she gazed up bewilderedly into his angry eyes.

'Your singer, I presume?' he ground out harshly, his fingers biting into her shoulders. 'It must have been. That's why you couldn't talk with me around. Well, you'll be able to whisper sweet nothings to each other in the morning, but while you're here that's *all* you'll do.

You won't be seeing your no-talent *friend* until you uncle is well. Will asked me to see that you didn't and I intend to abide by his wishes.'

'You—*damn* you!' Juliet spluttered, then managed to untangle her tongue. 'Just who do you think you are? You can't tell me what to do! I don't care what Uncle Will said. *You* won't tell me who I can or can't see!'

'Oh, but I just did,' Raul whispered, his jaw tight as his dark gaze raked over her flushed face. 'But don't worry. I'll be here to keep you from getting too lonely. In fact, I'd be happy to start tonight. I always was attracted to you, even before Pablo met you, but I thought you were too young and inexperienced for me. You seemed like such an innocent and I didn't want to frighten you with my ardour. That was my mistake. You weren't the sheltered little girl I thought you were and now that you've been living with a man for almost a year, I certainly don't have to worry anymore about frightening you. Do I?'

Recognising the ruthless intent in his eyes, Juliet twisted and squirmed futilely in an attempt to escape his painful grip but was quickly subdued. Raul's arms encircled her waist, one hand moving up to tangle in the thickness of her hair, tilting her head back as he lowered his own.

'No!' she gasped softly. 'Raul, don't!'

'A warning, Juliet,' he whispered huskily as his mouth descended.

Expecting brutality, she was not prepared for a gently brushing kiss that unnerved her completely. Instinct made her struggle again but Raul slid his long fingers through her hair, clasping the back of her head, holding her fast. Her heart jumped and her legs went weak beneath her as his teeth closed tenderly on the full soft curve of her lower lip, tugging, nibbling until her mouth opened slightly with her quickly drawn breath. Suddenly, she was gathered close against him, her lips captured with hard marauding swiftness. And the aching thrill that quickened inside her startled her so much that she propelled herself away from him, her cheeks crimson, her eyes wide with alarm.

'Remember, that was just a warning.

And I think you realise that it could have become the danger itself,' he muttered roughly, his eyes dark with indefinable emotions as he raked his fingers through his thick hair. 'I don't think you're a very faithful girl, Juliet. First you betrayed Pablo. And just now, I think you might have wanted to betray your rock singer. Maybe you will next time. And let me assure you there will be a next time if you give me any trouble while you're here. What just happened is nothing compared to what will happen if you try to see your boyfriend, knowing Will doesn't want you to. So, if you know what's good for you, you'll start thinking of your uncle for a change, instead of acting like a selfish, unfeeling little brat. You'll just have to survive without your lover for a while. But the sacrifice won't kill you.'

Juliet blanched. Embarrassment and resentment exploded in her and she could take no more of his abuse and hypocrisy. Bitterly ashamed of her insane response to his kiss, she had to lash out at him. 'Lover! You think Benny is my lover? Well, you're absolutely crazy! Within a month after we left Granada last year, he met and married a girl who happens to be very pregnant right now, seven months pregnant in fact. So it isn't likely that Benny's my lover, now is it, you—you...' Barely pausing to catch her breath, she swung back into her tirade with a vengeance. 'And don't you dare ever call me unfeeling again. You—you hypocrite! How can you call me unfeeling? *I'm* the one who didn't want a cold arranged marriage! And Pablo knew that. I didn't betray him! I told him from the beginning I wasn't romantically interested in him but he wouldn't leave me alone. He kept coming to see me and finally Uncle Will even got in on the act. He decided an arranged marriage made sense and you, *you* agreed to that! And you have the nerve to call *me* unfeeling! When I get married it'll be for love so that makes me more feeling than you'll ever be, you cold, emotionless...'

Unable to think of any insults vile enough to hurl at him, she turned and ran to the stairs, making it halfway up before Raul could react and call after her, 'Juliet, stop!' She heard his heavy footfalls as he took the steps two at a

74

time and fear of how he might retaliate made adrenalin pump through her. She sped on breathlessly, auburn hair streaming out behind her as she raced frantically to her room.

He didn't catch her. As he reached the landing, she was careening into her bedroom, slamming the door and locking it with violently shaking fingers. She collapsed back against the cool wooden panels, her breath coming fitfully. She pressed her palms against the madly racing pulses in her temples, tensing as she waited, expecting Raul to try to force his way in. But after a few minutes had passed and there was only silence in the hall outside, she walked across the room and flopped down on her bed, all energy depleted.

'God, what a disaster,' she groaned aloud. Raul thought she was a selfish spoiled brat and, despite her attraction to him, she thought he was a cold emotionless tyrant. Now they were stuck here together in the same house an Uncle Will had actually asked Raul to take care of her. That was like asking a lion to take care of a lamb and though the entire situation struck Juliet as rather ironically amusing, somehow, at the moment, she just didn't feel much like laughing.

CHAPTER 3

Juliet spent a restless night. It was nearly dawn when she drifted off to sleep and when she awoke, bright sunlight was streaming through her wide windows and across her bed. Her eyes felt positively gritty from lack of rest and though she was tempted to thrust her head beneath her pillow and stay in bed, she swung her feet onto the floor and got up instead. Even after a shower, she wasn't particularly eager to begin the day. The hours would pass too quickly; Raul would come back from the gallery this evening and she would have to face him again. If only she hadn't allowed him to goad her into such an emotional reaction last night, she would feel far less embarrassed now. His cool and haughty accusation that she was selfish and unfeeling should have been met with an equally haughty response, as if it didn't bother her one whit what he thought of her. It had been useless to try to defend herself anyhow; Raul would never believe she hadn't encouraged Pablo's attention last year.

'Oh, so who cares what he thinks,' she muttered weakly as she shed her robe. After putting on a cool grass green sundress with narrow corded straps and slipping on cork-heeled straw sandals, Juliet went downstairs for breakfast. She wasn't really hungry but she knew if she refused to eat, Rosita would lecture her all day and she certainly was in no mood for that. Intent on picking a short length of thread from the skirt of her dress, she had her head bent as she approached the dining room and when she looked up again as she reached the doorway, she came to an abrupt halt, her heart lurching. Raul stood at the sideboard, pouring coffee from an electric percolator into a delicate china cup. She had thought he would have already left for the gallery so finding him here was a disheartening way to begin the day. Feeling an intense need for more time to prepare herself to face him, she started to turn and flee back upstairs but as he looked up and saw her in the doorway, she realised she was trapped. Though her stomach contracted, she resolutely squared her shoulders and stepped into the spacious dining room.

Raul's dark gaze swept slowly over her, then he extended the lean brown hand that held the cup. 'Coffee, Juliet?' he inquired as nonchalantly as though last night's confrontation had never occurred. He gave her one of his slow lazy smiles that had always set her pulses pounding. 'You take it with sugar. Right?'

She nodded, surprised he had ever noticed and as she was forced to go to him and take the cup he held out, uneasiness mingled with confusion. His hand was absolutely steady but hers shook and when his rough fingertips grazed hers as she took the delicate china saucer, her trembling caused the cup to rattle conspicuously. She blushed. He smiled almost indulgently, adding considerably to her bewilderment. That smile

78

reminded her of the man she had liked too much last year, and not wanting to be reminded, she moved to the long gleaming mahogany table and started to take a seat. There was no opportunity to pull out a chair, however. Raul stepped close to perform that courtesy for her. Sinking down onto the embroidered silk seat, she eyed him suspiciously through the thick long fringe of her lashes. He was being far too nice and she had no idea why. It would have been gratifying to think he had actually believed her last night but she didn't really imagine that he had. Valaquez family ties were too strong to allow him to believe her rather than his own brother. So why was he being so pleasant this morning, she wondered uneasily, unable to relax. Her fingers trembled as she unfolded her linen napkin and she found herself sitting stiffly and unnaturally. She conquered the temptation to look at Raul as he sat down at the head of the table, to her right. When his knee brushed her own, she hastily tucked her feet beneath her chair, chiding herself vehemently for the shiver of awareness that danced over her skin with the brief physical contact.

Feigning a great interest in the coffee she unnecessarily stirred, she shifted uncomfortably in her chair, wishing she had waited just a little longer to come downstairs. If she had, perhaps Raul would have already left for the gallery. But she hadn't waited and, now, sensing she was being watched, she dragged her gaze up from the coffee still swirling in her cup.

A guarded look came over Raul's magnetic green eyes, although he smiled slightly, etching attractive creases into his lean cheeks beside his mouth. 'What is on your agenda today?' he asked, his deep voice pleasantly modulated, conveying none of the animosity it had conveyed with every word last night. 'Do you have any special plans?'

For a long moment Juliet could only stare at him, overwhelmingly aware of how good he looked. The crisp white shirt he wore with the grey vested suit accentuated his bronzed skin and thick dark hair, hair she had often wished she could run her fingers through. A sudden desire to reach out and touch it now surged through her but she suppressed that unreasonable longing and managed to shake her head. 'No special plans, except to visit Uncle Will, of course.' She lifted her shoulders in a slight shrug. 'Other than that, I'm not sure what I'll do. Maybe I'll be industrious and go through my closet. I need to pick out what I want to give to charity and what I'll want to take with me when I leave Granada.'

'You'll have plenty of opportunity to do that later since you won't be leaving for quite some time,' Raul declared flatly, rising lithely to his feet to walk to the sideboard again. He didn't elaborate on his imperious statement; he didn't need to and a couple of minutes later, he came back to the table again, placing a small plate containing two hot rolls and curls of butter on the table before Juliet. Then, he sat down again with his own plate of shirred eggs and thin strips of aromatic bacon.

Juliet stared at the rolls, a somewhat perverse rebelliousness rising in her. 'I'm not hungry.'

'Eat anyway,' he commanded blithely.

'You're thinner than you were last year.'

As his frankly appraising gaze passed over her, Juliet tensed. 'Despite spending most of your life in England, you're still very Spanish, aren't you? Now you've even adopted the Spanish penchant for plump women.'

Raul laughed softly at her indignant tone. 'Few men of any nationality want to hold women shaped like broom handles in their arms.'

'I have considerably more shape than a broom handle,' Juliet muttered defensively, then blushed as she belatedly recognised the intimation in his statement. 'Besides, I don't see that my shape is any of your concern anyhow. You won't be holding me in your arms.'

'You think not? We'll see,' he answered, his tone evocatively soft. 'But we'll settle that difference of opinion some other time. For now, just eat.'

Although Juliet felt like refusing flatly to take one bite, the aroma of Rosita's freshly baked rolls was tempting. She stared at the plate before her but at last, the demand for nourishment made by her healthy young body overcame her stubbornness. Buttering a roll, she glanced at Raul out of the corner of her eye then willed herself to ignore the slight triumphant smile that tugged at the corners of his strong yet sensuously shaped mouth. By the time she had nibbled her way through one roll, Raul had finished his meal. He leaned back in his chair and lit a cigarette without asking her permission, probably remembering that she had never minded his occasional smoking last year. Knowing he was watching her, feeling almost adolescently self-conscious because of it, Juliet folded her fine linen napkin, then clasped her hands together in her lap. The silence in the room was more than a little disconcerting and she wished he would say something, anything, to ease her tension.

Finally, he did speak. 'You'll be needing a car while you're here and I remember how you disliked driving Will's old Bentley. So I'll have the Lotus Esprit driven into town for you to use.'

'That's not necessary, thank you,' she responded stiffly, wanting no favours from him. 'I don't mind driving the

Bentley all that much.'

'The Bentley is too unwieldy; you'll be much more at ease driving the Esprit so I'll call out to Casa Valaquez today and have it brought here,' Raul repeated firmly. 'It's useless to argue, Juliet. I've decided.'

Juliet sniffed. His attempts to seem friendly weren't very convincing after the insults he had heaped on her last night and she wondered exactly what he was up to. If he thought offering her the use of his car would lull her into believing he suddenly wanted to be chummy, then he had better think again. She wasn't quite that gullible, even if he did possess a certain charm that was very nearly irresistible. Besides, he couldn't tell her it was useless to argue. She'd argue if she wanted to and her eyes issued a challenge as they met his.

'You're issuing your royal decrees again and I told you last night that I won't tolerate being bossed around,' she declared recklessly. 'So I won't borrow your car and that's final. I might bang it up and I don't want that responsibility. At least with Uncle Will's heavy old

Bentley, I could probably drive into a brick wall and never even put a dent in it.'

Raul's hand came out but even as Juliet flinched and drew away, his fingertips feathered coaxingly across her high cheekbones then up to trace her slightly arched brows. 'You'll enjoy driving the Esprit, Juliet,' he said softly yet insistently. 'And since I rarely drive it myself, it sits in the garage. So you'd be doing me a favour by using it. It isn't good for any car to sit too long without being driven.'

She was being conned and knew it but his coaxing tone and caressing fingers were far more persuasive than last night's threats had been, so much more persuasive that she found herself wanting to give in to him. Besides, she rationalised, she did hate driving the Bentley but driving the Esprit might be an exhilarating adventure. Since she was committed to staying in Granada anyway, she might as well derive some pleasure from the situation. 'Oh, all right,' she finally relented. She pulled back slightly, escaping the fingers that were causing her heart to beat too rapidly, then felt a ridiculous sense of loss when Raul's hand dropped away. Dismayed by her own ambivalent feelings, she looked at Raul cautiously, confusion warring with defensiveness in her amber eyes as they met his. She glanced away again quickly. 'I'll borrow the car but remember this was all your idea and don't get mad at me if I happen to have an accident in it.'

Raul leaned forward in his chair, his expression suddenly very serious. 'You think I would care about the car if you had an accident, Juliet?' he muttered, jade green eyes searching her delicate features. 'What kind of unfeeling monster do you think I am? Don't you know I'd be concerned about you, not the damn car, if you had an accident.'

Foolishly, she laughed at him and was immediately made to regret her response. Her eyes dilated and widened as her wrist was quickly enclosed in a vice-like grip. Her warming cheeks were fanned by his breath as he half rose from his chair and his dark angular face came down close in front of hers. She gulped. 'All right, I'm sorry I laughed,' she blurted out compulsively. 'It was rude.'

'And unjustified,' he added softly, releasing her wrist and sitting back in his chair again, his dark narrowed eyes drifting over her. He shook his head, then massaged the back of his neck with one lean hand. 'Juliet, you're such a foolish child.'

She thrust back her chair and stood. 'I don't have to listen to your insulting, condescending remarks,' she proclaimed heatedly, entrancing rose colour blooming in her cheeks. She tossed her head indignantly as he suddenly grinned. 'You—you are the most...' She never finished her scathing opinion because at that moment, Rosita bustled into the dining room, carrying a blue and white enamelled vase filled with fragile ivory rosebuds. As Raul also rose to his feet, the housekeeper eyed both him and the girl hopefully. Then she very nearly giggled as he took one of the roses from the vase, broke off part of the long stem, and catching Juliet's hand to hold her there, tucked the bud into her shimmering auburn hair. His hand dropped down to cup her cheek, his fingers stroking caressingly.

'Hmm, just as I thought,' he murmured, undaunted by Juliet's outraged scowl. 'Even the petals of a rose aren't as soft as your skin.' And he silenced her attempted retort by pressing a finger against her lips, then a faint warning glinted in his green eyes. 'But remember, I'm still not sure I should believe what you said last night. If you were telling the truth, then I've judged you too harshly. But if you were lying, I will find out about it and you'll suffer the consequences, I promise you. So if you're wise, you still won't see this Benny while you're here. Is that clear?'

'Contrary to what you believe, you're not a feudal lord and I'm not your obedient serf,' she retorted furiously, low enough so Rosita couldn't hear. Resentment burned in her eyes. 'Besides, Benny happens to be in Jaen—with Holly, his wife. But even if he were in Granada, I'd see him if I wanted to. So you might as well stop trying to order me around because I'll do whatever I damn well please.'

Raul laughed softly and gently tapped the end of her small straight nose. 'You'll reconsider, I'm sure,' he declared confidently. Then the teasing gleam in his eyes altered to something much more subtly disturbing as his hand curved into the insweep of her waist. 'I have to go to the gallery now but I can close it early this afternoon and drive you to the clinic to see Will, if you don't remember the way.'

'I remember, thank you. And I wouldn't expect you to close the gallery and take me, even if I didn't.'

His dark eyebrows raised as he smiled indulgently. 'Such independence,' he drawled. 'Well, after you visit Will, if you want to, you may come down to the gallery and see the changes we've made.'

'How magnanimous of you to invite me but I don't think I'll have the time to come.' She forced herself to shrug casually. 'Remember? I plan to go through my closet today.'

'Ah yes, well, I certainly wouldn't want to encourage you to neglect such an important duty,' he countered wryly. Then, incredibly, as his hand on her waist tightened with slight pressure, he tilted her face up with one finger beneath her small chin. His dark head lowered. He brushed a feather-light kiss across her forehead, then smiled mysteriously as she drew back, blushing hotly and unable to conceal her surprise. Dark green eyes, unreadable and piercing, held hers for a breathtaking moment before he slowly slipped his hand from around her waist and tugged a silken strand of her hair. He smiled. 'Until this evening, *mi pequena.*'

My little one. He had never called her that before, nor any other endearment for that matter and as Juliet watched him leave the dining room, she took a deep tremulous breath. A man that attractive had no right to utter such endearments so carelessly and especially not in such a deep caressing tone. Shaking her head in bewilderment, she looked away from the door, only to find Rosita giving her a smug grin.

'You are *afortunada, nina,*' the housekeeper declared gleefully. 'Senor Valaquez is not so angry at you. He is the forgiving man.'

He's a maddeningly unfathomable man, Juliet started to argue but didn't. Instead of challenging Rosita's idolising evaluation of Raul, she walked slowly out of the dining room and up the stairs. A slight frown knitted her brow as she thoughtfully tapped her finger against her lips. Did Raul have some nefarious ulterior motive for this unexpectedly friendly treatment of her? Remembering how ruthless he had been last night, she feared he must have. And she dreaded the day when she discovered exactly what that motive was.

CHAPTER 4

Benny called Juliet the next afternoon. As she was coming into the house after visiting her uncle, the phone rang. Since Rosita was nowhere in sight, she hurried to the table in the centre of the hall and lifted the receiver warily, hoping the caller wouldn't bombard her with a long monologue of rapid-fire Spanish. She had learned the language when she first came to live with her uncle. But Juliet had never been a proficient linguist.

Luckily the voice that responded to her cautious *hola* was distinctly American and blessedly familiar.

'Benny, how are you?' she asked enthusiastically, slipping her feet from her leather sandals and luxuriating in the coolness of the wood floor beneath her bare soles. 'I guess you and Holly are drawing crowds into the coffee house to hear you.'

'I have to see you,' Benny replied, his voice oddly strained. 'Can I come to the house now?'

'Now? But how can you? Aren't you calling from Jaen?'

'We're in Granada. Look, I'll explain everything when I see you. Can I come or not? I'm no more than five minutes away.'

Though she detected the urgent note in his voice and was concerned, she knew it would be foolhardy to invite him to the house. Rosita could be such a blabbermouth sometimes and if Benny came, she would more than likely tell Raul about the visit. Glancing around the hall as if she expected to see the housekeeper lurking in a corner, eavesdropping, Juliet lowered her voice to answer at last, 'I can't see you here but let's meet somewhere. How about the Court of the Lions at the Alhambra? Say in twenty minutes?'

'Fine. Don't be late,' Benny answered brusquely, then hung up without even saying good-bye.

More than a little worried by his strange behaviour, Juliet wasted no time leaving the house again and within fifteen minutes was driving up the narrow steeply graded road to the Alhambra. Its sturdy clay walls and thirteen square towers gleamed golden in the sun against the backdrop of snow-tipped Sierra Nevada mountains. Disdaining the new parking area, Juliet parked Raul's black Esprit by the thicket of trees that edged the road. Getting out of the car, she rushed to buy a ticket to the castle. The sun blazed down relentlessly on her bare head as she passed through a courtyard, showed her ticket to the gatekeeper, then entered through a door into a cool quiet gallery. It was like taking a step back in time and almost too bedazzling. Graceful slender columns supported filigreed arches. Wainscoting of geometrically arranged red, green and white tiles lined the lower walls while the upper walls and domed ceilings were decorated with plasterwork mouldings of floral motifs, painted gold or red or blue.

Although Juliet had visited the Alhambra before, the delicate beauty of the Moorish architecture enchanted her as much now as it always had. She would have liked to linger in the cool gallery; there was so much to see but this wasn't the time to explore. The Court of the Lions was some distance away and Benny might already be waiting for her. As she went on, past a long row of arched windows through which sunlight streamed, her cork-heeled sandals made only faint noise on the marble floor. The only other sound came from the splashing fountains in the inner courtyards and from the gentle movement of the cypress trees as a breeze occasionally drifted through them. Glancing at her wristwatch, Juliet quickened her pace. Two more minutes and she would be late and judging by Benny's urgent tone, he really needed to see her. Apprehension uncurled in her stomach so she hardly noticed the next sun-drenched courtyard she passed through. She did catch a glimpse of one of her favourite chambers with its domed ceiling of carved wood inlaid with ivory and silver. Finally, after wandering through several rooms of one of the royal residential apartments, she stepped out into the Court of the Lions.

She hesitated, glancing around the veranda-enclosed courtyard. Fragile, fluted columns cast long shadows in the bright sun. Four white marble walkways led to the sculptured fountain supported by stylised lions, which spouted streams of water from their small round mouths. A single column of water sprang up in the fountain's centre, creating rainbow-hued droplets that splashed back into the stone basin.

Benny was nowhere to be seen. Juliet walked to the fountain but as she dipped her fingers into the sparkling water, he appeared, looking quite haggard, his boyish face drawn, his skin ashen. 'What's wrong?' she exclaimed, laying her hand on his arm. 'What is it? Where's Holly?'

Benny raked his fingers through already rumpled reddish hair and gave a sigh that was half a groan. 'She's in the hospital.'

'Oh, no! But what's wrong? She hasn't—hasn't had the baby prematurely?'

'No, but she could,' Benny replied thickly, then pointed in the direction of a stone bench beside an ornamental yew tree. 'Let's go sit over there. Okay? I'm exhausted.'

After they had settled themselves on the bench and Benny had stared morosely at his feet for several minutes without speaking again, Juliet could stand the silence no longer. 'Tell me exactly what's wrong, *please*. Why might Holly have the baby two months early?'

'We had an accident in the van,' Benny began dully. 'Yesterday, after we talked to you on the phone and you sounded so lonely, we decided to start early this morning for Granada. We planned to take you away from here if you wanted to leave.' He paused a moment, clenching his hand into a fist on his thigh. 'I didn't sleep much last night, getting a cold, I guess, so Holly insisted on driving. Softhearted little fool swerved to avoid hitting a scruffy old stray cat. We hit a signpost instead and she was thrown against the steering wheel. Bruised her up pretty bad but she's all right.'

Juliet's face had gone pale. 'And the baby?'

'Heartbeat's still strong but for a while there were signs that Holly might go into labour so the doctor wants her to stay in hospital, in bed, for the rest of her pregnancy. Naturally, she's plenty upset.'

Juliet, however, was relieved and she patted Benny's arm consolingly. 'But the baby should be fine if Holly stays in bed, right? I know it's rotten luck but it could have been so much worse. Try to remember that.'

'We're both trying to,' he replied tiredly. 'But mostly I'm worried about her because she's so worried about how much it'll cost to stay in the hospital so long. I told her I'll get two jobs so we'll pay the bills somehow.'

Juliet dismissed his words with a wave of her hand. 'You won't need two jobs and you won't have to worry about the medical bills. My parents left me some money and I've never spent any of it. Uncle Will's held it in trust for me but now that I'm twenty-one, I can do whatever I want with it. So you tell Holly she doesn't have to worry about paying her hospital bill. I'll take care of that.'

'Oh, no you won't,' Benny retorted emphatically. 'No way. That's your money and...'

'And you and Holly are my friends and I want so much to help. Please let me.' As Benny argued and Juliet realised how stubborn he was going to be, she decided a little emotional blackmail would be justified in these circumstances. She allowed her lower lip to tremble and tears to fill her eyes. 'You've got to let me help. I feel responsible for the accident since you were on your way here to see me when it happened. If you don't let me help pay the medical expenses, I'll feel so guilty. I'll never forgive myself.'

Benny's hesitation was his undoing. After a few more minutes of her fervent pleading he acquiesced. 'It's crazy for you to feel guilty about the accident, but if you do, then I guess I have to let you *help* with the bills. But you'll just help. All right? I'll want to pay as much I can. Remember the coffee house where you and I met last year. I can get a job singing there again, I'm almost sure. The pay's not terrific but beggars can't be choosers.'

'Where will you stay while Holly's in the hospital?'

'Probably that little hotel where I stayed last year. It ain't what you'd call grand but it is cheap,' Benny said wryly, sounding more like himself. Then his expression sobered again. 'I shouldn't have loaded all my problems onto your shoulders when you have enough troubles of your own. How's your uncle?'

'About the same. His doctor says it may take him a while to recover completely.'

'So you're stuck here, huh? And how are things going with the macho Raul? Is he giving you a hard time?'

Juliet sighed. 'I really don't know what to make of him,' she said softly. 'That night I arrived back, he was so hostile he finally goaded me into telling him what I thought of him for trying to arrange a marriage between Pablo and me. But I'm sure he still really thinks I led Pablo on, then dumped him. What bothers me now is that Raul is being very nice to me, so nice that I'm getting very edgy. He has to have some devious motive for being that nice.' She smiled wryly. 'But even now, with this Mr Friendly act he's putting on, he keeps telling me in no uncertain terms that I'm not to see you. He doesn't quite believe you're married and he thinks you and I are much more to each other than travelling companions.'

Benny's eyebrows lifted. 'He's got everything wrong, hasn't he?' He smiled mischievously. 'Boy, if he only knew how willing I was last year to be more than your friend and how uninterested you were. It really broke my heart when I realised you only thought of me as your buddy.'

'Your heart sure mended fast enough after you met Holly,' Juliet countered with a grin. 'You never gave me another romantic thought.'

Benny smiled sheepishly. 'I guess the two of us were destined to be just friends. But I'm a little confused about Raul. Why should it matter to him what we are to each other? He's not still trying to arrange something between you and Pablo, is he?'

Juliet lifted her face to look up at the cool blue sky, and shook her head. 'Oh, I don't know what he has in mind. Maybe he just wants to boss me around for a while. After all, I probably insulted the entire Valaquez family by refusing to marry Pablo, then running off with you.'

'And you're going to go on letting him believe that? You're not going to try to convince him I am married to Holly?'

'Why should I?' Juliet countered rather resentfully. 'He doesn't want to believe anything I say. And if I did convince him, he'd probably try to rush me down the aisle with Pablo and I certainly wouldn't appreciate that.'

'But he can't force you to marry anybody so why do you care if he tries? Unless it bothers you that he's not romantically interested in you himself?'

Blushing slightly under Benny's too

perceptive gaze, Juliet muttered evasively, 'I don't want to talk about Raul anymore. Tell me, is Holly allowed visitors? Could I go see her?'

'Sure and she wants to see you; she told me to tell you to come as soon as you could.' Suddenly, Benny hopped up from the bench. 'Well, I'd better go. I want to stop by the hospital before I go see if I can beg my old job back at the coffee house.'

'Try not to worry too much,' Juliet said softly, standing also. 'I'm sure both Holly and the baby will be all right and if you need money, just call me. Okay?'

Benny nodded, then surprisingly he grasped her shoulders and gave her a gentle kiss on her lips. 'You know you're a great kid,' he muttered, then rushed away before she could respond.

As Juliet watched him walk beneath an archway into the shadows then disappear through the door to the King's Salon, she shook her head sadly. He and Holly didn't deserve trouble like this and, in actuality, she did feel rather guilty that the accident had happened on their way to see her, when they had called her yesterday, she should have made a concerted effort to sound more cheerful. Then they wouldn't have felt the need to come to Granada to rescue her and this entire mess would never have occurred. But it had and she released her breath in a long shuddering sigh of regret.

'Parting is such sweet sorrow,' a deep sarcastic voice spoke from behind her. When she spun around, eyes wide with surprise and dismay, Raul shook his head. 'I must say, Juliet, your Benny doesn't look like the Romeo type. He looks more like a reject from the hippie generation.'

Juliet closed her eyes, trying to control the tumultuous beating of her heart. A tightening constriction in her throat prevented her from speaking but, really, there wasn't much she could say anyway; Raul was right. Benny had looked disreputable today, his jeans and faded shirt wrinkled, as if he had slept in them, and his hair, which was overdue for a trim anyhow, had stood up on end because he had repeatedly raked his fingers through it. And he had also been rather bleary-eyed due to the cold he was catching. This had been the worst possible time for Raul to see him but she had no intention of apologising for her friend's appearance. If Raul wanted to think she had poor taste in companions, then let him.

'Are you going to stand there with your eyes closed all day?' Raul prompted at last, his tone grim. 'Or are you going to face me and admit you lied last night. Your Benny is no more married than I am.'

Juliet came alive, her head jerking up, her eyes opening, fury flaring in them. 'He most certainly is married. And I'm plenty tired of you calling me a liar! Benny has a wife and I'm not going to tell you that again.'

'If he's married, then why this secret rendezvous with you?' Raul asked caustically though his lean features remained infuriatingly serene. 'Or is that a foolish question? Does he have both a wife and a mistress, namely you?'

Since Juliet refused to dignify such an insane allegation by answering it, she instead muttered resentfully, 'What are you doing here anyway? How did you

104

find me? Did Rosita overhear me on the phone and call you?'

'Believe it or not, I didn't come here to deliberately disrupt your rendezvous with your lover,' Raul said bitingly, tossing his suit coat back over one shoulder then thrusting his other hand into his right trouser pocket as his dark gaze raked mercilessly over her. 'I just happened to stumble over the emotional parting scene. I've been with the director of the museum here. I have a client who has in his possession a clay urn that belongs in the Alhambra. He wants to sell; the museum wants to buy and I'm negotiating the terms.'

'Oh, I see,' she muttered, glancing away. Unreasonably, she was disappointed he hadn't come here specifically to drag her away from Benny but that was a foolish reaction and she berated herself for it. After all, she knew very well he didn't care enough about her to inconvenience himself. Wishing she didn't care about him either, she half turned away but was unable to suppress a soft sigh. 'Well, I didn't realise the gallery was in the business of selling artifacts too. Things must have changed. Uncle Will only handled paintings and sculptures. I suppose this new business is your idea?'

'Yes. Now, enough of this trite nonsense,' Raul murmured close to her ear. Taking her hand in his, he swung her around to face him again, his jaw clenched. 'If you recall, I promised retribution if you saw Benny. You chose to ignore my warning so now...'

His words trailed off suggestively and his message was quite clear. Though Juliet quaked inside, she drew herself up to her full height, which unfortunately didn't seem considerable compared to his. Nevertheless, she squared her jaw and shoulders simultaneously and forced herself to look directly up at him. 'Don't be ridiculous, Raul,' she said more tauntingly than she meant to. 'You're not going to do anything to me in a public place like this and I know it.' She gestured toward a group being led through the courtyard by a tour guide. 'See. With all these people around, you don't dare...'

'I will dare, Juliet,' he growled menacingly, taking a step closer to her. 'I don't appreciate being lied to. So if you know what's good for you, you'll just admit Benny isn't married. It's obvious he isn't. I certainly didn't see a pregnant woman with him.'

Enough was enough; it was too much actually and Raul's mocking words only succeeded in reminding Juliet that Holly was in the hospital and that the life of her unborn baby might very well be in danger. Tears sprang to her eyes and before she could blink them away, Raul saw them.

'What the...'

'Oh, will you just shut up?' she muttered bleakly, turning away from him. 'Whether you believe me or not doesn't much matter to me right now. I'm much more worried about Holly. For your information, she's Benny's wife and he met me here to tell me they'd had an accident. She's in the hospital right now and she might have her baby two months early. She's my friend and I'm worried about her so I don't feel like being abused by you. So would you just go away and leave me alone. Please.'

Raul stepped around in front of her and perhaps it was the trembling of her lips that convinced him. 'Damn,' he muttered violently, reaching out to brush her hair back from her cheeks. 'All right, I believe you. Even you wouldn't make up such an elaborate lie. What I don't understand is why you're still with Benny. And I certainly don't understand how you can be friends with the girl he dumped you for. Isn't it a little awkward to travel with an ex-lover and his wife?'

Juliet's shoulders sagged and her grim laugh was more a soft moan. 'You idiot, Benny is a friend. That's...'

'You American girls have such a casual regard for intimate relationships,' Raul scoffed, shaking his head. 'Friends can change to lovers then back again to friends the next day, without anybody ever feeling deeply involved.'

Realising it was useless to try to convince him that Benny had never been her lover, Juliet moved away from him, then sighed when he followed. She was too utterly weary of arguing with him to even resist when amazingly gentle fingertips brushed away the crystalline teardrop that fell from the thick fringe of long, dark brown lashes onto her cheek.

'Come with me; we'll walk in the garden,' he insisted softly, cupping her elbow in one large hand to guide her toward a door beyond a keyhole archway. 'There are too many people in here.'

Though Juliet considered protesting, one glance at his firmly carved features changed her mind. There was a determination in his eyes that squelched any opposition.

Glaring sunlight struck them and the heat of the day enveloped them as they entered a terraced inner garden bordered by cypress and myrtle trees. Though Juliet began to drag her feet balkingly as she was directed past a splashing fountain with waters cascading coolly into a rippling pool, Raul only smiled down at her and pulled her closer to his side. His muscular arm encircled her waist as he took her up the mosaic tiled terraces into the dark, private copse of bordering cypress trees. In the shaded seclusion, Raul tossed the suit coat he carried onto the ground, dropped down to his knees on it, and pulled her down to him. He produced a freshly laundered white monogrammed handkerchief. 'I really hope your friend Holly will be all right. And the baby too,' he murmured gently, then proceeded to dry Juliet's cheeks with the soft square of fine cloth. As she pensively chewed her lower lip, he pressed the handkerchief into her left hand, then with an incomprehensible whisper, caught her chin between his thumb and forefinger, tugging slightly, tenderly coaxing her lips to part as she took a quick breath.

Suddenly, everything was different. The swaying branches whispered above them and, with the occasional singing of the birds and the tinkling music of the cascading fountain, provided the only sounds in the abrupt intense silence that surrounded them. Juliet's senses awakened to a new, keener awareness. The red of the roses and the white of the delicate jasmine in the garden became, in an instant, much more vibrant. Their fragrance mingled with the slightly piney scent of rosemary and perfumed the air. Her heart seemed to stop beating as she saw the warming gleam of desire that flamed in the dark green depths of Raul's eyes. It was as if nothing else existed except this garden paradise and them but her common sense wouldn't let her become totally lulled into submission by the exotic surroundings. As Raul's hands suddenly spanned her waist, drawing her to him so that she was half reclining across hard thighs and he lowered his head, she was prepared to fight him tooth and nail if he tried to kiss her. But it didn't quite work out that way. Once again, his mouth moved over hers with such gentle teasing persuasion that common sense had no chance to prevail. Her soft lips clung to his, parting as his teeth nibbled and tugged slightly on the full lower curve and the kiss became a powerful sensual force she had no strength to resist.

It was insane but his mere touch seemed to have some hypnotising effect on her. She relaxed against him involuntarily, her heart leaping as he gathered her closer, his powerful arms enfolding her in warmth. Her trembling hands pressed against his chest but he was undaunted by such ineffectual resistance. One caressing hand moved along the in-curving contour of her waist, his finger-tips stroking into the tantalising arch of the small of her back, his thumb brush-ing the cushioned slope of her breast.

A shiver danced over her skin. Her fingers clutching his shirtfront spread open over his chest, warmed by the com-pelling heat of his flesh, felt even through the fabric. Her senses spiralled as she inhaled the mingling scents of lime and tobacco. And as she intuitively moved nearer, his mouth took complete posses-sion of hers. Startled yet aroused by the touch of his tongue tasting hers, she was swept upward in the tumultuous dawning of desire. Last year, she had often day-dreamed of Raul kissing her but even her wildest erotic imaginings hadn't pre-pared her for this. His kiss was a deliber-ate seduction, an intimate searching possession that made her ache to be much closer to him. Now, only this moment mattered; everything else, even his tyrannical unfair behaviour toward her, ceased to exist. Beyond rational thought, she surrendered to emotions far stronger than any will to resist. Her small trembling hands fluttered hesitantly upward to encircle the strong bronzed column of his neck, her thumbs grazing over the contouring tendons.

'Juliet,' he whispered, his voice excitingly low and rough as he gathered her closer still with swift undeniable urgency. As her softness yielded to the harder stronger masculine line of his body, one questing hand slipped up to cover the mound of one breast and when the firm warm flesh surged responsively against his palm, he groaned softly.

His touch was electric. As Juliet's slender bare arms went around his neck, she delighted in the shafting awareness that shot through her body when strong fingers curved into her throbbing cushioned breast. Other men had tried to bestow such familiar caresses; Pablo had tried often but she had always brushed his hand away with mild irritation. Raul's touch was different, so very different. She liked it. The demand his hard lean hands conveyed sent shivers dancing over her skin and aroused a central throbbing aching inside her. Her soft lips parted wider and were captured by the firm yet sensuous shape of his. Her mouth opened slightly, invitingly. His kiss hardened, then became a deepening, spellbinding exploration that weakened her limbs with intensifying warmth. And as his fingers tangled in the thick hair on her nape, she was kissing him back with a passion that was rising to meet his.

It was the clatter of footfalls on the tiles around the fountain that brought Juliet back to the real world a moment later. And when she heard a tour guide droning on in memorised English, she dragged her lips from Raul's with a breathless murmur of protest. Still cradled in his arms, she opened drowsy amber eyes, met the debilitating triumphant gleam in the green depths of his and blushed crimson. When she struggled to escape his arms, he released her immediately and she sat up, her head bent, her silken hair falling forward to conceal her face. She felt thoroughly confused and somewhat ashamed and when Raul's fingertips feathered over her nape, she jerked away.

'Let's not play games, Juliet,' he said softly. 'You're a very responsive young woman and you've been without a lover too long. We could have a very satisfying relationship while you're here in Granada.'

Juliet scrambled to her knees, the colour draining from her face as she stared at him. 'Are you suggesting that w-we have a casual affair?' she stammered. 'Wh-what kind of person do you think I am?'

'I think you're a very modern young woman and I don't want you to be lonely while you're here,' he said with provoking calm, as if he were deliberately baiting her. 'So my suggestion that we keep each other company wasn't meant as an insult.'

'Well, I *am* insulted!' she retorted recklessly. 'And you can just go straight to hell! I wouldn't choose you to keep me company if you were the last man on earth. And I haven't been without a lover too long. I've never had...' Her words halted abruptly. She couldn't tell him she'd never had a lover—that admission would be far too revealing and make her wanton response to him too significant. She had no desire to let him learn that his touch affected her in a way no other man's ever had. Raul was already difficult to handle, as it was. Clamping her lips firmly together, she jumped to her feet but the muscles of her throat constricted painfully as Raul stood swiftly and caught her wrist before she could escape. Her eyes widened with bewilderment as she stared down at the lean fingers curving around her small wrist. 'Wh-why are you doing this?' she asked huskily. 'Yesterday you were pretending to be nice but today, you're—you're being horrid.'

'I can be nice or I can be "horrid," ' he answered bluntly. 'How I treat you is all up to you, Juliet. And I don't believe you really think I've been horrid today. You enjoyed the past few minutes as much as I did so why try to deny it?'

With a careless shrug, he released her and as she turned away, she was aware of him reaching down for his coat and tossing it over one shoulder. For a tense moment, his gaze seemed to bore into her back but she refused to look at him.

'We'll go see Will tonight at eight, as usual. Be ready.'

His commanding tone was the last straw. A biting retort sprang to her lips but before she could turn and utter it, he was walking away. She glared after him, her fists clenched at her sides but when he didn't even glance back at her, her shoulders drooped slightly and she released her breath in a long shuddering sigh. Absently, she reached up for the slender low-hanging branch of willow that brushed her shoulder and with an audible oath of frustration, she snapped off one narrow long leaf. As she watched Raul walk out of sight, she wondered why his erroneous opinion of her upset her so much. She shouldn't care what he thought of her. After all, she had no reason to be fond of him either. He was too busy, too conceited—a super sophisticate totally devoid of warmth.

Raul proved her wrong that evening. He *was* capable of warmth, at least in his attitude toward Will McKay. He actually seemed fond of the older man and the affection Juliet detected in his green eyes during their visit to Will nearly took her breath away. And she also noticed with some dismay that Raul treated all the nurses with such irresistible charm that every one on duty that evening seemed to find some excuse to stop by Will's room while Raul was there. Juliet watched the teasing exchanges between him and the younger women with increasing discontent. Why didn't he treat her the way he treated them? Though he obviously appreciated their femininity, his attitude conveyed no hint of disrespect or insult. After he engaged in a half-serious flirtation with a particularly lovely raven-haired your nurse, Juliet sat staring at him when the girl left. Obviously sensing her bewildered appraisal, he finally looked up, his unfathomable eyes issuing a challenge until she nervously chewed her upper lip and averted her gaze.

'Well, Raul, has the doctor told *you* when I might get out of this wretched bed?' Will McKay asked querulously, inadvertently easing some of the tension Juliet felt. 'He won't tell me anything. He acts like it's none of my business how long I have to lie here with my leg dangling in the air.'

Raul smiled understandingly. 'It won't be much longer, Will. Try not to be impatient and remember, you'll still have to take it easy for quite some time after you're released from the clinic.'

'But the gallery. I need...'

'Don't worry about the gallery. I'll handle everything.'

'You can't neglect your other responsibilities indefinitely though,' Will argued. 'I never expected you to keep the gallery open personally so if you want to close it until I'm well again, I'll understand.'

'That won't be necessary,' Raul assured him. 'I'm bringing in someone to keep the gallery open, someone very capable so you have no reason to worry.'

Visibly relieved, Will nodded, then gave Juliet a wan smile and reached out a thin blue-veined hand. 'I'm sorry to be such poor company, child, but I am feeling rather tired.'

Smiling back at him lovingly, Juliet patted his hand, then tucked it back beneath the crisp white sheet covering him. 'You're not poor company. You just need a lot of rest.'

'So we'll leave you to get some sleep,' Raul added, getting up from his chair to stand beside the bed. He nodded perfunctorily at Juliet. 'Ready?'

Not really, she thought but she stood anyway. After brushing a kiss against her uncle's cheek, she preceded Raul out of the room, down the long corridor and through the reception area into the cool night air. The lush clinic grounds shimmered in the light of a cream-coloured moon and the fragrances of roses and bougainvillaea mingled sweetly. It was a lovely night but as Juliet slipped into the leather seat of Raul's BMW, she was really too uneasy to appreciate the beauty around her. What had happened between them that afternoon in the garden made it impossible for her to relax and she could only hope he would be enough of a gentleman not to mention the incident.

He didn't. Actually, he didn't say anything at all to her until they were back in Granada and he was parking the car before one of the city's swankiest hotels.

'The assistant manager from our gallery in Madrid arrived this evening and will be going home with us for dinner so we can discuss business,' he announced matter-of-factly. 'I told Rosita I'd be bringing a guest.'

'I suppose this means you'll be moving out of the house,' Juliet murmured, carefully examining her fingernails, not certain whether she felt disappointed or relieved. 'I mean, since this assistant manager will be taking care of the gallery, you won't need to stay in Granada, will you?'

Raul smiled rather mockingly. 'You seem to be forgetting Will asked me to take care of you. So no, I won't be moving out of the house. I'll be able to conduct most of my business by phone from there. Sorry if that upsets any plans you might have had.'

'I had no plans you could have...' Her reply was cut short as Raul got out of the car and closed the door before she could finish speaking. With a sigh of sheer exasperation, she folded her arms across her chest and slouched down in her seat. When her own door was opened a few seconds later and Raul stood beside it silently, as if expected her to get out, she thrust out her jaw. 'I'll wait here,' she muttered without looking at him. 'I don't imagine you'll be long, will you?'

'No, not long but you'll go in with me anyway,' he declared, reaching in to curve his hand around her upper arm. When she shook her head, his fingers tightened and he pulled her out despite her muttered protest. He added nonchalantly, 'I don't leave little girls alone in my car at night.'

Refusing to be baited, she didn't bother to answer but as they entered the plushly carpeted hotel lobby a moment later, she moved away from him, toward the cosily arranged brown leather sofa and chairs that faced the desk. After Raul spoke to the clerk, as he walked toward where she was now sitting on the sofa, she avoided looking at him by meticulously arranging the folds of the skirt of her ice-blue gauze dress. To her surprise, he sat down on the sofa beside her, settling back against the cushions and stretching his long legs out in front of him. During the next few minutes they waited in silence, but Juliet couldn't resist the temptation to observe him surreptitiously out of the corner of her eye.

Suddenly he smiled, one of those warm friendly smiles *she* had rarely, if ever, gotten from him. As he rose lithely to his feet, she followed the direction of his gaze and watched as a beautiful woman, probably in her late twenties, stopped in the centre of the lobby and stretched black silk-clad arms out to him. She was Spanish, with lovely dark eyes and a flawless olive complexion. Though she was quite tall and slim, the draped bodice and clingy skirt of her dress accentuated some very generous curves. Raul embraced her only briefly but she didn't remove her long slender hands from his shoulders until she kissed his lips lingeringly. He certainly didn't seem to object, Juliet noticed, wrinkling her nose discreetly. Then as he took the woman's hand and led her back toward the sofa, she bit back the disgruntled sigh that rose in her throat. She had no desire to meet one of his lady friends.

Unfortunately, Raul made the introduction anyway. 'Jimena, this is Will McKay's niece, Juliet. Juliet, Jimena Ruiz, the assistant manager of our Madrid gallery.'

Juliet was somewhat surprised. It had never occurred to her that the assistant manager would be a woman, especially a woman who looked the way Jemena did. Her black silk dress was undoubtedly a high fashion original and the narrow-strapped snakeskin shoes she wore probably cost a small fortune. Actually, Jemena looked as if she would be more at home in a fashion show than in an art gallery but Juliet disguised her surprise, said hello, and smiled.

Jemena's answering smile was more haughty than friendly, then she turned all her attention to Raul again, clinging to his arm tenaciously as if she thought he might float away if she released him. As Juliet stood and the three of them left the hotel and walked to the car, Jemena spoke to Raul in Spanish, effectively excluding Juliet from the conversation. It didn't matter. As the older woman automatically slipped into the front passenger seat, the supercilious look she gave Juliet needed no translation anyway. Conceding graciously, Juliet flashed a bright smile as Raul opened the back door for her and she got inside, shunning the helping hand he held out.

As Raul drove toward Will McKay's house, Jemena chattered away nonstop but finally he did remember Juliet was in the car. 'Speak English, please, Jemena,' he requested politely. 'Juliet can't translate that quickly.'

'Indeed?' Glancing back at Juliet, Jemena lifted perfectly arched black brows questioningly. 'But your uncle has lived many years in Granada, has he not, Senorita McKay?

'Juliet's been in school in the States most of the time,' Raul answered for her, then added succinctly, 'And for the past year, she's been travelling over Europe.'

'Ah, yes, with the boyfriend who is the rock singer.' Jemina smiled snidely. 'You are the girl who was engaged to Pablo—I remember now.'

'I was never engaged to Pablo, Senorita Ruiz,' Juliet responded tersely. 'He completely misunderstood our relationship. I never wanted to be more to him than a friend.'

'Well, there are friends and there are friends,' Jemena said suggestively, her laugh low and seductively husky as she brushed her hand against Raul's lean cheek. 'Is that not right, *querido?*' When he only smiled at her and didn't answer, she continued. 'I am so happy that you called me to manage the *galería* here. I missed you so much last week when you did not make your monthly visit to Madrid.'

By the time they reached the house a few minutes later, Juliet was wishing Jemena would start speaking Spanish again. If she was only going to whisper sweet nothings into Raul's ear, Juliet was not the least bit interested in what she had to say.

Unfortunately, the conversation during dinner was no more inspiring. Jemena chattered incessantly about the parties recently given by her obviously innumerable art circle friends. Since Juliet was unfamiliar with all except a few of the names the older woman mentioned, she was bored nearly to tears. And by the time the meal blessedly ended and Rosita served coffee to the three of them in the *sala,* she had to hide a yawn behind her hand. Looking up rather guiltily, she found Raul watching her. Warmth gathered in her cheeks as a smile tugged at the corners of his mouth.

Apparently noticing this exchange, Jemena regained Raul's complete attention by snuggling closer to him on the sofa. 'It is getting late, *querido,*' she murmured too sweetly. 'Perhaps you should tell me everything I will need to know about our gallery here so I will be prepared tomorrow morning.' Then she turned toward Juliet, thinning her lips into a patently false smile. 'You will not mind if I speak Spanish now, will you, Senorita McKay? I would be much more comfortable and since we will only be discussing business, you would be bored anyway.'

Nothing could bore me more than the last two hours with you have, Juliet thought uncharitably but she smiled and nodded and placed the cup of untasted coffee on the table beside her chair. 'Please do whatever makes you comfortable,' she replied as she stood. 'I think I'll go up to my room anyway, if you'll excuse me. I'm feeling a bit tired.'

'Young people do need their sleep,' the older woman agreed, with a coy irritating little laugh. 'And we would not want to keep the senorita up past her bedtime, would we, *querido?*'

Raul was standing also now and as Juliet walked across the *sala,* she was beginning to think he wasn't going to say anything, though he was watching her intently. Unusually self-conscious, she fumbled with the ornate handles of the double doors.

'Sleep well,' he called softly. *'Buenas noches,* Juliet.'

Surprised there had been no hint of the usual mockery in his deep voice, Juliet turned and gave him a rather shy smile. *'Buenas noches,* Raul.'

His own slight smile deepened. 'Your inflection is excellent. Perhaps you would like me to help you work on your Spanish?'

'I would like that,' she answered, covering her astonishment at the offer. 'But I'm sure you're much too busy to waste your time teaching me.'

Before he could reply, she walked out of the room but as she pulled the doors closed behind her, Jemena was tugging at Raul's hand and saying as he sat back down beside her, 'Of course you do not have the time to give the senorita Spanish lessons, *querido*. That is a job for a professor, not a business entrepreneur.'

'That is a job for a professor, not a business entrepreneur,' Juliet mimicked wickedly beneath her breath as she walked up the stairs. There was something about Jemena she didn't like at all and it wasn't simply her condescending attitude. And she certainly wasn't gullible enough to believe that the two of them would spend much of their time tonight discussing business, the way they were snuggled up together on the sofa.

As Juliet walked into her bedroom, the sudden memory of those few minutes she and Raul had shared in the garden that afternoon came unbidden to her mind. She stretched out across her bed, propped up on her elbows, her chin cupped in her hands, wondering if he would kiss Jemena the way he had kissed her.

'Why should you care what he does?' she asked herself impatiently, then turned over onto her back with a sigh, knowing the answer. Fool that she was, she was jealous and actually loathed the mere thought of Raul kissing any woman other than herself.

CHAPTER 5

'But, Raul, it's really not necessary,' Juliet repeated stubbornly, absently twirling a strand of hair. 'Besides the fact that Uncle Will and I would be just fine right here, I really don't think your grandmother would be particularly happy with me staying in her home. I told you I know she's never cared for me.'

'I decide who does and who does not stay at Casa Valaquez,' Raul declared, his jaw taut, his green eyes beginning to glitter with impatience. 'My grandmother accepts that fact.'

Juliet laughed humourlessly. 'Oh, yes, I'd forgotten. With your father still in England on diplomatic service, you're master of the house, aren't you? Sort of like a feudal lord? Does that mean if I ever disobey you, you'll toss me in your dungeon?'

'Don't be flippant,' he cautioned, his voice low as his hand shot out to cover hers on the tabletop, squeezing her slender fingers between the hardness of his. 'Disobeying me won't get you tossed in a dungeon, Juliet. I can think of much more pleasurable ways to deal with you.' When rose colour flooded her cheeks at his blatant intimation, he smiled sardonically and released her hand. 'Now, I'm saying this one last time—after leaving the clinic, Will is going directly to the *casa* to recuperate and you'll go with him. That's my final decision and I'm not going to argue with you about it.'

'Do you realise how pompous you sound when you say something like that?' Juliet replied recklessly. 'Are you so superior that I have no right to disagree with anything you say?'

For a moment, Raul only surveyed her intently but instead of glowering angrily at her for such audacity, his dark gaze at last softened and the slight smile he gave her was almost sheepish. 'You're right and I'm sorry if I sound as if I thought I was superior to you. Of course you have every right to disagree with me. It's only silly, trivial arguments that I refuse to participate in but since this is obviously important to you...'

'It is important.'

'Even so, I'm afraid this is one argument you can't possibly win because I know taking Will to Casa Valaquez will be best for him.'

'That's your opinion. I disagree with it wholeheartedly. Rosita and I could take very good care of Uncle Will right here.'

'I don't doubt that but there will be other people to help you care for him at the *casa*,' Raul explained, pressing one finger against her lips as she started to protest. 'You can't deny that, Juliet. Nor can you deny that Will would be much more comfortable out of Granada during the hottest part of the summer. With that cast on his leg, he'll be particularly susceptible to the heat.'

'But we have air conditioning here.'

'But at Casa Valaquez, he'll be able to sit outside in the shade of the cypresses. Here, he would have to stay inside all the time,' Raul persisted, his voice lowering as his fingertip began to feather slowly, coaxingly across her lips. 'There's always a nice cool breeze from the plain at the *casa* but you have to admit that the heat in town can be almost unbearable at times, don't you? Hmm?'

'Yes, but...' With the low seductive tenor of his voice and his persuasive touch, Juliet felt her resolve begin to weaken considerably. What he said made sense, at least for her uncle, but if he went to Casa Valaquez, she would have to go along too, since she'd promised to stay with him until he was well again. And in his own domain, Raul would probably be even more domineering than he was now, which would cause more friction between them. Besides, there was his grandmother, a very formidable elderly lady with cold obsidian eyes that had always conveyed disapproval of Juliet. All in all, Juliet could think of many things she would rather do than spend a few weeks subjected to Raul's demands and Senora Valaquez's disdainful glare. Yet, she did owe Uncle Will a great deal and he would be more comfortable away from the heat of the city....

Obviously, Raul sensed her uncertainty. 'You'll go,' he said flatly. 'It's all settled.'

'But Rosita,' Juliet murmured weakly. 'She'll be lost in this house all alone. I don't think I should leave her.'

'I never expected you to leave her. She'll go along, of course, to help care for Will.'

Juliet met Raul's penetrating gaze with a slight shrug of her shoulders. 'Well, you've boxed me into a corner, haven't you? You have an answer for every argument I make so what else can I do besides agree to go with Uncle Will?'

'Not a thing; I knew I could convince you,' Raul said softly, cupping her small chin in one tan hand. 'You'll do what's best for Will because you care about him.'

Juliet's eyes widened with surprise. 'Well, what brought about this change of opinion? Just the other day you called me a "selfish unfeeling little brat." '

'Maybe I understand better now how trapped you felt last year. If you really did try to discourage Pablo...'

'I did,' Juliet interrupted emphatic-

134

ally. 'But he wouldn't listen and Uncle Will wouldn't listen and...'

Raul's hand dropped away from her face while some of the warmth faded from those mesmerising green eyes. 'Running away was no answer though,' he said icily. 'You could have discussed the problem with me.'

Juliet stared at him disbelievingly. 'And what good would that have done? Pablo told me you were all for our marriage, so talking to you about my problem would have been like talking to the moon.'

Raul pushed back his chair and stood towering over her, thrusting his hands into the pockets of his trousers. 'Pablo tends to interpret other people's words and actions the way he wants to. I never agreed to an arranged marriage between you and him, Juliet. He told me he had proposed and you had accepted so there was nothing I could do except offer my congratulations. Contrary to what you think of me, I don't think I'm an all-powerful lord. Pablo is my younger brother but I don't control his life. I wouldn't presume to arrange a marriage for him.'

Juliet rose slowly to stand on legs suddenly quite weak with relief. 'You mean you didn't...'

'Nothing changes the fact that you decided running away was far easier than simply refusing to marry Pablo,' Raul interrupted coldly, buttoning his suit coat over the matching tan vest. 'And I'm still disappointed in you for making such an immature decision. Now, if you'll excuse me, I have some business at the gallery.'

Juliet watched as he strode out of the dining room, then she sank back down on her chair, knowing she really couldn't defend herself. What he had said was true. It had been foolish to run away from her problem last year. She already regretted having done it since it made him see her as a silly child who chose to evade disagreements rather than to resolve them. She might have to admit to *herself* that one of the main reasons she had left with Benny last year was her mistaken idea that Raul approved of her arranged marriage to Pablo but she could hardly tell Raul that. Such a revelation would only embarrass him and humiliate her, so she supposed she would simply have to resign herself to his low opinion of her or try to change it by proving she was now more mature than she had been last year. No easy accomplishment, she thought with a sigh as she rested one elbow on the table and cupped her chin in her palm. Even so, she couldn't feel totally disheartened. At least she now knew that Raul was not as unfeeling as she had presumed. He hadn't approved of an arranged marriage between Pablo and her and that realisation somewhat eased the nagging feeling that she had been betrayed by Raul last year.

Three days later, Juliet turned the Esprit between white stone gateposts and onto the winding drive that led to Casa Valaquez. Endless rows of gnarl-trunked olive trees stretched out on each side, their leaf-laden branches spreading out wide beneath the hot sun. Life sustaining water from the Sierra Nevadas became silvery ribbons in irrigation ditches and sparkled in the molten gold sunlight.

Beside Juliet, in the passenger seat,

Rosita clasped her hands together and sighed with sheer happiness as she gazed out her window. 'It is so beautiful, *nina*. It was always my wish to work in a house in the country like this but...' She shrugged resignedly. 'I became the maid in a house in Granada when I was fourteen and the city has been where I live always. But coming to care for Senor Will in a place like this will be like a *vacacion*. Si?'

'Si,' Juliet murmured, smiling at the housekeeper. Then she turned her attention to the road again, hoping Rosita wouldn't detect the uncertainty she herself was feeling. Although she could understand Rosita's excitement, she felt far less confident that this little visit to Casa Valaquez would be like a vacation. Considering Raul's unflattering opinion of her and his grandmother's haughty disapproval, Juliet feared her time here might seem more like a term in a penitentiary than a holiday. She had made the commitment, however, so there was no turning back now.

After a sharp bend in the pebbled road, they approached Casa Valaquez, a white, rambling two-storied stucco structure set in a circle of shading cypress trees. To the side of the house, toward the back, were the stables and Juliet smiled as she saw a lanky yellow dog wriggle beneath the bottom rail of the paddock fence, then lope off into the distance across the lush green grass. Twice before, she had visited Raul's home, once with her uncle for dinner and once when Pablo had dragged her out here one afternoon to go riding. Though the house was lovely and the grounds exotic, she hadn't felt comfortable here on those two occasions, mostly because Pablo had been driving her crazy with his unwanted declarations of undying love and also because of Senora Valaquez. Though Raul's grandmother had been polite, Juliet had sensed a certain reservation in her manner and since she expected the same sort of reception today, she certainly wasn't eager to move in with a pile of luggage, as if she meant to put down roots here.

Staring at the house with great misgivings, Juliet gulped as she parked the car on the circle drive. 'I don't see why we had to bring everything we own,' she muttered to Rosita as she cut the engine. 'Senora Valaquez will probably faint when she sees all this luggage. She'll think we've decided to spend the rest of our lives here.'

'Is not so much,' the housekeeper argued with a careless wave of her hand. 'Is just Senor Will's clothes and yours and mine. Why you worry?'

'Who's worried?' Juliet retorted wryly, then shrugged. 'Well, I suppose we might as well get this over with. Why don't you go knock on the door?'

As Rosita hopped spryly out of the car and disappeared into the shadows beyond the fretted arch entrance, Juliet got out also and began taking suitcases out of the back. She was halted in her task by a manservant dressed all in black.

'Allow me, senorita,' he murmured without smiling. 'I will see to your luggage. The senora awaits you inside.'

Just my luck, Juliet thought with a wry smile as she reluctantly walked across the mosaic tiled patio supported by fluted columns festooned with trailing bougainvillaea vines laden with fragrant scarlet blooms. Going on beneath the fretted arch, she entered the inner courtyard and stopped for a moment to admire the central stone fountain and the hanging baskets of brightly coloured flowers that decorated the wrought iron railing of the second floor balcony. An orange tree in each corner of the courtyard provided shade and a sweet citrus fragrance and Juliet appreciatively inhaled the faintly perfumed air.

At that moment, panelled double doors that opened onto the huge main hall of the house were opened and Senora Valaquez stepped into the courtyard, forcing her patrician features into a stiff smile. 'Welcome to Casa Valaquez, Senorita McKay.'

Juliet stepped forward hesitantly. 'My uncle and I appreciate your hospitality, senora.'

De nada, the senora said with a grand, dismissive wave of her hand. 'It is nothing. *Mi nieto,* my grandson, thought that the fresh air here would hasten your uncle's recuperation. I hope that it will prove so. Now, if you will come inside, I will show you to your room.'

Juliet gestured uncertainly. 'Uh, our

housekeeper, Rosita...'

'She is being shown to her room by our housekeeper. We have put her next to Senor McKay down here on the first floor, where he can move around easily on his wheelchair.'

'A good idea,' Juliet agreed in a murmur as she stepped past Raul's grandmother into the immense main hall. Marble tiles of white and gold covered the floor and the white plastered walls were met with intricately carved mahogany wainscoting. The ceiling was domed and embellished with plaster mouldings. Ancient brass lamps were mounted on the walls beside huge gilt framed mirrors on each side of the hall that reflected the foot of the marble staircase that curved upward to the second floor. A tracery of delicate wrought iron comprised the balustrade and banister and stepping up along the staircase, narrow window embrasures in the wall were covered by more wrought iron, shaped into a matching scroll design.

Though Juliet had seen it all before, she looked around again with a certain amount of awe. Then she caught a glance of sharp jet black eyes sweeping over her denim skirt and casual yet neat pale blue knit shirt but she pretended not to notice the slight distaste those eyes conveyed. 'You have such a beautiful home, senora,' she said instead. 'I've always admired it.'

Alicia Valaquez acknowledged the compliment with only a curt nod. 'Now, senorita, I will show you to your room. It is upstairs.'

'Oh, but I thought I'd be close to Uncle Will,' Juliet blurted out, then gestured apologetically. 'I mean, since his room is on the first floor, shouldn't mine be too?'

'I thought that too,' Senora Valaquez informed her coolly. 'But Raul insisted that you would be more comfortable upstairs. He said your uncle would be fine with the maid and the nurse.'

'Nurse?' Juliet exclaimed softly. 'I didn't realise Raul intended to hire a nurse for Uncle Will. Was that really necessary?'

The senora stroked her thick silver hair which was coiled into a smooth coronet on her crown and stared down her thin aristocratic nose at Juliet. 'If my grandson did not think a nurse was necessary, I am certain he would not have hired one. If you do not agree with his decision, then you should speak to him.'

'Could I? I mean, it's not that I *disagree,* exactly. I just think I should discuss the matter with him. Is he here right now? Could I speak to him?'

'He is here, yes, but he is very busy in his office. I would suggest you wait until dinner tonight to speak with him. He is working now and you would not wish to disturb him, would you?'

'That's the last thing I wish to do, I assure you,' Juliet answered with a wry smile that unfortunately wasn't returned. Heaving a silent sigh then, she followed the senora up the marble stairs and along a wide carpeted hall into the north wing of the house.

Raul's grandmother stopped at last and opened double doors to the most beautiful bedroom Juliet had ever seen. As she stepped inside, her espadrilles sinking down in thick white carpet, her eyes widened in pleasant surprise.

Though the furniture was heavy and dark, typically Spanish, the room's overall decor was light and airy. Aquamarine silk drapes billowed in the breeze that drifted through the French windows that led to the flower-bedecked balcony and they matched the quilted satin coverlet that covered the high wide bed. Cut-glass vases containing fresh red rosebuds graced the gleaming tops of the bureau and ivory-inlaid vanity.

'How lovely,' Juliet said softly. 'It is magnificent, senora.'

'I am pleased you like it,' Alicia Valaquez responded with another of her stiff unenthusiastic smiles. 'Now, I will leave you. Fernando will be up with your luggage in a moment and I will send your maid to help you unpack.'

Juliet nodded, then sighed with relief as Senora Valaquez went out and closed the double doors behind her. Without her dampening presence, Juliet felt free to explore her new accommodations and after a quick look at the original painting of an orange grove that hung on one wall, she wandered out onto the balcony which overlooked another larger courtyard. Potted palms lined the tiled apron of a huge swimming pool, with its azure waters sparkling invitingly in the sunlight.

'Is nice here, eh, *nina?*' Rosita asked as she stepped onto the balcony to join Juliet. 'You like to swim, si? Maybe you wear a teeny little bikini and catch Senor Raul's eye, eh?'

As Rosita cackled gleefully, Juliet dodged the elbow that tried to poke her ribs, then shook her head admonishingly. 'You're impossible, Rosita. I don't have a teeny little bikini and even if I did, I wouldn't wear it to catch any man's eye, especially Raul's.'

'But you would like for him to see you as a woman, eh, *nina?*' Rosita persisted too perceptively. 'If you do not wish to wear the teeny bikini, then you will have to catch his eye in another way. Si?'

'I have no idea what you're talking about,' Juliet lied, spinning around on one heel to walk back into the room. Spotting her luggage sitting on the carpeted floor, she used it to temporarily divert Rosita's attention.

Unpacking was the perfect diversion. During the next twenty minutes, Rosita was far more concerned with shaking wrinkles out of Juliet's dresses than she was in discussing Raul Valaquez. When the last pair of shoes had been tucked neatly into the vast closet, she placed her gnarled hands on scrawny hips and smiled with satisfaction. 'Now, Senor Will is settled in; you are settled in. So I will go downstairs and unpack my own clothes.'

'And I think I'll go visit Uncle Will. Maybe he'd like for me to push his chair out into the courtyard. I'll walk down-stairs with you and you can show me exactly where his room is.'

'Senor Will is sleeping,' Rosita in-formed her. 'The nurse say the ride here tired him.'

'Oh. Well, he needs all the rest he can get.' Staring out the balcony doors, Juliet tapped her forefinger thoughtfully against her cheek. 'I think maybe I'll take a walk then, until he wakes up from his nap.'

After walking down the balcony stairs with Rosita, Juliet strolled across the flower-studded courtyard, past the swim-ming pool, beyond the far border of verdant cypress trees. As she walked across the drive, the glaring sun bore down relentlessly on her bare head so it was a pleasure to reach the shade provided by a sprawling chestnut tree growing by the paddock fence. Leaning on the railing, Juliet rested her chin on her hands and smiled at the lanky yellow dog chasing an equally lanky, long-legged black colt around the grassy paddock, a game both animals seemed to enjoy immensely.

Suddenly, heavy hands descended on Juliet's shoulders and turned her and found herself staring up into a dark face, similar to Raul's and perhaps more classically handsome, though not nearly as intriguing. 'Hello, Pablo,' she murmured with a gentle smile. 'How have you been?'

'How can you ask me that, *mi amante?*' he answered in a dramatic whisper, his black eyes reproachful and heavy lidded. 'You have broken my heart and you ask me how I've been. I have been miserable this past year; that is how I have been.'

Juliet fought a smile. 'I bet your

misery didn't stop you from taking out other girls the past eleven months, did it?'

'There have been girls, yes,' he admitted with a careless shrug. 'But I only went out with them to help me forget you, help me forget how you hurt me by leaving the way you did.'

As his hands went down to clamp around her waist, Juliet sighed and placed her own hands on his arms. 'Look, Pablo, I think maybe you're exaggerating how much I hurt you last year,' she said kindly but firmly. 'I *had* told you often enough I wasn't interested in a romantic relationship and frankly I think you only wanted me because I didn't fall at your feet and worship you the way all the other senoritas seem to do.'

'That isn't true, *mi amante,*' he muttered, releasing her to turn and rake his fingers through his hair. After adopting a tragic pose by bending his head and staring morosely at the ground, he glanced sideways at her as if to see if this performance was being taken seriously. 'I loved you, *querida*. And now that

149

you're here again, I realise I still do. I'll love you forever.'

'You're being overly dramatic again,' she said flatly. 'You've tried all these tricks on me before and they've never worked. I know you're not in love with me because you're too much a playboy to be in love with anyone. Why don't you just admit that you want me because I'm the first girl you've ever met who wasn't eager to marry you? If I accepted your proposal, you'd run like a scared rabbit but since I refuse, you find me intriguing.'

'Try accepting and see what I do, *amada,*' he bluffed outrageously, turning swiftly to haul her into his arms. 'See how fast I run if you say you'll marry me.'

Juliet had to laugh up at him. 'Pablo, you're impossible,' she said, spreading her hands open against his chest to maintain a protective distance between them. Then when an answering smile tugged at the corners of his mouth, she reached up to pat his cheek affectionately. 'Even if you do drive me crazy sometimes, I can't help but like you. So why don't we stop all this silly nonsense and just be friends.'

'Because it isn't friendship I want from you,' he muttered, his smile fading to be replaced by a petulant downcurving of his lips. Throwing her off-balance momentarily by yanking her closer, he proceeded to clamp his mouth down over hers.

Since she had been the unwilling recipient of his kisses before, Juliet knew just what to do. She held herself stiffly in the circle of his arms, her lips pressed firmly together until her lack of response made him so impatient that his kiss became furiously rough, in his vain attempt to use sheer force to part her lips. Infuriated, Juliet dragged her lips away from his, her eyes glittering with irritation as she glared up at him. 'Enough is enough,' she said tersely. 'Let me go right now, Pablo.'

Amazingly, he did. But his black eyes conveyed a sullen, almost childlike stubbornness as they met hers. 'I don't understand you,' he muttered sulkily, thrusting his hands deep into his trouser pockets and kicking at the exposed root of a tree with his toe. A cloud of dust rose, then settled on the highly glossed leather of his Gucci shoe but he didn't seem to notice. 'Why are you being so difficult? Other girls don't mind my kisses.'

He looked so much like a spoiled little boy who had dropped his candy that Juliet almost felt sorry for him. 'Other girls are romantically interested in you but I've told you and told you I don't feel that way,' she said gently. 'If you'd just stop pretending you're madly in love with me, maybe we could be friends.'

'No, never,' he retorted peevishly. 'I won't give up until you agree to marry me. If you'd just give me half a chance, I know I could make you forget that stupid singer you ran off with last year. You've been wasting yourself on him, Juliet. He's a no-talent, impoverished...'

'You happen to be talking about someone very dear to me,' she interrupted, angry colour flooding her cheeks. 'Now, I think you'd better go, Pablo, before I really lose my temper with you.'

He suddenly chuckled confidently and leaned down to brush a kiss across her lips. 'You are so stubborn, *amada,* but you don't fool me. You wouldn't be here at Casa Valaquez right now if you hadn't decided you prefer me to that singer of yours.'

Juliet could only lift her eyes heavenward in disgust, then breathe a disgruntled sigh as Pablo strode blithely away. He hadn't matured one bit in the past year but she had, and this time she wouldn't run away to escape his unwanted attention. If necessary, she would stop trying to be so nice to him and tell him in no uncertain terms why he never would appeal to her. She didn't want to be so blunt but it looked as if he might force her to be. What a stupid, irritating situation, she thought as she slipped her hands into the pockets of her denim skirt. As she turned to stare across the paddock again, a rueful little smile hovered on her lips. Now, if it were only Raul instead of Pablo who was so eager to make her fall in love with him...

'Do you get your thrills from life by teasing young men, Juliet?' Raul's deep voice interrupted her thoughts. As she spun around to face him, his hands gripped her upper arms then slid down-

153

ward to remove hers from her pockets. He moved closer, pressing her against the paddock fence, his eyes glittering dangerously as he lifted her trembling hands up and pinned them against his broad hard chest. 'You aren't really interested in Pablo but you aren't kind enough to simply tell him to leave you alone, are you? I was watching you with him. You don't get rid of a man by touching his cheek or smiling up at him, all wide-eyed and seemingly innocent. You only make him want you more and you know that.'

At the injustice of his accusation, Juliet blushed hotly and struggled to free herself from his iron-hard grip. Her attempts to escape were futile, however, and after a moment, she ceased resisting to stand stiffly before him, her eyes sparkling. 'You always think the worst of me, don't you?' she accused huskily. 'What do you suggest I do to make Pablo leave me alone? I've tried telling him I'm not romantically interested in him but maybe you think I should slap his face or do something else equally dramatic so he'll finally get the message. I was only trying to be nice to him; I don't want to hurt his feelings but here you are, accusing me of being a tease. Well, I'm not!' Her voice broke on the last word and her chin wobbled slightly as the anger in her eyes vanished to be replaced by rather vulnerable appeal. 'Why can't I do anything to please you? What have I ever done to make you dislike me so much? Do you suggest I try to have a personality transplant? Or would you still dislike me, even if I could change myself completely?'

Raul's lean features hardened. 'Don't try your wiles on me, Juliet. You may get more than you bargained for. You know very well that I don't dislike you. I disapprove of you but I don't dislike you. In fact, I think I like you much more than I should.'

'You don't either,' she whispered bleakly, her voice revealingly tremulous. 'You—you act like you hate me.'

With a sudden roughly muttered imprecation, Raul pulled her to him, his muscular arms encircling her waist. Green eyes flared with passion as he gazed down at her and as her lips parted, his fingers tangled almost roughly in the silky hair that tumbled down her back. 'God, you really know how to wrap a man around your little finger, don't you?' he groaned. 'How can a boy like Pablo be expected to resist you, when I can't resist you myself?'

'Raul, *please,* you're wrong about me, I...'Juliet's words broke off with a soft gasp as he swiftly lowered his head and tantalised her with firm seeking kisses over the madly beating pulse in her throat, up along the smooth line of her jaw. She trembled as shivers of awareness radiated out over every inch of skin in response to his caressing touch. The warmth of his flesh seemed to sear her through the thin fabric of his white shirt and her hands slipped inside his unbuttoned vest to stroke his lean sides. Her breath caught as he pressed burning kisses into the slight hollows of her cheeks, against her close eyelids and along the creamy skin of her throat. Whispering her name, he caressed the delicate contours of her ear with the tip of his tongue, then nibbled the soft fleshy lobe until she moved eagerly against him. Making her wait, he alternately kissed first one corner then the other of her mouth. And when her small fingers tangled in the thick dark hair on his nape, his hard lips covered hers with hungry compelling swiftness. Juliet moaned softly; a keen aching flared to life deep within her and kindled fires that warmed and weakened her lower limbs as her slender arms encircled his neck.

With a soft groan, he led her beneath the low boughs of the chestnut tree and lowered her to the soft bed of grass. His marauding lips explored the parted tenderness of her and his hand was still tangled in her hair, pillowing her head. The lean strength of his muscular body pressed her down into the springy mattress of turf and one long leg pinned both hers with evocative weight.

Unfamiliar desires coursed through her, like fire in her veins as his tongue tasted hers. Her mouth opened slightly, eagerly and she arched against him.

'I *need* you,' he whispered huskily, lifting his dark head only to retake her lips, urgently at first, then with slow compelling gentleness, his plundering mouth possessing hers. His teeth closed on her lower lip, then the satiny skin of her throat, nibbling tenderly.

Her body seemed to melt against his warmth as his hand trailed along the rounded side of her breast, down to her waist, and lower, to the gentle outsweep of her hips. Her heart leaped as he breathed her name against the madly beating pulse in her throat. Almost of their own volition, her fingers slipped inside his shirt, her nails catching in the fine dark hair on his chest as she traced the muscular contours of flesh and bone. He was so invitingly warm, so over-whelmingly male that she delighted in touching him as much as she delighted in being touched. *'Coqueta, atormenda-tora,'* he muttered huskily, his lean hands grazing upward to cup her breasts. His fingers pressed gently into the cushioned fullness; his palms brushed slowly back and forth over the straining aroused peaks. A tremor shook her slight body and his lips hardened on hers for a tanta-lising moment, then he lifted his head slightly. Leaning on one elbow beside her, he brushed her tousled hair back from her cheeks. As her eyes flickered open, then were lost in the hot glow burning in his, he pushed aside the straps of her shirt, baring creamy smooth shoulders to kisses that he pressed into the delicate hollows. His lips sought the slight curving of her breasts above her bodice, then the scented shadowed hollow between, arousing desires in her she had never before experienced.

Trembling fingers explored his lean face, tracing the sensuous outline of his lips and as he caught one fingertip between his teeth, her drowsy gaze was captured and held by the spellbinding message of his. 'Kiss me again,' she whispered compulsively. And he did, with dizzying thoroughness, gently twisting her soft lips beneath his. She was yielding completely to his superior strength, almost lost in the moment, until his hands on her hips pressed her against the hardening ridge of his body, alerting her to the danger she was inviting. Inexperienced as she was, she knew what his response meant and she also knew she couldn't satisfy the desire his body was conveying. She struggled instinctively. 'Don't. *Don't!*' she whispered imploringly. 'Raul, please, let me go.'

'*Atormentadora,*' he muttered again, more accusingly this time, but he released her and sat up. Raking his fingers through his hair, he allowed his dark gaze to sweep over her as she sat up too, then a self-derisive smile played over his lips. 'Yes. You *do* know how to wrap a man around your finger. You know I can't criticise Pablo for wanting you, when I can't keep my hands off you myself.'

Juliet winced and reached out to him but he rose lithely to his feet and strode away, without a backward glance. As she watched him go, she stood also on unsteady legs, then leaned wearily against the rough trunk of the tree. A desolate expression settled on her delicate features and she closed her eyes with a soft moan. What was happening to her? How could she be so drawn to Raul when he thought she was a heartless little flirt, a tease? Pride alone should make it easy for her to resist his touch but it never worked that way at all and she was miserable. If only he felt more for her than a mere physical attraction,

160

she wouldn't feel ashamed of her response to him. But he didn't and as she reminded herself of that fact, she drew a deep shuddering breath. Unshed tears burned behind her eyes; she felt as if she had been through an emotional wringer. And *he* had called *her* the tormentor.

CHAPTER 6

Will McKay strummed his fingers on the armrests of his wheelchair. As he stared out across the courtyard toward the pool, he shook his head and smiled ruefully. 'So it was Pablo who was the villain in this situation. But I suppose I'm to blame too for believing him when he said you were in love with him but afraid to marry him because you didn't think you would ever fit into such an aristocratic wealthy family. I thought your fears were foolish and that's the only reason I tried to persuade you to accept his proposal—because I thought you really did want to marry him. You silly

161

child, I never would try to push you into a loveless arranged marriage.'

Juliet leaned forward in her rattan chair to squeeze his hand, releasing her breath in an exaggerated sigh of relief. 'That's the best news I've heard in a long time. I really was confused last year when you kept insisting I marry him. You've always been such a romantic; then, all of a sudden, you *seemed* to be pushing me into an arranged marriage and you were so insistent about it, that I just decided to leave. I love you and I hated arguing with you all the time.'

Will smiled at her but his lips trembled slightly and there was a suspicious dampness in his eyes. At last, he cleared his throat and nodded. 'I love you too, child. You must know that. I would have been a lonely old man the past nine years without you. I want you to know how grateful I am to you for the happiness you've given me.'

'Oh, Uncle Will,' Juliet murmured, her own voice thick with emotion as he stroked her cheek. 'You have no reason to be grateful to me; it's the other way around. I owe you everything. Without you, I would have been a real orphan.' Her expression became regretfully pensive and she chewed her lower lip. 'I just wish I hadn't run away last year. I should have stayed; we could have talked and straightened out our misunderstanding. I'm really sorry now that I left the way I did.'

'I'm sorry too, and I hope you didn't get involved with that disreputable rock singer simply because you were upset with me,' Will said, his tone sharpening. 'You should have known your relationship with him wouldn't last.'

'Oh, no, not you too,' Juliet groaned, then shook her head emphatically. 'Uncle Will, I never was involved with Benny the way you obviously think. He was and still is just a very dear friend. Why does everybody assume he and I were—uh, living together for the past eleven months?'

'You mean you weren't?'

'No! Absolutely not!'

'Oh, thank God,' Will breathed, relaxing back in the wheelchair. He raked his fingers through his thinning grey-brown hair, then gave Juliet a somewhat stern stare. 'But I don't think you should be surprised that everyone assumes you and this Benny fellow were romantically involved. What else could we all think? When a young man and woman run off together, it's usually because they think they're in love. Isn't it?'

'Well, yes, I guess so,' she conceded reluctantly, then spread her hands in a resigned gesture. 'It just never occurred to me that everyone would jump to that conclusion, maybe because I've never had any romantic feelings for Benny.'

'I'm glad to hear you're not completely lacking in good taste then,' Will responded with an unusual lack of tolerance. 'That is a very shabby young man. And I guess he sings obscene lyrics to the accompaniment of loud, disharmonious noise he calls music.'

'No, he doesn't as a matter of fact. He happens to be a very talented guitarist and his repertoire of Old English and Early American ballads and folk songs is extensive. He's a very popular performer in coffee houses, especially now that Holly's singing with him.'

'Who's Holly?'

'Benny's wife. He married her about a month after we left Granada last year,' Juliet explained, then proceeded to tell him all about her travelling companions, ending with Holly's confinement in the hospital.

By the time she had finished, Will's opinion of Benny had changed completely. 'Well, I can see I misjudged that young man,' he said with an apologetic grimace. 'I guess it was that unkempt hair and those patched jeans that gave me the wrong impression. Think you can forgive an old man for being so prejudiced?'

'I think I can,' Juliet assured him. 'I suppose we all have our little prejudices.'

'Umm, I suppose,' Will murmured absently, stroking his chin with his thumb and forefinger. He shifted his position, taking care not to jostle his leg cast. 'Well, I'd like to do something for Benny and Holly. If she's going to have to stay in the hospital for several weeks, the bill's going to be outrageous. Could I— do you think they'd let me help them pay it?'

'I doubt it,' Juliet answered honestly.

'Benny wasn't even very receptive to my offer of help. But I finally persuaded him to let me use some of my trust fund if they really need money.'

'Your trust fund?' Will exclaimed, shaking his head. 'No, honey, you come to me if Benny and Holly need help. I don't want you making withdrawals from your trust fund.' He smiled teasingly. 'After all, it'll make a very nice dowry.'

'If I have to pay a man to marry me, then I'll just stay single, thank you,' she replied pertly, then pretended to be very hurt. 'Besides, I didn't know I was such a disaster that I'd have to buy myself a husband.'

Her uncle laughed. 'Judging by the way Pablo chases after you, you have nothing to worry about. I'm sure he'd be willing to buy you, if Raul would be willing to give him the money.'

'Hah! Well, then don't expect Pablo to be making any cash offers,' Juliet announced rather resentfully. 'Raul wouldn't give him a peso to buy *me.*'

Will eyed her speculatively. 'You sound as if you think Raul doesn't like you? Why should you think that? I always thought he acted very fond of you.'

'Maybe he was a little fond of me. Last year. But—oh, it doesn't matter,' Juliet evaded, forcing a cheery smile to her lips. 'I've just thought of the perfect way to help Benny save a little money. We could let him stay at the house in Granada while we're staying here. That way, he won't have to pay for a hotel room. Would you mind if he stayed there?'

'I think it's a fine idea,' Will agreed happily, forgetting about Raul as Juliet had hoped he would. 'In fact, Benny would be doing me a favour by staying there. Even in Granada, there are bur- glaries so it would be less likely to happen to us, if Benny stays at the house.'

'Terrific. If I tell Benny that, he'll be more likely to accept the offer.'

'Fine,' Will said with a satisfied smile. 'Well, now that's settled, how about playing some poker?'

Juliet grimaced comically. 'You wouldn't be willing to play Crazy Eights instead, would you?'

'No. Poker. We won't bet since you're

not a very proficient player yet.'

'That's an understatement if I ever heard one,' Juliet quipped, watching warily as her uncle took a deck of cards from the side pocket of his wheelchair, shuffled them, then dealt them five cards apiece.

'Now, this is called five-card draw,' he informed her. 'Remember?'

'That much I remember,' she answered wryly. 'After that, I'm lost.' Picking up her cards, she wrinkled her nose disgustedly. She had nothing except three hearts so she discarded a spade and a club and when Uncle Will dealt her two more cards, they weren't hearts so she still had nothing, not even a measly pair.

Will won that hand with a pair of threes and during the next half hour, Juliet won only twice, once with a pair of tens and once almost by default because she held the high card when neither of them had hands worth anything. At last, however, she was lucky. Holding a pair of aces and a pair of queens, she thought she would undoubtedly win.

Will, however, laid down three nines. 'Sorry, honey,' he said sympathetically.

'But three of a kind beats two pairs.'

'Are you sure?' she muttered, staring at the cards on the wrought iron table. 'That doesn't seem fair.'

Will chuckled indulgently, shuffled the cards and dealt again. This time, Juliet broke the cardinal rule of poker. Discarding one of the four spades she held, she hoped to be dealt a seven to fill out a possible straight. She didn't get the seven and when she laid down her cards in disgust, Will glanced up at her suspiciously. 'You didn't discard a spade before, did you?' he asked hopefully and when she nodded, he groaned. 'Oh, honey, why did you do that? One more spade and you would have had a flush and a flush always beats a straight.'

'It does? But I thought a straight beat a flush. Oh, I'm all confused.'

Will shook his head admonishingly, adding, 'And never, never draw to an inside straight.'

'A what?' she exclaimed bewilderedly. 'Oh, this is ridiculous. I don't even know what an inside straight is.' As Will started to patiently explain, she shook her head and threw up her hands in defeat. 'It's useless, Uncle Will, today at least. Maybe we could practice again tomorrow. Right now, couldn't we play something I understand, like Go Fish?'

'Go Fish?' he exclaimed softly, obviously not enthusiastic. But at last he nodded. 'Oh, all right but just one...' His words halted and he smiled as Senora Valaquez stepped out into the courtyard and walked across the flagstone toward them, smoothing the skirt of her mauve linen dress.

'*Buenas tardes,* Senor McKay, senorita,' she said with a polite yet stiff little smile. 'I wanted to come ask how you are feeling this afternoon. But I see you must be better, since you are playing cards. You are playing poker perhaps? That is a game my husband Fredrico and I sometimes played.' She pursed her lips into a moue. 'I must confess I was never very good at it.'

'That makes two of us,' Juliet announced wryly, then impulsively added, 'Would you like to join us, senora. We're about to play a game much simpler than poker, called Go Fish.'

'Go Fish?' the senora queried, frowning slightly. *'Que es* Go Fish? Is it a difficult game to learn, senor?'

'Hardly,' Will answered, chuckling. 'The only objective is to make pairs. Please sit down and join us and I'll explain.'

To Juliet's amazement, Alicia Valaquez did join them and after a brief explanation of the simplistic rules, the game began. But they weren't allowed to finish. Will's nurse, an enormous woman with a perpetual scowl strode purposefully into the courtyard and made a beeline for his wheelchair.

'Is time for siesta, senor,' she commanded rather than informed, pulling his chair away from the table the moment he laid down his cards. 'Doctor say you need much rest.'

Will shot Juliet an apologetic glance. 'Sorry to stop the game just when you were winning, honey.'

Juliet gestured dismissively. 'Ah well, I think I'll survive without winning this one game. Besides, Nurse Lopez is right. You should rest.'

Will had no chance to do more than lift his hand in a wave as he was

hurriedly whisked away by his stout pro-
tectress. With his departure, there was a
sudden silence at the wrought iron table.
As Juliet scooped all the cards into a neat
stack, she sensed Senora Valaquez was
watching her and glanced up with a
hesitant smile.

''You are fond of your uncle, are you
not, senorita?' Alicia Valaquez asked
abruptly, though her tone was somewhat
less unfriendly than usual. 'You seem to
have a very warm regard for him.'

'I love Uncle Will,' Juliet said simply.
'He's been very good to me.'

'Then why did you leave his house last
year?' the senora asked bluntly. 'Surely
you knew he would be very upset?'

'Now, I realise I shouldn't have left,'
Juliet admitted, rising to her feet as
Senora Valaquez did. 'Our problem was
really just a misunderstanding which we
should have discussed but we didn't.
And I went away because I didn't want to
upset him by arguing with him.'

'And this argument would have been
about Pablo, si?' the older woman questioned, her tone hardening. 'You did not
wish to marry my grandson and your

uncle wanted you to?'

'So I thought but he thought I was in love with Pablo and I—well, I just wasn't,' Juliet told her gently, not wanting to insult her. 'I guess that was just a misunderstanding between Pablo and me.'

Senora Valaquez didn't look pleased. 'The men of my country have volatile emotions, senorita,' she said tersely. 'It is not wise for any young woman to trifle with the affections of a passionate man.'

'Oh, but I didn't. I...'

'But your excuse is that you are so young, I suppose,' Alicia Valaquez interrupted, then conceded begrudgingly, 'At least you are fond of your uncle. That is commendable.'

As Raul's grandmother turned and glided away, Juliet smiled ruefully. Since that was as close as she would probably ever come to getting a compliment from Senora Valaquez, she supposed she should cherish it, even if it had been given reluctantly. With a sigh, she picked up the deck of cards and walked into the house, wondering how to occupy herself now that her uncle was napping. This

173

morning she had gone for her daily swim and it simply seemed too hot to go for a walk so she decided she didn't have much choice except to go to her room and read. As she wandered along the main hall, gazing down at the lovely muted gold and white tile flooring, she wasn't watching where she was going and suddenly ran directly into Raul as he stepped out of his office. The collision caused her to drop the deck of cards and as they scattered on the floor at their feet, Raul grasped her upper arms to steady her.

'I'm sorry,' she murmured rather breathlessly, gazing up at him. Even after being at Casa Valaquez for over two weeks, she still felt quite ill at ease in his presence. And being held close enough to him to feel the heat emanating from his body now made her doubly aware of his vital male magnetism and her own unconquerable susceptibility to it. Easing free of his grasp, she knelt down to begin gathering the scattered cards, chewing her lower lip as he came down on his heels beside her to help. When they had retrieved every card, Raul stood again, drawing her up with him but still he said nothing, though his dark gaze drifted lazily from her small sandaled feet upward to the flaming auburn hair that framed her appealingly small, upturned face.

'Well, uh, I—I was just going to my room,' she announced squeakily, disconcerted as usual by his appraisal. 'Thanks for helping me pick up the cards and I'm sorry I bumped into you. I guess I wasn't looking where I was going.'

As she started to turn away, Raul caught one small hand in his. 'Is something wrong, Juliet?' his voice low and melodious. 'You look a little forlorn.'

'I...No, nothing's wrong.'

'You're sure? Your friend Holly isn't worse, is she?'

'Holly? Oh no, she's feeling better now, though she hates being stuck in that hospital bed,' Juliet said rather weakly, surprised that he even remembered Holly's name. Then she shrugged. 'But I guess she's just feeling restless, like I am. We're both accustomed to being busy.'

'Busy?' Raul questioned, raising one dark eyebrow. 'How busy can you be while you're riding around in a van?'

Juliet gazed down at his thumb brushing slowly back and forth across the smooth sensitive skin on the back of her hand, wishing she wouldn't be so unnerved by such meaningless caresses. Without looking back up at him, she lifted her slight shoulders in another shrug. 'We weren't hoboes, Raul. Actually, we didn't spend all that much time on the road. I made bookings in towns as close together as possible. Holly and Benny spent most of their time rehearsing while I kept up with our income and expenses and got as many bookings in advance as I could.'

'I see,' he said flatly, giving no indication of whether or not this new information impressed him. But there was an almost wry note in his voice with his next question. 'Why did Benny and Holly rehearse? A great deal of rock music sounds very impromptu.'

'Benny and Holly aren't into rock music,' Juliet said rather wearily, then gave him the same explanation she had given her uncle. She glanced up at him almost belligerently when she had finished. He only smiled. 'Sort of modern-day troubadors eh? Are they good?'

'They're very good,' she said loyally and truthfully. 'Benny has a rich baritone voice and Holly's a superb soprano. You wouldn't believe how they can harmonise.'

'I'd like to hear them some time,' Raul said, the creases in his lean cheeks deepening when he noted her expression of surprise. But then his smile faded and he lifted her hand, idly playing with the tips of her fingers. 'Now why don't you tell me why you're feeling so restless here. When you're not with Will, you could swim or go riding, or even take the Esprit and drive into Granada.'

'Oh, I know, but all those things are such leisurely ways to spend every day. I guess I just don't feel very useful except when I'm keeping Uncle Will company.' She paused as an idea formulated in her mind and before she could lose her nerve, she blurted it out. 'But you're busy, Raul. Maybe I could help you. With all those galleries, you must have a lot of paperwork. You wouldn't have any filing or typing I could do, would you?'

Raul's eyes narrowed enigmatically as

he shook his head. 'Senorita Domecq handles all that for me. Remember?'

Unhappily, Juliet did. Senorita Domecq was his middle-aged secretary who always dressed in grey, never talked and moved wraithlike, sort of like a ghost through the house, but Raul had once mentioned that she was a supremely efficient employee. Giving him a disappointed smile, she nodded. 'Well, I suppose I'll just have to think of some other way to occupy myself, won't I?'

For a long moment, he didn't answer but his dark gaze held hers and finally he squeezed her hand slightly then released it. 'If you're really serious about helping me, there is something you could do. Do you have any plans for tonight?' When she shook her head, he inclined his. 'Good. Then you will go to a party with me.'

'A party?' Juliet exclaimed softly, absolutely flabbergasted he would consider taking her out for a social evening. She stared at him, her disbelief unhidden. 'I don't understand how I'd be helping you with your work by going to a party.'

178

'Because I'm only going for business reasons,' Raul explained. 'A local patron of the arts is honouring a young painter who's making quite an impression on most of the European critics. I'd like to talk to him about placing his work in our galleries.'

'Oh. I see. But why would you want to take me? Why not Jemena Ruiz? I'm sure she'd be of more help to you than I would. And besides—I'm really not much of a partying person.'

'All the better. You'll be perfect then because I'm getting weary of these parties and tonight I only want to talk to Luis Diego, then leave. If I ask Jemena to go with me, I'll never get away. She never tires of going to parties.'

'So you want to take me because I won't object to leaving early?' Juliet ascertained, aware of the slight sense of disappointment nagging at her. 'Why don't you just go alone then?'

'No,' Raul replied curtly, his expression darkening. 'I don't want to go alone to this party, especially, and since you did volunteer to help me with my work, I'm taking you. Be ready at nine, please.

We'll arrive late and leave early to make up for it. Agreed?'

'Well, I...'

'Agreed,' he pronounced, the look in his eyes brooking no argument as he strode back to his office without another word.

After watching him close the door, Juliet lifted her shoulders in a slight shrug and did the only thing she could do under the circumstances. She went up to her room to decide what would be appropriate to wear that evening.

Seeing Raul, so darkly attractive in a cream-coloured casual suit and a tobacco brown shirt open at the collar, Juliet was glad she had chosen to wear something simple. Actually, she had to admit to herself that she had chosen the forest green floor-length jersey mainly because it was the same colour as Raul's eyes but the choice had been appropriate anyway. With a scooped neckline and cap sleeves, the dress was neither too plain nor too fancy and it accented her softly curvaceous body enough to make her feel very feminine while at the same time demure. And as she walked down the curving marble staircase, to join Raul in the vast hall, he too seemed quite aware of her femininity. Bold green eyes swept over her as he held out his hand when she reached the next to last step.

'*Preciosa,*' he murmured, holding her gaze as she blushed slightly at the word that needed no translation. Then he led her out through the courtyard into the star-studded night. A black Mercedes gleamed in the light of a full cream-coloured moon. After he had opened the passenger door for her, then came around to slide his long legs beneath the steering column, Juliet surrendered to aroused curiosity. 'Isn't this your grandmother's car? Where is yours?'

'In the garage for a tune-up.' Raul smiled mischievously. 'Abuela begrudgingly consented to let me borrow hers tonight, a rare honour, I assure you. She doesn't like for anyone else to drive it.'

'I noticed her driving away the other day and was a little surprised that she doesn't have a chauffeur.'

'She enjoys driving too much to let anyone do it for her.' Raul laughed softly. 'She is something of a...What is it they say in America? A speed devil?'

'Almost. A speed demon,' Juliet supplied the correct terminology, then shook her head musingly. 'It's hard for me to imagine your grandmother tearing along the road in her car, though. She's so—so sedate.'

'Oh, but she's not quite as stiff-laced as she sometimes seems.'

'Obviously not,' Juliet said wryly. 'And I guess I did get a glimpse of her warmer side this afternoon. She actually played cards with Uncle Will and me. And he teased her quite a bit, almost flirted, and I think she really enjoyed it.'

Raul nodded. 'I'm not surprised. Abuela can be quite the *coqueta*.' Looking away from the straight ribbon of road that stretched out before them, he eyed Juliet speculatively. 'If she was willing to play cards with you, she must not disapprove of you as much as you thought she did.'

'I wouldn't go so far as to say that,' Juliet murmured, then hastily changed the subject. 'I've been meaning to ask you: what's your full name? I mean,

Spaniards always have a long string of them but I've never known what all yours are. Do you mind telling me?'

'Why should I mind?' Raul answered, turning his attention back to the road with a rather bored shrug. 'If you're really interested, my name is Raul Esteban Rodrigo Valaquez Madrigal, Madrigal being my mother's maiden name which is always added at the end, an old custom of respect.'

'Well, that's some name, quite a mouthful,' Juliet said teasingly, then added, 'I just wondered if I should start calling you Don Raul. The servants do.'

Raul glanced at her again, his eyes narrowing. Then a slight, suggestive smile curved his lips. 'I think we can dispense with such formalities, don't you, Juliet, considering some of the moments we've shared?' When she tensed and swiftly looked away to stare out her window, he laughed softly, almost triumphantly. 'Now, since you didn't succeed in changing the subject, why don't you answer my question? Are you finding my grandmother less disapproving of you than you thought she would be?'

'Not really,' Juliet murmured honestly, twisting her hands together in her lap. 'She did express some surprise that I'm fond of Uncle Will; she even went so far as to say my affection for him is commendable. But, she still obviously thinks I played fast and loose with Pablo.' Biting back a sigh, when no response from Raul was forthcoming, she had to assume that he agreed with his grandmother. For a moment she was tempted to try to defend herself again, but finally, she decided she would be wasting her time. Raul had made up his mind about her and nothing she could say would change it. Subsiding against the armrest on her door, she stared morosely out at the blocks of modern apartments that heralded the suburbs of Granada.

A minute or so later, Raul swung the Mercedes off the road into a circular drive before a gleaming high-rise building. As he lifted himself out of the car, a boy with a friendly beaming smile loped over to take the keys and stand patiently by the open door while a doorman, resplendent in an ivory and black uniform, helped Juliet out on the passenger side.

Inside the building, as Juliet and Raul crossed the luxuriously appointed, gold-carpeted lobby toward a bank of elevators, she looked around curiously then lifted her eyebrows as he guided her to the open elevator set a little apart from the rest. As Raul pushed one of the control buttons, the doors glided closed noiselessly then they were whisked upward to the opulent entrance foyer of the penthouse. A white jacketed man-servant, apparently there to intercept possible gatecrashers, bowed stiffly and murmured a welcome as they stepped off the elevator. Then he moved swiftly to open double doors behind which could be heard the muffled chink of innumerable glasses and the buzz of many voices talking at once.

'I guess art patrons do have to be wealthy,' Juliet remarked innocently, then wondered if she had said the wrong thing as Raul's strong jaw and his hand cupping her elbow tightened simultaneously as he replied, 'Our hostess, Janine Elcano, is a very wealthy widow and it is of course very chic to become a patron of the arts.'

Juliet detected what she imagined was a slight hint of sarcasm in his tone but she couldn't be sure and didn't dare question him as they proceeded into a vast room filled with small groups and milling people. A squeal of delight accompanied their entrance and in half a second Raul was being embraced by a tall svelte woman in her thirties with natural platinum blonde hair and expertly made up baby blue eyes. She *was* chic in a slinky black silk dress supported by narrow rhinestoned straps. Long crimson-tipped fingers spread across Raul's shoulders as she leaned back after kissing him to smile beckoningly.

'Darling, you're late,' she cooed, pursing her crimson glossed lips into a little pout that detracted not at all from her natural beauty yet nonetheless made her look rather silly. 'I was beginning to think you weren't going to come. I know you don't care for these parties of mine, but I did promise you we could be alone after the masses had departed. I'm so glad you decided to come.'

Something almost perverse made

186

Juliet cough softly and as the woman, obviously Janine Elcano, turned her baby blues in her direction, she smiled then glanced at Raul.

'Janine, this is Senorita Juliet McKay,' he said with something like relief as he extricated himself from the woman's clinging hands. 'Juliet, our hostess, Senora Janine Elcano.'

'Senorita,' the older woman said stiffly without even a forced smile. 'Welcome to my home.'

Though the welcome was blatantly insincere, Juliet pretended not to notice and only smiled. The hostess, however, was not to be outdone. Glancing across the crowded room with a slight frown, she at last gained the attention of a young man and when she beckoned imperiously, he trotted over to her.

'Rex, darling, would you entertain this young lady while I talk to Raul a moment,' she asked, her voice nearly dripping with saccharine sweetness as she looked at Juliet. 'Rex is my cousin, visiting from the States so the two of you should have a great deal in common.' Then with a considerably more enthusiastic smile for Raul, she attached her hands around his arm as if he were a lifeline and started to move away.

'Excuse me, Juliet, but Janine knows I wish to speak to Luis Diego,' he said softly. And as he walked away with his possessive hostess, he added, 'Don't you, Janine?'

After seeing Janine gaze up at him with another pout, Juliet turned to smile at Rex. He smiled back then looked her over and obviously after finding her attractive enough, took her hand between both of his and began stroking it too familiarly. 'How'd you get hooked up with Raul Valaquez?' he asked nosily. 'You're a little young for him, aren't you?'

'How long have you been in Spain?' Juliet evaded his question, squelching the desire to snatch her hand away. Instead, she merely slipped it slowly from his grasp. There was something about Rex she didn't find at all appealing. Though he was handsome enough, tall with dark brown hair and his cousin's baby blue eyes, there was little sign of intelligence in his features. And he looked at her with one of those half-sneering smiles that seemed to say she should be falling at his feet in adoration. Deciding she could do without his dubious attention, she commenced a chatter that was certain to send him on his way. 'Don't you just love Spain?' she enthused. 'I do. There's such a timelessness about it, don't you think? And I'm just fascinated by the Moorish influence on the country's history. Aren't you?'

'Uh, well, I guess so,' Rex muttered, shuffling his feet uncomfortably as he looked around. Then he snapped his fingers and stepped away from her. 'You won't mind if I leave you for a minute, will you?' he asked hopefully. 'I just spied a friend of mine I haven't seen for a while. Be right back.'

Smiling to herself as he scurried away, Juliet looked around the room. A thick white carpet cushioned her feet and there was a preponderance of chrome and glass tables and white upholstered furniture, with colour accents provided by canvases on the walls that were splashed with bold reds, greens and blues. She glanced around and after seeing Raul talking to a young man with a clipped black moustache, she headed down the steps into the sunken conversation pit. Sections of a white velvet sofa surrounded a glass and chrome table. The three men and two women who were sitting there were engaged in conversation and didn't even glance in her direction as she sat down. Despite Janine's *haute couture* black silk dress, Juliet didn't feel she had come too casual. Other guests had taken much less care with their appearance than she had. Some of the men were in jeans and flowing shirts and a few of the women wore baggy trousers and flowing shirts they might well have borrowed from the men.

On the table before Juliet sat a modern sculpture. A circle of plaster with a hole in the centre, it seemed to be a fairly good representation of an upright doughnut and after she lost interest in trying to find a deeper meaning in it, she began to people-watch.

An hour and a half later, she was becoming very bored. All these people seemed the same and from the snatches of conversation she had heard made by the guests who were English or American, they all seemed to have a very high regard for their intelligence, a sort of superiority complex that suggested that they thought they were a step above the common man. During the time she had sat on the sofa, only one person had spoken to her, an Englishwoman all in black. 'Do you sculpt or paint?' she had asked. When Juliet had said that she did neither, the woman had responded with an 'Oh, *really?*' that sounded as if she had never met such an untalented creature. Then she had quickly departed. Not that Juliet much cared. All in all, this gathering reminded her of a snobbish college clique and she could certainly understand why Raul didn't adore these parties. She herself would rather have been with Rosita, who was real and had common sense to complement an innate intelligence.

Unfortunately, Rosita wasn't at the party and since Raul was still talking to the moustachioed man, Juliet settled more comfortably on the sofa, only to become the unwilling witness to an argument. The Englishwoman in the black caftan, her greying brown hair bunched in a topknot on her crown was sitting on the sofa opposite Juliet. And she was visibly bristling, her dangling copper earrings dancing as she shook her head at the man seated beside her.

'Really, Devery, you're becoming more and more like those bloody American critics who go into a swoon every time a realist comes along,' she was saying crossly. 'What is so bloody fabulous about this Diego chap? Simply because he paints old decrepit sheep sheds and baskets of olives sitting on stone steps doesn't mean he's God's latest gift to the art world.'

'Perhaps you don't really understand realistic painting, Margaret,' Devery countered blandly, his own accent distinctly British. 'There was an excellent programme on the telly the other night about the impact of realism in art. Of course it was narrated in Spanish but you know the language well. Did you happen to see it?'

'Most certainly not,' Margaret snorted. 'You know I never ever watch the telly.'

'Pity,' Devery retorted. 'You might

have learned something about realistic painting.'

'Well, really, Dev, you sound as if you think I'm totally ignorant. I happen to know quite a lot about realistic painting, certainly enough to know its highly over-rated. And this fuss made over this Diego boy is a perfect example. I say he lacks imagination. His paintings look like photographs. Who cares about olives in a basket? Maybe the public thinks that's art but I don't think Diego is the genius everyone makes him out to be. His forms are too sharp, too definite, lacking in warmth.'

'What rot,' Devery responded succinctly. 'He's a master of light and texture. One can almost believe he could pluck the smooth firm olives from the rough woven basket. And the way he uses light and shadow to add more realism is exquisite. And I'm not alone in thinking he might well be our modern-day Rembrandt.'

'Too harsh,' Margaret persisted heatedly, waving her gaunt hands excitedly. 'Why should anyone buy a painting so detailed that it looks like a photograph?

One would save a great deal of money by buying an instant camera.'

Devery laughed heartily. 'This all sounds a bit like envy. Are you sure you believe Diego is untalented or are you actually perturbed at yourself because you haven't the willpower and patience to do more than dapple in pastels and create blurred images? Hmm, Margaret? Why don't you admit you might have been a much more successful artist if you weren't too lazy to add detail to your work?'

'I'll admit no such thing!' she cried defensively, jerking her head so violently that her topknot of hair bobbed. '*I* create moods; I'm an impressionist! And do please stop calling me Margaret when you know damned well I prefer to be called Mag or Maggie.'

'Ah yes, Mag,' Devery quipped. 'That's more in keeping with the Bohemian image you like to project, is it not?'

As answer, Mag merely sniffed at him, spun on one heel and marched away, her copper necklace swinging back and forth across her flat chest.

194

Juliet yawned, noticing that as Devery walked away he was smiling with almost perverse satisfaction. Then as she quickly stifled the yawn that threatened to follow the first, she was joined on the sofa by a young man in his late twenties. Smiling, he handed her a glass filled with iced amber liquid, which she accepted with murmured thanks.

'Ah, you're American. So am I,' the man said giving her another genuinely friendly smile. 'The name's David Judson; maybe you've heard it. I've been watching you sitting here all alone and thought it was high time you had some company. Do you mind?'

Juliet didn't mind at all. There seemed to be something different about this man, perhaps a real quality in his personality that she found refreshing. During the next ten minutes as they talked, he mercifully never once played the pseudo intellectual and only after they had discussed their impressions of Spain, did he bring up art.

'I'm a portrait painter,' he said modestly, allowing his gaze to wander over her for the first time. 'And I know this might sound like a come-on but I think you'd be a terrific model. That russet hair and creamy complexion and those luminous eyes...' He paused, then grinned charmingly. 'What do you say? Would you be willing to let me paint you?'

Juliet hesitated, her mind occupied with the name David Judson, which rang a bell in her memory. Then she realised she had heard of him and that he was one of the most respected portrait painters in the States. So she supposed she should consider it quite an honour that he had asked her to be the subject for one of his works. 'You really think I'd do?' she questioned rather shyly. 'I mean, I'm certainly no raving beauty.'

'There's a quality about you,' Judson assured her earnestly. 'And if I could capture that quality on canvas, I'd have a masterpiece, I'm sure of it. So, how about it? Will you come to my studio and let me paint you? Please.'

Juliet gestured uncertainly. 'Well, I don't know. I...'

'Sorry, Judson, Juliet hasn't the time to be one of your models,' Raul interrupted curtly from behind them. As she jerked around to look up at him, his green eyes burned into her. Then he came around, took her drink from her hand, and unceremoniously drew her up to stand before him. 'Time to go, Juliet.'

She had no chance to utter a word as she was hauled away but she did manage to cast an apologetic glance back over her shoulder to David who simply shrugged resignedly in response. And before she could protest Raul's impolite behaviour, they were waylaid by Jemena Ruiz, who was dazzling in a white satin lounging suit.

'Are you leaving so early, Raul?' she asked querulously. Then she glared at Juliet as if she was certain their precipitous departure must be the younger girl's fault. She stepped around in front of Raul, her slender hands sliding down his arms. 'Do not go just yet, *por favor, querido*. I have hardly talked to you at all. You have spent almost all evening with Diego and of course Janine has monopolised the remainder of your time so...'

'We must go,' Raul interrupted firmly,

still holding Juliet's hand in a vicelike grip. *'Buenas noches,* Jemena. I'll probably see you tomorrow.'

Though the older woman scowled and called after him in staccato Spanish, he went on, his pace so brisk that Juliet practically had to trot to keep up with him. By the time he impelled her onto the elevator and they began the rapid descent, she was getting riled. What right did he have to treat her so rudely when she had sat on that sofa for nearly two hours, waiting patiently for him to conduct his business? He actually acted angry at her now, though she couldn't imagine why. Half afraid to ask, she said nothing until the Mercedes was brought around to the entrance and they had gotten inside. Yet, in the confines of the car, the silence between them became unbearable.

Finally, she could stand the tension no longer and blurted out, 'Well, what's wrong? Did Luis Diego give you a difficult time?'

Raul gave her a withering look. 'On the contrary, he agreed to place his work in our galleries.'

'Then what's the matter?' Juliet exclaimed confusedly. 'You almost act mad at me and I certainly haven't done anything. Or—have I?'

'We won't discuss this now, Juliet,' he decreed. 'We'll talk at the *casa.*'

'But...'

'At the *casa,*' he nearly growled, his voice so low and menacing that she automatically kept silent.

For the remainder of the ride home, Juliet cast furtive glances at Raul's strong profile, wondering with some trepidation what in the world was going on. By the time he parked the Mercedes before Casa Valaquez and herded her through the moonlit courtyard and into the main hall, she was feeling rather queasy with apprehension. There was a tension about him that hinted at a barely leashed fury and appalled her though she knew he wasn't justified in taking out his ill humour on her. Their footsteps clattered on the tiled floor until he stopped her at the foot of the staircase and both his hands descended heavily on her shoulders. His eyes glittered like green ice shards, impaling hers as his grip tightened.

'You will not go to David Judson's studio,' he muttered at last. 'Is that understood?'

'Well, no, not really,' she replied, striving to sound cool and composed despite the jerky beating of her heart. 'Why shouldn't I go? And why should you try to tell me I can't? If I want to pose for David, that's my business. Not yours!'

Raul's expression darkened grimly. 'But don't you think it's Will's business too? He certainly wouldn't be pleased.'

'Why ever not? I think he'd be very excited if David painted me.'

'Are you out of your mind?' Raul exploded, his fingers pressing into the delicate hollows of her shoulders. 'Will would be horrified. *Madre de Dios!* I paint as a hobby so let me do your portrait. I certainly won't display it conspicuously so you'd be wiser to let me paint you if you're so eager to pose nude.'

'*Nude!*' Juliet squeaked, her face paling then flaring scarlet. '*Nude!* You mean like—*naked?*'

200

Raul sighed wearily. 'You mean you didn't know that's what Judson had in mind?'

'I still don't know that,' she retorted, managing to control her jangled nerves. 'I don't believe you. I've heard of David Judson and he does *not* paint nudes.'

With a muffled curse, Raul raised his eyes heavenward. *'Poco idiota,* little fool,' he translated unnecessarily. 'David *Hudson,* not Judson, is the renowned portrait painter.'

'What?' Juliet gasped. 'You mean...'

'I mean Judson is a notorious womaniser. He calls himself an artist but he's far more interested in getting involved with his models than in painting them.'

Juliet could have died of humiliation right there on the spot. Feeling like a perfect imbecile for allowing herself to be conned, she bent her head, her silken hair falling forward to conceal her burning cheeks. And when Raul reached out to cup her chin in one tan hand, she flinched and tried to move away from him.

He wouldn't allow her to escape. One muscular arm encircled her waist as he

201

tilted up her chin, forcing her to face him. His expression softened, conveying a certain tenderness. 'You're not so worldly-wise after all, are you, despite...' He shook his head, his narrowing gaze searching her face as his hand dropped from her chin and his fingertips feathered along the rounded neckline of her dress. As she trembled, her eyes widening, he drew her slightly nearer. 'You are a puzzle, Juliet,' he whispered huskily. 'Sometimes you manage to appear so naive, so innocent, so very vulnerable.'

Juliet drew in a sharp breath, her nerves on fire from his evocative touch. 'Raul, I—I...'

He released her abruptly, thrusting his hands into his trouser pockets. 'Go to bed, Juliet,' he commanded. 'I'll see you in the morning.'

Foolishly she hesitated. 'But I...'

'Damn it, go!' he repeated hoarsely, his eyes blazing as he took one menacing step toward her. 'Go now before I decide to discover exactly how vulnerable you are.'

Faced with that threat, Juliet went, in

a hurry. She sped up the stairs, her heart hammering in her breast because she knew only too well that where Raul was concerned, she was vulnerable indeed and probably lacking in the strength it would take to deny him anything he might ask of her.

CHAPTER 7

As Holly sighed heavily and stared out the window, Juliet leaned forward in her chair, toward the bed. 'Is there anything I can bring you that would make the time pass faster? Do you want some more books? How about some romantic novels? You like romances, don't you?'

'Romance is what got me into this situation,' Holly replied glibly, patting her burgeoning abdomen. 'But yes, bring me some and anything else that might keep me occupied. I'm about to go nuts in this place.'

Juliet stroked her cheek thoughtfully with one forefinger. 'How about some soft yarn. You could crochet the baby some booties and sweaters.'

'I've crocheted enough booties and sweaters already to outfit every baby born in Spain this year.'

'Oh. Well, have you made a blanket yet? You could really make something pretty. And after you finish that, I'll bring you some embroidery paraphernalia. You're artistic. You could create your own designs and make some very lovely pictures.'

'Whatever,' Holly said with a rather impatient dismissive gesture. 'Now enough about what I *could* do to occupy my time. I'm tired of thinking about it. I'd much rather hear what you're doing. What's it like to live the easy life on the grand Valaquez estate?'

'Boring sometimes,' Juliet answered candidly. 'I'm like you, I guess, accustomed to keeping busy, and I really don't have much to do with looking after Uncle Will. He has this hulk of a nurse, who rarely ever smiles and who acts like she owns him. I guess she's acting in his best interest when she's always whisking him away for naps but he's getting tired of her bossiness, which means he's feeling much better. So maybe she won't be there much longer and Rosita and I will have more to do.'

Idly pleating the edge of her crisp white sheet, Holly smiled wryly. 'I'm surprised you don't have enough to do at the *casa*. I thought you'd be spending all your time trying to stay out of Pablo's clutches. Or isn't he still chasing after you?'

'Occasionally he sneaks up on me but, luckily, Raul keeps him pretty busy out in the olive groves. I think he's supposed to be learning all about olive growing from the foreman.'

'And Raul? Do you see much of him? How's he treating you these days?'

Moving restlessly in her chair, Juliet sighed. 'I really can't answer that,' she said, a note of bewilderment in her voice. 'Sometimes he's nice to me; sometimes he isn't. I can't figure him out.'

'And how do you feel about him?' Holly persisted gently. 'I know you were much more interested in him than in Pablo last year, romantically interested, I mean. So, are you still attracted to him?'

205

Juliet laughed humourlessly. 'If you'd ever seen Raul, you wouldn't have to ask me that. I don't imagine there are many females who aren't attracted to him.'

'But I've always had the feeling you felt more for him than just a casual attraction. I still have that feeling. Am I right or wrong?'

'Oh, damn, I don't know,' Juliet murmured, meticulously arranging the folds of her gauze skirt. 'Sometimes, when he's ordering me around, I feel like hitting him. But—then, all he has to do is touch me and all my irritation seems to dissolve and I want to throw myself in his arms. Nobody else has ever made me feel that way before and its very confusing.'

'Falling in love *is* very confusing,' Holly said softly. 'Especially the first time. And this is the first time for you, isn't it, Juliet? You've never been in love before?'

'I'm not in love now either!' Juliet protested with revealing vehemence. And when she was unable to meet Holly's knowing gaze, she bent her head, concealing her eyes with the thick fringe of her lashes. Lifting her shoulders in a resigned gesture, she realised she couldn't fool Holly and abandoned all pretence when she spoke again. 'Well, I guess I am afraid I'm falling in love. And I don't *want* to! Not with Raul. He—he doesn't approve of me or even like me very much. So I'm just asking for trouble by feeling about him the way I do.'

'But if Raul is very nice to you sometimes, he must like you a little,' Holly argued. 'And you just said you feel like throwing yourself in his arms when he touches you and I can't believe you'd respond that way if he wasn't showing you some tenderness.'

Juliet hesitated a moment, then shook her head, as if she was reassembling her thoughts. 'Well, even if he is tender sometimes, the only thing he feels for me is a slight physical attraction and that's not enough.'

'But...'

'Oh, let's stop trying to analyse this situation,' Juliet interrupted wearily. 'Even if Raul did like me a little, nothing would ever come of it. How could he ever be very interested in me when there are oodles of much more sophisticated women eager to become seriously involved with him? Against that kind of competition I don't stand a chance, so let's stop talking about Raul. All right?' Sitting up straight in her chair, she glanced at her wristwatch. 'Besides, I'd better go now and let you rest. And I do want to see Benny before I go back to the *casa*. I can help him move his belongings out of the hotel and into our house.'

'If you *can* get him to move into the house,' Holly said, with a dejected sigh. 'As I said a while ago, I think it's a great idea but Benny probably won't agree. He'll think of it as charity.'

'But he'll be doing Uncle Will a favour by staying there,' Juliet repeated her earlier explanation. 'So I can't see how Benny could feel he's being offered charity.'

'Oh, you know how stubborn Benny can be. I think he needs to prove to himself that he can take care of his family without anybody's help. That's why he's exhausting himself by singing at the coffee house every night, then going back there early the next morning to help clean up so he can make a little extra money. But he's never going to make enough to keep up with the bills I'm running up here.' Holly's voice quavered then lowered to a frightened husky whisper, 'You wouldn't believe how much it's costing to be in here, Juliet, and they're already asking us to begin paying. Neither my family or Benny's can afford to help us much and I—I just don't know what we're going to do.'

As Holly started crying softly, Juliet jumped up by the bed to pat her friend's hand comfortingly. 'Please don't get yourself all upset,' she murmured, her own voice hoarse. 'Worrying isn't going to help the baby and besides, you have nothing to worry about. I told Benny I'd be glad to use some of the money my parents left me to help you two pay the hospital bill.'

'Benny never mentioned that to me,' Holly said, drying her cheeks with the tissue Juliet handed her. 'But I guess he didn't because he'd be too proud to take your money.'

'Well, that's just too bad; he'll take it anyway,' Juliet declared emphatically. 'Now, how much do you need?'

'But...'

'How much?'

Holly hesitated only a moment. 'The bill here's already over two thousand dollars. And that's too much money for you to...'

'You let me worry about what's too much and what isn't.' Half-turning, she picked up her purse from the chair. Turning back, she squeezed Holly's hand and smiled reassuringly. 'I'm going to the bank right now and draw out the money. Then after I give it to Benny, I'm going to insist he move into our house. So I want you to stop fretting and get some rest. Everything is going to be just fine, you'll see.'

Holly smiled wanly. 'I don't know if Benny will let you do this, Juliet. He's one of the most stubborn people I've ever known.'

'Well, he's about to find out I can be as stubborn as he is,' Juliet announced confidently and, after straightening Holly's bedcovers, she smiled a good-bye and left.

At the Granada branch of an American bank twenty minutes later, the manager himself handled Juliet's transaction. Since she had never made a withdrawal from her account before, he seemed a bit curious about why she had suddenly decided to use the money. But, obviously, her answers to his questions satisfied him because he didn't delay in giving her the amount she requested.

After leaving the bank, Juliet went to Benny's small hotel and found him in the administrative lobby. He looked tired, too tired even to push back the shock of hair that grazed his forehead but he managed to smile when Juliet joined him at the registration desk where he was handing the clerk the key to his room.

'Where are you going?' Juliet asked. 'Are you in a real hurry?'

'Well, sort of. I was going to the hospital to see Holly. Why?'

Juliet made a great show of twisting the straps of her purse nervously. 'Well, I was hoping I could talk to you for a few minutes up in your room. I have to ask a favour of you.'

Obviously convinced by her tone that she was serious, Benny nodded, retrieved his door key, then allowed her to precede him up the stairs to the second floor. Though his room was tiny and cramped, the plain furniture was sturdy and everything was spotlessly clean. He only had to remove a paperback book from the only chair so Juliet could sit on it, while he sat down on the edge of the bed. 'Well, go ahead, Juliet, ask your favour,' he prompted. 'You know I'll do anything I can for you.'

'Oh, I was hoping you'd say that. But actually this is a favour for Uncle Will. He's just worrying himself sick about his house being burglarised while we're staying at the *casa*. You know, burglars can't resist an unoccupied house, so I told him I'd ask you to stay there and sort of keep an eye on things for us. Do you think you could?' She smiled hopefully at him. 'Please. I hate for Uncle Will to be constantly fretting about burglars and actually, you could benefit from the arrangement too. You'd be closer to the hospital and, besides, you could save the money it costs to rent this room. What do you say? Will you do it?'

For a long moment, Benny only stared at her, saying nothing. Then he rose to his feet and paced back and forth beside the bed. 'You're not just making up this whole story, are you, to help me out by saving me room rent?'

'What a suspicious mind you have,' Juliet retorted. 'I assure you I'm not making up anything. Uncle Will *is* worried about burglars and, quite frankly, I'm disappointed in you for not believing me. I thought you trusted me more than that.'

'Oh, I do trust you, Juliet, you know that,' Benny insisted, ruffling his reddish hair by running his fingers through it. Shaking his head at her, he smiled. 'But I also know what a tender-hearted little thing you are. You'd make up any kind of story to get me to accept your help.'

'Hmmph, well, I'm not making up this story and even though Uncle Will was very relieved when I told him I was sure you'd move in and keep an eye on the house, if you don't want to help us, then...'

'I didn't say no, did I?' Benny exclaimed, glancing around the cramped room with a grimace. 'To tell the truth, I'm getting claustrophobia in here. It wouldn't be so bad to have a house to myself and if I'd really be doing you a favour in the process...'

'Oh, you would, you would,' Juliet assured him eagerly as she stood. 'So you'll do it then?''

'Well, sure. Why not?' Benny acquiesced, then smiled at her with a certain amount of relief. 'When would you want me to move in?'

'Today. Right now, in fact,' Juliet said, tossing her purse on the chair. Unwilling to give him time to change his mind, she glanced around the room. 'Where's your luggage? I'll help you pack and we can move you out of here and into the house before you go visit Holly. Okay? She'll be pleased to hear you're doing me a favour and saving money, don't you think?'

Faced with such logic, Benny couldn't disagree and, fifteen minutes after he took two suitcases from the tiny closet, all his belongings were packed. He checked out of the hotel, then followed in the van as Juliet drove the Esprit to her uncle's house.

'Wow, this sure beats my room in the

hotel,' he commented as she opened the door to the upstairs guest room. Setting down the suitcases on the thick lemon yellow carpet, he wandered over to the window that overlooked the courtyard. 'View's better too. There, when I looked out my window, all I saw was a sagging stucco wall.'

'And here you can use the kitchen,' Juliet reminded him, hoisting one of the suitcases up on the chest at the foot of the bed. 'You can buy groceries and that'll be cheaper than having to eat out.'

Benny nodded agreeably then frowned as she opened his suitcase. 'Hey, you don't have to help me unpack. I can do that after I get back from the hospital.'

'Oh, I don't mind helping,' Juliet said, not adding that she wanted him settled in before she brought up the subject of money. And indeed, they had put away most of the contents in the second suitcase before she picked up her purse and removed a long slip of paper, which she handed to him.

He only glanced at it, then shaking his head emphatically, tried to thrust it back into her hand. When she refused to take it, he uttered an oath. 'This is a four thousand dollar cheque. And if you're trying to give it to me, I can't accept.'

'But you promised to let me help you financially. Are you breaking that promise now?'

'I said you could *help*—not that you could hand me a fortune.' He tried again to hand her the cheque. 'Come on, Juliet: this is too much. I can't take all this money from you.'

'You need it, don't you?' she countered as gently as possible. Laying her hand on his arm, she smiled understandingly. 'Look, I know you'd rather handle everything yourself but this is one of those times when that just isn't possible. You can't work around the clock trying to keep up with your bills. You'll only succeed in making yourself ill and what good will that do Holly? She's already very worried about you.'

'God, don't you think I know that?' he mumbled, pressing his palm against his forehead. 'And I know I'm to blame for this whole crazy mess.'

'How can you possibly say that?' Juliet objected. 'How could you be to blame for what was purely an accident?'

'An accident that wouldn't have happened if I'd had good sense months ago. Don't you see? I should have taken Holly home to the States a long time ago. I could've gotten some kind of regular job there; we could've had a permanent home. Instead, I've dragged her all over Europe in that rickety van. And that's no way for a pregnant woman to live.'

'Benny, you're being too hard on yourself,' Juliet said comfortingly. 'You sound as if you dragged Holly around against her will but you know better. She wanted to stay in Europe so if you're going to blame yourself for everything, then you'll have to blame her too.'

'Maybe we are both to blame,' he muttered guiltily. 'Both of us should have been adult enough to know that we couldn't continue our vagabond existence after the baby was born. I only wish I'd realised that fact months ago. This child is mine, my responsibility. And, somehow, after he's born, I'm going to have to give him a secure life and that probably means going back to the States. Unfortunately, there's not a lot of call for people with master's degrees in music, so God only knows what kind of job I'll be able to find.'

'Let's not worry about that right now,' Juliet advised. 'At the moment, the main concern is that Holly get proper care until the baby's born. And that means she has to pay her hospital bill so she can stay there. Don't you agree that's *really* all that matters right now?'

'Well, yes—but *four thousand* dollars! Damn it,' he muttered, waving the cheque. 'I can't take this much from you. It's not necessary. Holly's bill isn't even that high.'

'Yet,' Juliet reminded him. 'But it will be, so keep what's left when you pay the bill today, then pay them more next week. If you pay them regularly, they'll stop hassling you. And don't forget that I'll give you more, whenever you need it.'

'You can't give us all your money, Juliet!'

'Don't be so difficult,' she pleaded. 'For gosh sake, you and Holly are my best friends. If I can't use my money to help you, then what good is it?'

'Oh, hell, you have an answer for

everything,' he groaned but finally nodded. 'All right, I'll take the money.'

She breathed a sigh of relief, then grinned at him. 'I'm glad and not only because I want to help. But that happens to be a cashier's cheque and I know you wouldn't have wanted me to keep carrying it around. I mean, someone might have tried to rob a poor little defenceless girl like me.'

'Defenceless, my foot,' Benny retorted, laughing reluctantly. 'You're as sly as a fox. You would have made me take the cheque by pretending to be afraid to carry it with you. You certainly know how to play all the angles, don't you?'

'I try my best,' she countered.

Benny's expression abruptly sobered again. 'But this *is* just a loan. You remember that. I intend to pay back every penny.'

'Whatever you want,' she agreed, giving him a cheeky smile. 'I'll even charge you interest, if you insist. And you probably will.'

'You bet I will,' Benny said seriously as he placed the cheque in his well-worn wallet. Looking back up, he smiled gratefully. 'You're a good kid, Juliet. I don't know how to thank you.'

'Then don't try.' Pressing her hand against his shoulder, she headed him toward the door. 'Just go see Holly and I'll finish your unpacking. But wait! We forgot something.' Scrounging through her purse, she found the key to the house and handed it to him. 'I won't be here when you get back.'

Benny nodded, leaned down to clumsily brush a kiss across her cheek, then walked quickly from the room.

After hearing the van's noisy departure, Juliet finished hanging the last of Benny's shirts in the closet. As she started back across the room to get the empty suitcases to store them, she heard the front door close, then heavy footsteps ascending the stairs. She halted mid-stride for only a second, then went on, deciding Benny must have forgotten something. As she snapped shut the clasps on one suitcase, however, she realised she hadn't heard the van return and that decrepit old engine had a recognisable knock. Since she hadn't heard it, she suddenly knew it probably wasn't Benny who was in the house. With that realisation, her heart began hammering in her ears and she spun around to face the doorway just as Raul stepped through it, his considerable height and the breadth of his shoulders seemingly diminishing the size of the room.

'Oh, thank God, it's you,' Juliet breathed, pressing her fist against the ache in her chest where her heart palpitated violently. 'I thought you were an intruder when I realised I hadn't heard the van return. Benny's van, I mean. He just left.'

'I know,' Raul answered, his deep voice gruff. 'I waited until he left before coming in.' When Juliet only frowned questioningly, he gave her an unpleasant smile and moved with the menacing ease of a big cat toward her, stopping within touching distance. But he didn't touch her. Instead, he allowed his gaze to flick over her, then added caustically, 'Will's recuperation and your friend's stay in the hospital coincided perfectly, didn't they? Now, you and Benny have a nice place for a rendezvous and you don't have to worry about his wife possibly interfering.'

Juliet took a sharp breath, ignoring the ache in her chest his words caused. 'If you're going to start in on me again, I'm leaving,' she announced stiffly. 'I'm tired of your ridiculous accusations and this time, I'm not even going to try to defend myself.'

As she snatched up her purse from the bed and tried to sweep past Raul, his arm shot out, caught her around the waist, and pulled her relentlessly against him. He easily subdued her futile struggle to free herself. 'Can you defend yourself?' he asked, the coolness in his green eyes belying his soft tone. 'Or are you just unwilling to make up a lie?'

'I don't tell lies!' she protested, then sighed. 'Yes, I could defend myself but I see no point in trying. You wouldn't believe me anyway. You never do.'

'Why don't you try me again,' he said with an infuriating smile. 'Maybe this time, you'll convince me.'

Provoked by his mocking tone, Juliet pushed her small hands against his chest but only succeeded in inciting him to use more force. One lean hand tangled in the fiery cascading strands of her hair while his arm tightened, bringing her so much closer against him that her slight body was actually arched toward him. 'Be still,' he commanded huskily, clasping the back of her head in his large hand. 'If you do have some explanation for you and Benny being in this house together, I want to hear it. And I want to hear it now. So begin.'

For a moment, Juliet pressed her lips together firmly, determined not to explain anything to him but something unrelenting in his stern expression changed her mind. No longer able to meet his harsh gaze, she bent her head, fixing her own bewildered gaze on the buttons of his light blue shirt. 'I...Benny's going to stay here,' she began, her voice so soft Raul had to bend down closer to hear. 'It'll save him the cost of a hotel room and Uncle Will won't have to worry about the house standing empty, inviting burglars.'

'Will knows about Benny staying here?' Raul questioned, his voice rather uneven, somehow making his slight accent even more appealing. 'You're saying Will agreed to this arrangement?' When Juliet nodded, his hold on her became infinitely gentler and his fingers threaded through her hair so evocatively that she compulsively lifted her face to him. A hint of a smile tugged at the corners of his mouth. 'I seem to have misjudged you again,' he said softly. 'I don't know what it is about you that makes me jump to conclusions.'

Juliet swallowed with difficulty, nearly mesmerised by the sudden warmth in his eyes. Then she shook her head, trying to dispell the dangerous weakness that threatened to sap the strength from her limbs. 'I—I guess you just don't like me very much so—so you don't trust me. But that really isn't very fair.'

'No, it isn't,' he agreed incredibly, his intent gaze narrowing as he slowly lowered his dark head. 'But it isn't because I don't like you that I don't trust you. As I've said before, I think I like you too much. But I can't trust you, Juliet, because you're so young you still play games with men. You played games with Benny and with Pablo and now, you're trying to play a game with me. But, Juliet, I'm not a man to play games with.'

Though she wanted to defend herself, his warm caressing breath against her cheek sent a shiver of awareness feathering along her spine and banished all coherent thought. Her eyes widened, softened with vulnerability, then were captured and held by a sudden warming gleam in his that defied analysis. His wide shoulders blocked the light from the window and suddenly that beloved dark face and those eyes became all that was real in the world. As she drew in a startled breath, her softly curved lips parted slightly and his brushed slowly across her cheek to touch them, lightly at first, then with a swift graduation of intensity that swept her up in a tide of irresistible passion. His lips hardened, possessed hers with undeniable hunger and without gentleness and she found delight in a sheer physical strength so superior to hers. Dizzying pleasure claimed her as his hand roamed freely, exploring the tantalising curves of her slight body and with the pressure of his taut muscular thighs grazing hers and the hot upsurging evidence of his desire, she intuitively moved against him, eliciting his soft groan.

His mouth lifted, hovered just above hers and his eyes were alight with passion as he muttered roughly, *'Atormentadora,* this time you will give me what you make me want so badly. Won't you, *mi amada?* Say yes.'

'Raul,' she breathed, fear shafting through her. But it was such a pleasurable fear that she could only seek his lips again without giving him an answer, at least in words.

Obviously interpreting her silence as acquiescence, Raul murmured her name triumphantly and winding her hair around his hand, tilted her head back and trailed blazing kisses along her jaw, down the slender length of her smooth neck. Curiously unsteady fingers unfastened the fabric buttons of her white sleeveless blouse and he held her slightly away from him as he slipped the soft garment from her shoulders, down her shapely arms, and off completely.

She heard his sharply indrawn breath

226

as he allowed the blouse to slip between his fingers and fall to the floor. She closed her eyes, unable to withstand the searing heat of his gaze as he observed the rapid rise and fall of breasts barely concealed by a wisp of a white lace bra but she could offer no resistance as he unbuttoned her skirt, then lowered the zipper and it joined the blouse on the floor. Strong hands spanned her waist, his fingers probing her spine. And suddenly, even the wispy lace bra was removed and she was standing before him in only a satiny white half-slip. Her eyes flickered open again and she trembled as his dark gaze seemed to be devouring her.

'God, Juliet, such exquisite skin,' he whispered, drawing her closer as he lowered his head, his lips seeking the scented hollow at the base of her throat, then moving slowly downward as his lean hands came around to cup the cushioned fullness of her breasts.

Knowing what he was about to do and more afraid of him than she had ever been, Juliet uttered a soft cry and pressed herself against him, unmindful of the buttons of his shirt digging into her flesh.

He buried his face in her touseled hair, his hand stroking from her shoulder downward over one breast as he murmured close to her ear, 'Juliet, *mi pequena,* why are you so shy with me? You needn't be. I promise I'm going to be very gentle.'

The protest she would have made found no voice as he swiftly swept her up in his arms and carried her across the room to the bed. After tossing back the white quilted coverlet, he put her down gently, his gaze trailing over the length of her body with hot intensity. He removed the leather sandals from her feet and as he stepped out of his own shoes, his fingers feathered up one shapely slender leg to her thigh, just above her knee.

As she trembled, her wide eyes held by his, his jaw tightened. He shed his blazer, then his light blue shirt. In the shaft of sunlight, his smooth skin gleamed like bronze and his broad shoulders and hair-roughened chest were shaped by muscular contours. Juliet lay immobile, looking up at him, appalled by her need to touch him. Yet, when he began to undo the buckle of his belt, she moved her head back and forth on the pillow.

'No!' she gasped weakly, only able to breath again when his fingers stilled and an amazingly tender expression softened his features.

'All right, *mi pequena,*' he whispered, coming down onto the bed beside her. 'I don't want to rush you.'

Yet, she sensed the leashed urgency in him as her hands came up involuntarily to press against his chest, as if she meant to fight him. And the gesture was futile. He allowed no resistance. Though he was gentle, he caught both her wrists and pinned her arms back above her head in one large hand as the other sought the warm firm flesh of one breast. Her eyes closed and she moaned softly as his fingers took possession, stroking, encircling and brushing over the roseate peak until it was ruched and surging tautly with his questing touch.

'Yes, you do want me,' he said softly. 'Almost as much as I want you.'

Any denial she might have uttered was silenced as he kissed her again, his lips teasing the soft fullness of hers, his strong teeth nibbling tenderly as the weight of his lean body pressed her into the soft mattress. He released her wrists then but she was beyond attempting to resist him. As he turned over onto his side, taking her with him, his hands on her hips arching her warmth against the throbbing hardness of his body, she became all boneless acquiescence. Her hand drifted up to lay against his cheek, her trembling fingers tracing the contours of his ear and the strong tendons of his neck.

With a muffled exclamation, he pressed her shoulder back and lowered his head. His mouth closed around the dark peak of one breast, burning the sensitised skin and as flames of need consumed her, she entwined her fingers in the thick dark hair on his nape.

His lips came up to take hers again, the tip of his tongue entering the opening flower of her mouth and suddenly she no longer wondered if she loved him. She knew she did. The nearly overwhelming physical and emotional need she felt to surrender completely to him made her certain she would never love any man the way she loved him. His every touch scorched her skin and her own hands moved feverishly over his broad back. Their legs entangled but as his thigh encountered the barrier of her twisted half-slip, he effortlessly removed the offending garment. And it wasn't until his finger slid beneath the waistband of her panties that the self-protective instinct at last overwhelmed the womanly desires he had awakened.

Juliet tensed, tugging at his hand even as conflicting emotions tore through her. 'Raul, please, I can't,' she murmured tremulously. 'I'm sorry but please...'

'God, Juliet, you're driving me crazy,' he muttered roughly but he turned onto his side. Propped on one elbow, he brushed her tousled hair back from her face, his narrowed eyes enigmatically dark and searching. 'You weren't playing a game this time. You wanted me to make love to you but you couldn't go through with it. Are you that afraid of me, Juliet?'

Chewing her lower lip, feeling a great need to cry, she could only nod.

'But why?' he asked softly. 'Why

should you be afraid of me?'

Since she couldn't tell him she was in love with him and knew he didn't love her, she offered no answer at all and felt a very real sense of loss as he levered himself up away from her to stand beside the bed.

'You won't always be afraid of me,' he promised huskily, rebuttoning his shirt as his gaze drifted up over her bare breasts to linger on her parted lips. After stepping back into his shoes, he caught up his blazer and tossed it across one shoulder, then strode toward the door. He stopped, turned back to look at her and smiled gently. 'We could have something very wonderful together, Juliet, and we will. You know as well as I do that it's inevitable.'

With that, he was gone and with him all the warmth she had previously felt. Shivering, she reached for the quilted coverlet and pulled it up over her head as she nuzzled her cheek against the pillow. He was right. Some deep intuition told her he would become her lover eventually. It *was* inevitable and she knew it. Yet, she also knew that an intimate re-

relationship with him without his love would never be enough. And she was very much afraid she would forever yearn for what she could never have.

CHAPTER 8

The next Tuesday afternoon, Juliet decided to go riding. For a day in mid-June, it was only moderately hot. Though the sun blazed down as usual, a brisker cooling breeze drifted across the Vega plain. And Juliet felt a great need to escape the *casa*. It had been four days since her encounter with Raul at the house in Granada, and though she hadn't spoken to him alone since then, she still felt very vulnerable whenever she saw him. The memory of that day's events seemed almost a tangible thing between them and, now, his every glance in her direction made her look away shyly. She simply wasn't worldly enough to smile blithely at a man who knew with such certainty that he would become her lover someday.

She had tried telling herself that she simply wouldn't allow him to become her lover but such resolutions were rather meaningless, considering how she invariably responded to him. In that bed with him on Friday, she had come so close to complete surrender that now she was afraid to be alone with him again.

After dressing in jeans and a cool knit tank top, Juliet waylaid the housekeeper in the hall outside her room. When they had confused each other thoroughly by speaking in a pidgin mixture of fractured English and Spanish, Juliet had comprehended enough to know that Raul was busy in his office. Relieved that there would be little chance of running into him out on the grounds of the estate, she went back through her room, down across the courtyard, and on to the stables. No one was there, not even the stable hand. Passing between the double rows of stalls, she admired each of the perfectly groomed horses that were napping the lazy afternoon away. The fresh smell of grain reminded her of the riding lessons she had taken in boarding

234

school. Twelve years old and rather small for her age, she had always been intimidated by the sheer size of the animals. Now, though she was no longer afraid of horses, she chose to ride the golden mare in the last stall because she knew her to be gentle and easily managed.

Florera whinnied softly and tossed her cream-coloured mane as Juliet surreptitiously fed her a lump of sugar, all the while glancing around, hoping she wasn't being observed. She felt sure Raul wouldn't appreciate her giving such unwholesome treats to one of his thoroughbreds, though she didn't see that it could hurt to do so occasionally. After slipping a bridle over the mare's sleek, fine-boned head, Juliet led her out of the stall and saddled her herself, inhaling the rich leather scent of the gleaming saddle. As she bent down to adjust the stirrups, Florera playfully nudged her derriere, probably hoping to discover more sugar in the back pockets of her jeans. The soft brown nose, however, nudged a bit too hard. Caught off balance, Juliet had to grab for the saddle to keep from falling and, unfortunately, just at that moment,

Raul entered the stable, smiling indulgently at her very unequestrian pose.

Feeling clumsy and inept and very nervous now that he was here, Juliet steadied herself with as much dignity as she could muster. She returned his smile wanly, unnecessarily smoothed her hair, then hooked her thumbs in her back pockets. 'I was about to go for a ride,' she murmured, though that fact was perfectly obvious. 'You don't mind, do you?'

Shaking his head, Raul walked toward her, his muscular thighs straining the khaki fabric of his pants with each long stride. In a safari shirt with the top two buttons unfastened, he looked more approachable somehow, less menacing, and as Juliet finally managed to get her breathing under control, he stopped close in front of her. 'I don't mind if you go riding. But I would like to talk to you about something first.' When she inclined her head agreeably, he propped his elbows on the top railing of the stall and leaned back slightly, his dark gaze never leaving her face. 'The manager of your bank called me this morning,

236

knowing that Will is recuperating here. He was afraid maybe Will didn't realise you had withdrawn four thousand dollars from your account. I told him I would take care of the matter so that's what I'm doing. Would you care to tell me what you need four thousand dollars for?'

Juliet was incensed. 'He had no right to divulge my transaction with his bank,' she said indignantly. 'That's privileged information and he could be in a lot of trouble for being such a blabbermouth.'

'He was only thinking of Will,' Raul said patiently. 'And, besides, you're avoiding the question. Why did you withdraw that much money?'

Gesturing impatiently, Juliet turned around, pretending to adjust a stirrup but Raul wouldn't allow her to escape his inquisition so easily. Lightly gripping her arm, he turned her back around to face him again.

'Obviously, you didn't buy yourself a new car with the money or I would have noticed,' he said, his voice deceptively low. 'And unless you bought a very expensive piece of jewellery, I can't imgaine what you did with four thousand dollars. Or maybe I can. Perhaps you gave it to your boyfriend, Benny.'

Juliet clenched her hands into fists at her sides. 'Benny is *not* my boyfriend.'

'But you did give him the money,' Raul said tersely. 'Didn't you?'

'So what if I did?' she retorted. 'What business is it of yours? Why should you care what I do?'

'I care that you're still so attached to him,' Raul said grimly. He widened his stance, resting lean brown hands on his hips. 'Don't you wonder what kind of man would take so much money from a young woman?'

'A desperate man!' Juliet shook her head, something like disappointment darkening her amber eyes. Turning away from him, she took up the reins, thrust her left foot in the stirrup and propelled herself up onto the saddle, where she sat for a moment, small chin out-thrust as she looked down at him. 'I guess I was mistaken in thinking you could be a compassionate person. In case you haven't noticed, Raul, not everybody in the world is as wealthy as you. Benny certainly isn't and to keep Holly in the hospital, he has to pay the bill. He didn't want to take that four thousand dollars; I practically had to force him to. And finally he accepted the fact that he really didn't have any other choice. So that's the kind of man who would take money from a young woman—one who's been pushed against the wall and has nowhere to turn, except to a friend.'

Without waiting for Raul's reaction to her explanation, Juliet tugged on the reins and rapped her heels sharply into Florera's flanks. Pivoting smoothly, the mare took off in a loping gallop and Juliet exited the stable without a backward glance. As they headed down the dusty road that dissected the olive groves, the warm wind whipped her heated cheeks and lifted her thick russet tresses off her shoulders so that her hair streamed out behind her. Feeling the need to move quickly, she urged the mare onward at a faster pace until it seemed they were literally skimming over the gritty surface of the roadbed. The horse's swift easy stride somewhat eased Juliet's irritation and exhilaration took its place.

The widely spaced olive trees with their heavy spreading branches provided patches of blessed shade on the sun-dappled road. So it wasn't until they left the groves behind and the road petered out that Juliet realised she had left her straw hat in the stable. Though the day seemed cooler than usual, the sun still beat down on her head until she was beginning to feel uncomfortably hot. After the wild galloping ascent of the sloping grove, she didn't want to tire Florera further. She slowed the mare to a trot as they followed a narrow trail that wound between the hills and out-croppings of rock. Sun dried grasses swayed in a gentle breeze. This was un-tamed Andalusia. Without irrigation channels, vegetation was sparse. The greyish-brown earth only hinted at green and solitary trees were scattered here and there over the landscape. Spying a clump of hardy yellow-bloomed wildflowers that had sprung up in the shadow of a huge jagged rock, Juliet pulled back on the reins, bringing Florera to a halt, then dismounted.

After winding the reins around the

branch of a scraggly bush, she picked one yellow blossom and tucked it into her hair above her ear. Protected from the full rays of the sun in the shady spot, she leaned back against the rough rock surface and gazed pensively at the serrated, saw-like peaks of the Sierra Nevadas. Yet, her enjoyment of the scenery was marred somewhat by the memory of the confrontation she had just had with Raul. She plucked a long spike of golden grass, idly twirling the stem between her thumb and forefinger and as she was searching her brain for some way to improve Raul's opinion of her, the man himself came into view.

Astride a large black stallion called Diablo, he rode toward her, handling the spirited horse with the same seemingly effortless efficiency he exhibited in everything he did. He wore no hat but hers swung from the pommel of his western saddle. He didn't look at her as he dismounted, then tethered Diablo near Florera, giving the stallion enough rein to graze on the tender shoots of nearby wild turnip plants. Catching her hat by the ribbons, he allowed it to dangle from his fingers as he walked to her, diminishing the distance between them with only a few swift long strides.

As he stood silently before her for a long tense moment, Juliet swallowed uneasily, but it wasn't the argument they had just had that made her feel so vulnerable. It was the very real aura of male magnetism that exuded from him that was disturbing her right now and she wished he would say something, anything, to ease her tension.

'You forgot your hat,' he said at last, his voice without inflection. But he was very gentle as he adjusted the hat on her head, then tied the narrow navy grosgrain ribbons beneath her chin. In doing so, his hard knuckles grazed her jaw and when she drew back compulsively, his hands dropped down to span her waist. He smiled. 'You should never come out riding without protection for your head. You're not accustomed to such intense heat and, besides, your fair skin could easily burn in this sun. And you don't want more than that very charming sprinkling of freckles across your nose. Do you?'

Though Juliet shook her head, she gazed up at him bewilderedly, wondering what had caused this turnabout in attitude. And obviously, her confusion was quite apparent.

'You should have told me why you gave Benny the money before accusing me of lacking compassion. I'm not a mind reader, Juliet,' he said wryly. 'And, frankly, where your friend Benny is concerned, I seemed to have developed this peculiar intolerance, almost an active dislike.'

'Why?' Juliet breathed, disconcerted merely by his nearness. 'How could you dislike him? You don't even know him.'

'I think it's fairly obvious why I'm not fond of him,' he answered cryptically, then shrugged. 'Well, anyway, I'm sorry I assumed he had some frivolous reason for taking your money. It just never occurred to me that he needed to pay his wife's hospital bills. But I am well aware that everyone in the world isn't as fortunate as I am financially. Surely you don't believe I live in my ivory tower and never notice those who have more difficult lives.'

'I didn't think you did,' Juliet murmured. 'That's why I was so surprised you had no sympathy for Benny.'

'As I said, I don't read minds,' Raul reminded her. 'But I've said I'm sorry. Do you accept my apology?'

'Of course I do,' she answered, happy to do anything that would preclude another argument with him. 'Why don't we forget the whole misunderstanding?'

'It's forgotten,' Raul said softly then abruptly released her waist to take a step back from her. Slipping his hands into his pockets, he scrutinised her for several seconds, as if he were searching for something in her uplifted face. Then those magnificent green eyes turned away to stare beyond her and he almost sighed. 'I realise now how loyal you are to your friends', he announced suddenly. 'But I also know the extent of your personal finances. And you're not going to be able to support your friends indefinitely. So what will they do? Raising a child can be expensive.'

'Benny said they'd probably go back to the States after Holly has the baby. He realises he'll have to get a permanent job so they can settle down but he doesn't know what kind of job it'll have to be. As he said, there's not a great demand for people with master's degrees in music these days.'

'And if they do go home, what about you, Juliet?' Raul asked very quietly. 'Will you go with them?'

Something in his manner made Juliet shift her feet uncomfortably. 'I don't plan to go anywhere until Uncle Will's well again. After that, I suppose I'll go back to the States but not until January, when the second semester starts at college.' Even as she said the words, she realised how difficult it would be when she did have to leave Spain and Raul. Though he didn't return her deep feelings, there was something comforting about being near him. Yet she couldn't live a life of leisure with her uncle forever. A girl had to make her own way these days, she thought rather ruefully, bending her head so that the rim of her hat concealed her eyes. Suddenly, her heart skipped several beats as Raul stepped close again, so close that his hard thighs brushed hers. He cupped her chin in one hand, tilting her face up, his narrowed gaze again strangely searching as he looked down at her from his considerable height.

'Will would be much happier if you stayed in Spain,' he almost whispered, his voice appealingly rough. 'But I suppose you wouldn't want to do that?'

Responding to his serious tone, Juliet answered seriously. 'I don't think I could just loaf around forever, letting Uncle Will support me. Besides, everyone expects young women to take up careers these days. I wouldn't want to be a misfit.'

A muscle in Raul's strong jaw ticked with fascinating regularity. 'But do you *want* a career?'

I want you, she longed to say but knowing she couldn't, she simply forced a smile. 'I think I'd like to do something to help disadvantaged people, so there are a great many careers to choose from. I just have to decide exactly what I want to do.'

'You don't have to have a college degree to help other people,' Raul said. 'Truly caring about them is far more important than formal schooling. Abuela has no degrees but that hasn't stopped her from helping others. Many of the children around here would be suffering from malnourishment if she hadn't instructed their mothers in the basics of good nutrition and then seen that the families received the food they needed.'

'I'm sure her caring has made many lives much better,' Juliet said sincerely. 'And I envy her the resources that allow her to do it. But I'm afraid I'll have to get a job that pays and allows me to be of service to others. And to get one of those you almost have to have a college diploma so I have little choice except to go back school.'

Raul's eyes darkened to a deep forest green and for a moment he seemed on the verge of saying something, but apparently changed his mind. Instead he glanced down at the gold Piaget watch on his wrist. 'I must get back to the *casa*. I'm expecting a call from Madrid,' he told her, cupping her elbow to direct her toward the lazily grazing horses. 'You'll go back with me. I think you've spent enough time in the sun for one afternoon.'

Juliet didn't argue with him. By now, all desire for a longer ride had dissipated. As their horses picked their way over the rocky trail then broke into a canter on the road through the olive grove, she and Raul said little to each other but there was nothing really tense about the silence between them. Yet, Juliet did feel a vague sense of unfulfillment, as if something one of them needed to say had been left unsaid. The feeling persisted even as they rode into the stable but when Raul lithely dismounted, then reached up to lift her from the saddle, everything changed. The sense of unfulfillment altered to sweet anticipation as he brought her down close to him, allowing only the tips of her toes to touch ground before his arms enfolded her.

'Mi amada,' he whispered, burrowing his face in her hair. 'You're so beautiful.'

Another time, it might have hurt to hear him call her his love when he didn't love her, but at this moment she let herself luxuriate in the endearment. It was enough to be near him, to experience both his strength and tenderness. Detecting the evocatively familiar lime scent of his after shave, she relaxed against him, her arms encircling his neck. As she whispered his name, his lips found the racing pulse in her throat, then moved up to cover her own. The kiss teased, heightening the anticipation, then surged to a passionate taking of her mouth. A desire born of love quickened deep within her and keenly awakened every nerve in her body. Never had she felt so totally alive, so sensuously receptive that the lean hand curving into the small of her back and the other that gently cupped her nape seemed to sear her skin. The tip of his tongue tasted the sweetness of her mouth and she felt as if she were melting into him as dizzying pleasure swirled her senses.

'Juliet, I...' he began, then groaned softly as her lips eagerly sought his again.

Lost in the marauding power of his kiss, Juliet barely heard the footsteps on the concrete stable floor. But she was brought back to reality by a familiar feminine voice's furiously exclaimed, *'Dios!'* Raul reluctantly lifted his mouth from Juliet's. As her eyes opened, they met the hot glimmer in his. As he slowly released her and an appealing rosiness tinted her cheeks, he smiled slightly before turning to face Jemina Ruiz.

Juliet also turned, biting back a groan as she found not only Jemina glaring at her but Pablo and an unknown Spanish girl as well. Pablo's face was tight with anger. He took a step toward his brother. Then, without warning, he swung a fist.

'Pablo, no!' Juliet cried. But before she could move, Raul had already swiftly raised his arm to deflect the attempted blow. His green eyes raked over Pablo who stepped back, intimidated by a will far stronger than his. Yet, he didn't concede defeat gracefully. A string of strident Spanish pierced the silence until Raul interrupted with a curt command.

'Speak English. You're embarrassing Margarita with your indelicate language.'

'Damn you,' Pablo whispered violently, clenching and unclenching his fists. 'What right do you have to be kissing Juliet?'

'You're acting like a spoiled child,' Raul replied coolly. 'There's no reason for you to be so upset.'

Juliet felt rather ill, harldy able to believe Raul could so carelessly dismiss as nothing the few moments they had just shared together. And when Jemina Ruiz gave her a mocking triumphant smile, it was the final straw.

Juliet turned and fled the stable. She half ran across the pebbled drive in her haste to escape all of them, even the obviously confused Margarita. Desperate to reach the sanctuary of her room, she rushed between two of the cypresses that bordered the courtyard but she hadn't even passed the swimming pool before Jemina caught up with her.

'I will talk to you, senorita,' the older girl said venomously. Her sharp fingertips dug into Juliet's arm. 'Since the first time I saw you, I suspected you were the little fool. Now you have proven me correct. Do you believe Raul is seriously interested in you? *Idiota.* You are only a diversion for him, a silly little thing with whom he can dally.'

'Thank you for your analysis of his feelings,' Juliet answered sarcastically. As she tried to free her arm, Jemina's fingernails dug deeper into her flesh, but she refused to wince. 'Let me go.'

'In a moment. I am not yet finished.' Jemina sneered. 'You make me sick. You are one of those girls who can look so innocent even though you are not innocent at all. Perhaps that is what intrigues Raul. He knows you are experienced but you look so young and dewy-eyed.' She snorted. 'But he will not stay intrigued very long. So you would be wise to stay away from him. I tell you this for your own good.'

'I just bet,' Juliet retorted. And as fingernails clawed her arm before it was released, the remnants of her composure vanished. 'Why don't you go jump in the pool, Jemina? Or better yet, I think I'll push you in,' she threatened with incredible calm, stepping menacingly toward the older woman. 'I'd like to see what chlorine would do to that designer silk dress of yours. And I imagine your perfect coiffure wouldn't look so perfect after a dunking, would it?'

Jemina's almond eyes widened with surprise and some fear. Holding up one hand, she backed up, glanced over her shoulder, and, after seeing how near she was to the pool, she sidestepped hastily. Then she turned and scurried away, as if the hounds of hell were after her silk dress.

Juliet smiled grimly but soon delayed reaction set in, creating a heaviness in the centre of her chest as she wandered aimlessly into the house. She didn't really know why she suddenly felt so terribly depressed. Jemina hadn't told her anything she hadn't known already. Yet, somehow, the truth hurt more when another person told it, even if that person was a shrew like Jemina Ruiz.

Wandering across the main hall, Juliet decided to hide herself in the library. No one except Raul ever seemed to use the room and he usually did so only in the evenings.

After opening the ornately carved double doors quietly, Juliet slipped into the vast book-lined room. She had always liked it here. The comfortable leather furniture and sturdy tables and desks added a homey touch of stability and security, which was exactly what she needed at the moment.

Though the majority of leather bound volumes were naturally written in Spanish, there was an entire section devoted to English and American literature. After perusing the titles, she reached for a novel by Thomas Hardy, feeling his brooding view of life would certainly suit her present mood. But before she could take the book to a chair and sit down with it, Pablo threw open the library doors then shut them with a resounding bang after entering the room.

'You owe me an explanation,' he muttered as he approached Juliet. 'And I want you to answer this question for me: Were you not interested in me last year because you were in love with Raul?'

Hugging her book to her breasts, Juliet sighed tiredly. 'I told you last year I simply wasn't romantically interested in you. Raul had nothing to do with it. So no, I wasn't in love with him last year.'

'But now you are,' Pablo snapped. 'Aren't you?'

'Yes,' Juliet admitted candidly. 'I guess I am in love with him.'

'And is he in love with you too?'

'He certainly doesn't act like it,' she

retorted ruefully. Then her expression sobered. 'No, he isn't.'

'But you love him anyway. Is that it?' When she nodded, Pablo smote his forehead with the heel of his hand. 'I should have known it. So there is no chance for me, is there?'

'Pablo, please stop this game,' Juliet said beseechingly. 'You only think you want me because I'm not interested. That makes me a challenge, that's all. You know you don't really love me.'

'I know there's no use in loving you now, if Raul is my competition. But I could have loved you eternally.'

Juliet smiled indulgently. 'We're not even compatible. We never would be. Accept that. And try to be content with someone like Margarita. She is a lovely girl and she would certainly fit into your life more comfortably than I ever could.'

'What good is there in talking about us?' he muttered. 'If you're in love with Raul, I know you couldn't love me. He's much more dynamic than I am, more mature and stronger. Women flock to him; I can't compete.'

'You're younger,' Juliet reminded him

gently. 'Give yourself time and you'll be as—as magnetic as he is, I'm sure.'

'But not for you?' Pablo asked softly. 'I'll never have a chance with you?'

'No,' Juliet whispered. 'And I told you that last year.'

'And now I must accept it,' Pablo conceded with a slight smile. 'All right, I accept it. Or at least I understand. So I will leave you alone from now on. *Adios*, Juliet.'

Smiling slightly at his dramatic exit line, she allowed him to kiss her cheek. She watched him leave the room and shook her head indulgently. He was such a little boy; she couldn't stay mad at him. Drawing a deep breath, she sank down on a worn black leather chair but before she could open the book she held, the library doors opened again.

This time it was Raul who came in. Juliet's hands began to shake violently as he strode across the room to stand towering above her. 'I saw Pablo follow you in here,' he announced flatly. 'What did he say to you? Was he abusive?'

'N—not really,' she answered, her voice embarrassingly shaky. 'And I think

I finally managed to convince him he's only been interested in me because I've never thrown myself at him as many other girls do.'

'And why is that, Juliet?' Raul questioned seriously, his steady gaze enigmatic. 'My brother can be a charming young man so why doesn't he appeal to you? Is it because he is Spanish?'

'Because he is Spanish?' Juliet repeated blankly, then felt an incongruous desire to laugh. If only Raul knew that his being Spanish certainly hadn't prevented her from falling hopelessly in love with him...But he didn't know that and she couldn't tell him, so she shook her head instead. 'What would his being Spanish have to do with anything? I'm just not interested in him because—because, well, he just seems so young, I guess.'

Raul's tense expression altered slightly. He almost smiled. 'Pablo is older than you, Juliet.'

'But he *seems* younger. He's very flighty and I just take life more seriously, I guess.'

With a swiftness that set her pulses

pounding, Raul leaned down, his lean brown hands gripping the armrests of her chair. A sudden warmth in his green eyes seemed to envelop her. 'Do you take life seriously, *pequena?* Really?'

'Yes, I think I do,' she breathed nervously. 'Don't you believe that?'

'I'm trying, Juliet,' he answered cryptically. One hand came out to press gently against her cheek, then he straightened with something like a sigh of regret. 'We'll talk about this again soon,' he promised softly. 'But right now, I must catch that phone call from Madrid. You understand?'

Juliet understood nothing and could only gaze up at him with wide bewildered eyes. But when he murmured, 'Until later, *mi amada,*' and started to stride away, she called after him.

'Raul, I—I'm sorry if I've caused trouble between Pablo and you. I feel very bad about what happened—in the stable.'

Raul's gaze, dark and intense, roved over her. He shook his head. 'That wasn't your fault. Pablo simply has a hot temper but he rarely stays angry for long.'

'But he tried to hit you.'

'That wasn't the first time, I assure you,' Raul responded wryly. 'Even when brothers love each other, they don't always agree. So you are not to worry about what happened in the stable. Understood?'

'I don't know,' she murmured weakly. 'I still feel guilty.'

With an incomprehensible murmur, Raul took a step in her direction, then stopped and shook his head. 'You shouldn't feel guilty but I'll have to convince you of that later. The call from Madrid...' As she nodded and forced a wan smile, he hesitated again, then turned and quickly strode from the room.

With a soft heartfelt moan, Juliet closed her eyes but they flew open again as a voice spoke her name. Though Senora Valaquez was rising from the high-backed chair that faced the desk, in which she had been hidden from view, Juliet couldn't really be surprised. This quiet library had become as busy as Grand Central Station this afternoon.

'I did not intentionally eavesdrop,' Senora Valaquez said, as she walked toward Juliet. 'I confess I had fallen asleep in the chair and did not hear you come in. But Pablo entered so noisily and began talking before I could make my presence known. So I remained silent. I did not want to embarrass him or you.'

'I understand,' Juliet murmured, steeling herself for the disapproving sermon she feared would follow now. So she was astonished when Alicia Valaquez suddenly gave her an apparently genuine smile.

'I am rather glad I overheard you talk with Pablo,' the senora said quietly. 'I had assumed you deliberately played the tease with him last year, but when he did not deny that you had always tried to discourage him, I realised I had been wrong. I apologise for thinking badly of you.'

'It's all right, really,' Juliet said. 'I understand why you were so concerned about Pablo. He's your grandson and I can't blame you for being upset with me, if you felt I had deliberately hurt him.'

'Which I now know you did not do.'

The senora smiled gratefully. 'You were firm with him today but also kind.'

'I've never wanted to hurt his feelings,' Juliet offered. 'I like Pablo but...'

'It is Raul you love.' Senora Valaquez finished for her with a gentle smile. 'Yes, of course, I heard you tell Pablo that too.'

Imagining she detected sympathy in the woman's dark eyes, Juliet bent her head. 'I hope you won't tell Raul what I said?'

'Why should I? That is for you to do.'

Juliet smiled sadly. 'I can't tell him that. He'd be horrified.'

The senora's fine dark brows arched speculatively. 'Why are you so certain of that, *nina?* I suspect you do not know my grandson very well. Or you would not be so frightened of him that I could hear the fear in your voice when you spoke to him. He was being very nice to you, yet your voice trembled. Why? What is it about Raul that makes you afraid?'

Juliet spread her hands in a resigned gesture. 'Oh, you know.'

'I suspect I do. Now,' Alicia said softly. 'I was as innocent as you when I met Raul's grandfather so I too was afraid of him, though I loved him very much. So I understand what you are feeling.'

'Thank you for being so nice,' Juliet said sincerely. 'It's a relief to known you no longer dislike me, senora.'

Amazingly, the woman put out her hand and gently stroked Juliet's shimmering auburn hair. 'You may call me Dona Alicia if you wish, *nina,*' she offered. 'Now that we understand each other better, we can be friends. Si?'

'Si, I'd like that,' Juliet replied, finding some solace in the fact that at least Raul's grandmother's unflattering opinion of her had changed, even if his hadn't, and probably never would.

CHAPTER 9

Almost two weeks later, Holly's baby was born. In the hospital waiting room a little past midnight, Juliet looked up from the pages of the glossy magazine she was merely staring at. She shook her head as Benny paced in front of her for the millionth time, it seemed. 'Will you please sit down before you wear a hole in the carpet,' she said with a wry grin. 'You've been doing that since I got here at nine o'clock. Stop please: you're making me dizzy.'

'I can't stop,' Benny lamented, continuing his pacing as he raked his fingers through his untidy hair. 'When they called to tell me Holly had gone into labour, I was pretty calm—until I got here. Then when they told me it might take all night for the baby to be born, I just couldn't sit down and act like nothing was happening. How can I sit when Holly's all alone suffering all sorts of agonies.'

Sighing, Juliet closed the magazine she held. 'I don't imagine Holly's having a terrific time right now but don't blow everything all out of proportion. She's having a baby; women do that all the time. And the doctors won't let her suffer agonies and she's certainly not alone. She's being well taken care of and is probably a lot more relaxed than you are at the moment. So try to calm down,

Benny. Look at Senor Perez. His wife's having a baby right now too, but he's not pacing the floor like a caged lion.'

At the mention of his name, the rotund man beside Juliet opened his eyes, lifted his chin off his collarbone, and fought back a sleepy yawn. His warm brown eyes laughed understandingly at Benny but it was Juliet at whom he smiled. 'You say something to me, senorita?'

'No, not to you. About you,' Juliet explained. 'I was telling Benny that he should follow your example and relax. You don't seem unduly worried about your wife.'

'He had a few stiff drinks before he got here, I bet,' Benny interceded. 'He wouldn't be acting so calm if he hadn't.'

The older man laughed. 'Is not drink that has made me calm, senor. Is the experience I have. For Rosa and me, this will be baby *numero cinco.*'

'Five! You mean you've been through this hell four times before?' Benny exclaimed, horrified. 'How have you lived through it? Man, if I have my way, this will be our first *and* last baby. I couldn't stand the guilt of getting Holly pregnant again. It makes me sick to think about the pain she's having to endure right now.'

Senor Perez shook his head admonishingly, while lifting his shoulders in a fatalistic shrug. 'Women, they have the babies, senor. Men cannot do it. Is meant to be,' he philosophised. 'You have no need to feel the guilt.'

'Well, I don't happen to see it that way,' Benny shot back, tension making him uncharacteristically grumpy. 'This is my baby too, but Holly has to do all the suffering.'

'Benny, don't snap at the senor just because you're a nervous wreck,' Juliet said gently, catching her friend's hand as he paced by her. 'Sit down a minute. We'll talk.' When he reluctantly acquiesced and slumped down beside her on the orange vinyl sofa, she released his hand and smiled compassionately. 'Senor Perez is right, you shouldn't be feeling guilty. Holly wanted to have a baby right away so I don't know what you're blaming yourself for.'

'Oh, this whole pregnancy's been so

miserable for her. First she was sick in the mornings, then she had to stay in the hospital bed so many weeks and now, to top the whole mess off, she's having to go through labour pains.'

'That's usually the way pregnancies end,' Juliet reminded him wryly, but her slight smile faded when it wasn't returned. Her tone grew more serious. 'Look, I know Holly wouldn't want you to worry like this. You're wearing yourself out for no good reason. Isn't that right, Senor Perez?'

'Oh, si,' the older man replied with a wise smile. 'Is better to save your strength for when the baby goes home and cries all the nights.'

'Cries all night! Why should babies cry all night? Are they always sick?'

'Babies, they cry,' the senor philosophised again. 'Feed them. They stop for a while but soon they cry again. Is the way they are. You cannot change it.'

'Yeah, yeah is meant to be,' Benny mumbled, then jumped up to resume pacing again.

The next two hours passed slowly and Benny's unceasing movement began to make Juliet nearly as nervous as he was. Senor Perez's vigil was ended when a nurse came to tell him his wife had just had a healthy nine pound boy, his third son. After accepting Juliet's congratulations, he left the waiting room with a beaming smile on his way to call relatives to tell them the news.

As he disappeared into a phone booth down the hall, Benny turned to Juliet, horror widening his eyes. 'Nine pounds! Do you think something's wrong with it? Isn't that awfully small?'

'Lord, no. A nine pound baby is fairly large,' Juliet told him laughingly. 'I think most babies weigh less than that, about seven or eight pounds.'

'Oh, God, then what if our baby's nine pounds?' Benny groaned. 'That's too big. Holly's such a little girl. She can't have a nine pound baby!'

'Oh, will you be quiet,' Juliet pleaded. 'Stop looking for trouble everywhere. First nine pounds was too small; now it's too big. You've got to calm down, Benny. This will all be over soon and everything will be just fine. Someday, you'll look back at tonight and laugh at how nervous you were.'

'Huh, I doubt that,' he snorted as he stared glumly out the window. 'I'm not even sure I'll survive tonight so it won't be possible to look back on it.'

Juliet didn't answer. Nothing she said helped anyway. For the next half hour, she idled away the time by rearranging the contents of her purse, then making neat stacks of all the magazines in the waiting room. By the time she finished, Benny was reduced to muttering to himself as he continued walking back and forth across the room. Taking pity on him, she tried to initiate another conversation.

'Uncle Will said to tell you he certainly appreciates you staying at the house. It's a relief to him not to have to worry about break-ins.'

Benny halted mid-stride. 'How's he doing anyway? Leg mending all right?'

'Not fast enough for Uncle Will,' Juliet answered, smiling affectionately. 'He's very eager to get that cast off, mainly because he is about ready to murder that tyrannical nurse of his. He can't stand her.'

Benny frowned. 'Maybe I should be looking for a place for us to move if you think you and your uncle will be going back to his house soon. With the baby, Holly and I will need something bigger than a hotel room, maybe a little apartment. I just hope I can find something cheap.'

'You don't need to do that,' Juliet insisted. 'The doctor doesn't plan to remove Uncle Will's cast for several more weeks. So you and Holly will have the house to yourselves for a while and even after we move back, you won't need to leave. We'd both be happy to have you stay on.'

'Nope. We'll move out when you two come back. We wouldn't want to get in the way. I just hope I'll be able to find us a place inexpensive enough to allow us to save some money for our airfares back to the States.'

'You still plan to go back then?' Juliet asked, suppressing a sad little sigh when he nodded. 'I was sort of hoping you'd change your mind. I'm really going to miss you both.'

'We have to go though; it's the only

way for us to have a stable life.' Benny smiled teasingly. 'Besides, you won't have much time to miss us. Raul Valaquez will provide you with plenty of excitement, I'm sure.'

Juliet tried to smile in response, but couldn't quite succeed. 'I doubt I'll even see Raul very much after Uncle Will and I leave the *casa*. So I guess I'll just be at loose ends until I can get back into college for the second semester.'

'From what Holly told me about you and Raul, maybe you shouldn't be so sure you won't be seeing him,' Benny suggested. 'He might...'

'Senor Talmadge,' a nurse from the doorway interrupted. And when she beckoned to him, he simply stared at Juliet rather sillily.

'Well, go on,' she urged, waving him forward and following after, excitement rising in her. As Benny stopped before the nurse, gesturing nervously, she gave him a broad smile.

'You have a daughter, senor,' she announced, her English much better than Senor Perez's had been. 'The baby is little but that should be no trouble. She seems perfectly healthy.'

'And my wife?' Benny whispered urgently. 'Is she all right?'

'The little senora is perfect too,' the nurse assured him. 'She is tired now but there was no trouble with the delivery.'

As Benny swayed slightly, Juliet feared he might actually faint. After breathing a deep sigh of relief, however, he grabbed the nurse's hand and shook it so enthusiastically that the poor woman flexed it gingerly when he finally released it.

'I will return in a few minutes to take you to see the baby,' the nurse told him as she turned to leave. 'But it will be about an hour before your wife is returned to her room. Then, you may visit her also.'

Nodding, Benny spun around and enveloped Juliet in a nearly suffocating bear hug. 'Holly's fine; the baby's fine; they're both fine! Isn't it fantastic?'

'It's wonderful, Benny,' Juliet said raspingly, striving to catch her breath again. 'Congratulations, papa.'

'Papa. Me,' he whispered incredulously. 'I can hardly believe it.'

He repeated those words innumerable times during the next several minutes but when the nurse returned to lead them down the corridor to peer through the glass at the nursery, he suddenly became speechless. Yet when a bassinet was pushed up to the window, he gazed down at the flannel-bundled baby with awe.

'Gosh, she's tiny, isn't she. But look how beautiful she is. Don't you think she's beautiful?'

'Very beautiful,' Juliet agreed though she really couldn't tell. Obviously incensed, the baby was howling, her small red face contorted so much that her eyes were squeezed shut and her mouth was wide open. But Juliet was certain that in a more pacified frame of mind, Benny and Holly's daughter would be beautiful.

'She has thick black hair, like Holly's. See?' Benny commented happily, then muttered with disappointment when a nurse inside the nursery picked up the baby to pat her bottom comfortingly. Then she carried her away to sit down with her in a rocking chair in the far corner.

'You'll get to see her again,' Juliet

assured him as they walked back to the waiting room. And when he immediately collapsed onto the orange sofa, she smiled sympathetically. 'Why don't you stretch out and try to take a nap until you can see Holly? I think I'll leave now. You don't need me anymore; you'll want to see her alone. Tell her I'll visit tomorrow.'

'You're not driving all the way back to the *casa* now, are you? You shouldn't drive that far alone, Juliet. It's nearly four o'clock.'

'Well, maybe it would be wiser for me to just go to Uncle Will's house,' Juliet conceded. 'I told him I'd probably be at the hospital all night so he won't be worried about me. And it would be nice to get home in five minutes and fall right into bed. I'm tired.'

'I don't know what I would have done without you,' Benny said earnestly. 'Gone absolutely batty, I guess. Thanks for staying with me and trying to calm all my fears. I suppose I acted pretty silly.'

'Maniacal,' Juliet teased. 'But very, very normal for first-time fathers, I suspect. And you don't have to thank me

273

for staying. I wouldn't have missed this event for anything.'

'You're sure you'll be all right at the house alone.'

'I'm a big girl, Benny, and it'll be morning in a couple of hours anyway. I'll be fine. But I need the key I gave you. I'll leave it by the trunk of the potted ornamental yew tree by the door so you can get in later without waking me.' As he handed her the key and yawned behind one hand, she added, 'Now you take a nap. And for heaven's sake, comb your hair before you see Holly. She'll think you've been hit by a truck if she sees you the way you look right now.'

'Yes, mommy,' he quipped. 'I'll take my nap and comb my hair like a good boy.'

Juliet wrinkled her nose at him but his eyes were already fluttering shut so she tiptoed from the waiting room.

During the five minute drive to her uncle's house, Juliet's own eyelids began to droop. Benny's nervousness had been contagious and now that the excitement was over, she felt drained and more than ready for a few hours sleep. After parking the Esprit by the curb, she hurried to the front door, anxious to get inside. The dark moonless night was too eerily silent for her peace of mind. She turned the key in the lock, slipped into the hall, and firmly closed the door behind her, as she switched on the light. The long vigil at the hospital had made her a bit hungry so she went to the kitchen to slice off a morsel of sharp but smooth *Manchego* cheese. Tiredly nibbling it, she walked back through the hall and started up the stairs.

A sudden soft tapping on the front door halted her progress immediately. Her heart jerked against her breastbone and the last bite of cheese, which she had just swallowed skidded to a standstill somewhere in the vicinity of mid-throat. She swallowed repeatedly until at last the cheese continued its downward journey but her heart was still pounding rapidly as she stood immobile on the stairs, wondering if she had merely imagined she heard the tapping.

She hadn't. It came again, slightly louder this time. Pressing her fist between her breasts, she tiptoed down the stairs, knowing it wouldn't be Benny knocking. She had left the key where she had promised and, besides, he couldn't have seen Holly and left the hospital already. Moistening dry lips with the tip of her tongue, she moved toward the door and as she passed a side table she impulsively picked up a brass candle holder for use as a possible weapon. By the door, she took several deep voice-steadying breaths before softly calling, 'Who is it?'

'It's Raul,' his deep voice came back. 'Let me in, Juliet.'

Her fingers shook as she fumbled with the lock but she jerked open the door eagerly. As he entered the brightly lighted hall, she fought the desire to fly into his arms but it *was* good to see him. Until yesterday, he had been in Madrid for nearly a week and for several days before that he had kept himself so busy in his office at the *casa* that she had rarely seen him. Though she didn't mean to stare at him, she couldn't drag her gaze away. Dressed in casual khaki trousers and a dark green rugby styled shirt, he was so overwhelmingly masculine that she suddenly felt safer merely because he was in the house with her.

But why was he here?' she wondered, wrinkling her forehead questioningly. There was a certain drowsy look in his eyes that made her suspect he had just risen out of bed. But whose bed? Jemina Ruiz's? That certainly made sense because to leave Jemina's hotel to go home, he had to pass this house. Perhaps he had seen the Esprit and stopped to discover why she was here. The thought that he had probably spent most of the night with Jemina was rather nauseating, but needing to know the truth Juliet asked evasively, 'How did you know I was here?'

'Benny told me.'

'Benny? But how...'

'Will was worried about you so Rosita called the hospital about an hour ago and was told you must not be there because no once could find you in the waiting room.'

'That must have been when Benny and I were down by the nursery.'

'Probably. But Will had no way of knowing that so he got a little upset. He didn't like the idea of you driving back to the *casa* so late so he asked me to come look for you. When I didn't meet you on the road, I went to the hospital and Benny told me you had come here.'

'Oh. Well, I'm sorry Uncle Will dragged you out of bed unnecessarily,' Juliet murmured, 'I did tell him I might not be home all night. He shouldn't have been worried. I wish he hadn't bothered you.'

Raul tossed up one hand in a dismissive gesture. 'It was no bother. When Rosita told me she couldn't reach you at the hospital, I was worried too.'

'Were you?' Juliet breathed, her heart flip-flopping in response to the curiously strained quality she imagined she had detected in his deep voice. 'Really, Raul?'

'So, Holly had her baby,' he remarked, ignoring her question completely. 'Was it a boy or girl? I didn't ask Benny.'

'A girl with dark thick hair just like Holly's,' Juliet told him enthusiastically. 'You should see her, Raul. She's the tiniest thing.'

Dark green eyes swept over her as he

smiled indulgently. 'You sound very impressed. Was she that pretty?'

Juliet grimaced comically. 'Well, I'm sure she's pretty when she isn't crying but when I saw her tonight, she looked rather like a gnome, to tell the truth. But don't you dare tell Benny I said that. He thought she was the most magnificent child ever born, of course.'

'Of course,' Raul agreed wryly.

When he said nothing more and merely stood gazing at her intently, the drowsy look in his eyes became increasingly more disconcerting. Finally, Juliet gestured hesitantly. 'I suppose I should call Uncle Will and tell him I'm fine.'

'I suppose you should. And tell him that I'll stay here with you until morning so he has nothing to worry about.'

His proposal that they spend the rest of the night together alone in the house was stated calmly and matter-of-factly but the idea made Juliet tremble slightly nevertheless. Considering the passion that flared between them at times, she wasn't certain he or she, herself, could resist the temptation that might arise in such a situation. She shook her head.

'You don't have to stay. I mean, it's kind of you to offer but it really isn't necessary. As soon as Benny has seen Holly, he'll come home so I won't be alone.'

Raul stepped toward her, his expression hardening with impatience. 'You don't really think I'd let you stay here alone with Benny, do you?' he muttered. 'If you do, you're badly mistaken.'

'What's the difference in my staying here alone with him and staying here alone with you?' Juliet asked rather sharply, put on the defensive by his commanding tone. 'I can't see there's any difference whatsoever.'

'There's a big difference,' he answered calmly. 'He's a married man and I'm not. And I don't think Holly would be happy to hear the two of you had spent the night together.'

Juliet tensed, amber eyes flashing. 'What's that supposed to mean? Are you insinuating again that Benny and I...'

'I'm not insinuating anything,' Raul interrupted curtly. 'I'm merely stating a fact: Benny is a married man and here in Granada, it's not socially acceptable for a single girl to spend the night with a man who's married.'

'But it's all right for a single girl and single man to spend the night together,' she retorted. 'Is that what you're saying?'

'Let's just say it's a more acceptable arrangement,' he replied with infuriating aloofness. 'So I'm staying and that's that. Now, I suggest we stop this useless arguing and try to get some sleep. So,' he stared pointedly at the telephone. 'Are you going to call Will or shall I do it myself?'

'I'll do it,' Juliet muttered indignantly, sweeping past him to snatch up the receiver. It was Rosita she ultimately talked to, and although the housekeeper had to hear all about Holly and the baby, the call was relatively brief. After replacing the receiver, Juliet turned warily to face Raul again.

He was massaging the back of his neck with one lean hand, his dark face expressionless. 'I suggest we go to bed,' he said, his voice appealingly low and husky. But when her eyes widened, his took on an icy glint and he added sarcastically, 'In separate rooms, of course, if you'd be so kind as to show me to one.'

Tossing up her chin, she marched past him and preceded him up the stairs, down the hall one door past her own room. 'This is Uncle Will's room,' she told Raul. 'I hope you'll be comfortable.'

'I'm sure I will be,' he said softly, stepping forward as if he meant to enter the room. But he stopped before her and amazingly lifted a silken strand of her hair, rubbing it between his thumb and forefinger, as if testing its texture. But with her soft intake of breath, he released it again. 'Good night, Juliet.'

There was a strange tenderness in his tone that made it impossible to lift her gaze above the smooth brown column of his neck. She put out one hand as if to touch his arm, then decided against it. 'I'm sorry if I sounded ungrateful downstairs,' she blurted out compulsively at last. 'It's kind of you to stay here with me so Uncle Will won't worry.'

'Good night, Juliet,' he merely repeated, then stepped into the room and pushed the door shut behind him.

A minute later, in her own bedroom,

Juliet undressed slowly, unable to forget for a second that Raul was just next door. After slipping into a cool white lawn nightgown, she haphazardly washed her face and brushed her teeth. As she pulled back the quilted coverlet on her bed, she was certain she wouldn't get much rest at all for thinking about him being in the next room but as she slid in between cool blue sheets, her head hardly had time to touch the pillow before she was asleep.

She was dreaming about Raul and it was a happy dream. He was being incredibly nice to her and she felt a joyous sense of belonging. Yet it was a rather fragmented dream. First, they were walking hand in hand through the courtyard at the *casa,* then suddenly, they were standing together, looking through a nursery window, not at Holly's baby but at one that bore a striking resemblance to Raul, who was smiling down at her. It was as she smiled back at him that the dream faded and she was roused from sleep by a feather-light brushing back of hair from her face. As a result of the pleasant dream, a slight smile hovered when she opened her eyes and found Raul sitting on the edge of the bed beside her. It seemed right somehow for him to be there and she felt very little surprise even as his fingertips brushed across the sensitive nape of her neck.

'I've brought you coffee, Juliet,' he said softly, inclining his head toward the tray on the bedside table. 'It's rather late. I thought you might want to get up.'

'Not really,' she whispered. 'But what time is it?'

His fingers continued caressing her neck. 'It's nearly ten.'

'I suppose I should get up then, shouldn't I?'

He didn't answer. His narrowed gaze drifted over the fascinating contours of her body outlined against the sheet that covered her, then his eyes met hers again. 'Why were you smiling in your sleep?'

Perhaps it was lingering sleepiness that allowed her to tell the truth. 'I was dreaming—about you.'

The fingers against her nape ceased moving. 'A nice dream?'

'Yes,' she whispered, a sudden breathlessness roughening her voice. 'I—I think so.'

'What was your dream about? Will you tell me?'

'I can't remember exactly,' she lied, awake enough now to realise how dangerous it was for him to be sitting on her bed clad in only her uncle's terry bathrobe. 'Y-you know how vague dreams are sometimes.'

'But you remember enough about this one to know it was about me,' he persisted. 'So why can't you remember why you were smiling?'

She could only shake her head and become increasingly aware of an excitement that was mounting inside her, making her entire body grow heated though she was only covered by the thin sheet. 'I should get up. Is Benny here?' she babbled self-consciously. 'I—I didn't hear him come in. Did you?'

'No, but unless you snore outrageously loud, he must be here,' Raul said softly, mischievously. 'Because when I went down to make the coffee, I heard someone snoring loudly enough to wake the dead.'

Juliet had to smile. 'Holly's often said the same thing about his snoring. It's usually louder when he's tired. And he must be exhausted after last night.' Her words trailed off into a silence so unbearably nerve-wracking she had to break it again herself. 'I should get up. Th-thank you for bringing the coffee. I'll have a cup while I dress.'

'I thought we could have it together,' he murmured, a suspiciously teasing gleam in his jade green eyes. 'But if you'd like to get up and dress while you drink yours, I certainly won't object. I can't think of anything I'd rather do than watch you take off your nightgown.'

Juliet's cheeks flamed. 'Raul, please, go,' she murmured. 'It's crazy for you to be in here.'

'Is it?' He shook his head. 'I feel right at home and don't plan to leave...until you tell me what you were dreaming.'

She hesitated, then blurted out, 'It was a very choppy dream. We were walking in the courtyard at Casa Valaquez and...'

'And...'

'We were looking at a baby through a hospital nursery window.'

286

'Benny and Holly's baby?'

'P—probably,' she evaded, the inquisition beginning to make her tremble. 'I couldn't tell.'

'Really?' Raul's black eyebrows shot up. 'Surely you remember if the baby looked like a gnome. Did it?'

She giggled nervously and shook her head. 'No, the baby wasn't crying and was very handsome, actually.'

'Handsome? Hmm, since you use that particular word, the baby must have been a boy. Right?'

'I guess. Oh, I don't know! Why are you asking all these questions? Why do you care about my dream?'

'Because it was about me. I'm merely curious.'

'Well, that's all I remember about it so...'

'But why were you smiling?'

'Because in it, you were smiling at me!' she exclaimed softly. 'So why shouldn't I smile back?'

'Why indeed.' He laughed softly, then leaned down until his lips were brushing hers. 'I think it's very interesting that you dreamed you and I were looking at a baby in a hospital nursery, then smiling at each other, don't you? I think maybe you were dreaming that was *our* baby.'

Shaking her head, she shrank down against the mattress. 'Why should I d-dream something like that? I've never even thought about having a baby.'

'But you'd like to someday, wouldn't you, Juliet?'

'Well, sure, I guess so but...' A kiss silenced her, a kiss that began lightly, caressingly, then suddenly became a ravishing possession. The strength of the firm warm lips that parted hers forcefully became all that was real in the world until his hands trailed over her sheet-covered body and his touch became devastatingly real too. Her skin caught fire everywhere his hands made contact and suddenly, even the thin sheet seemed a barrier she no longer wanted between them. 'Come to bed, Raul,' she whispered urgently, unable to prevent herself and as he slipped beneath the sheet, her slender arms swiftly encircled his neck. He was so warm, so muscularly lean that she couldn't fight the weakness that invaded her body as his weight pressed her down into the soft mattress. Catching her small face between his hands, he lowered his head, his lips parting hers hungrily until her slender young body was arching against him.

'Juliet, God, I want you; *te quiero,* ' he whispered hoarsely, his breath hot as he pressed a burning kiss into the hollow at the base of her throat. 'And you're not afraid of me, not so afraid that you'll say no this time. Will you? Say yes, Juliet. Let me love you. Don't say no.'

'I don't want to say no,' she confessed, her fingers tangling in his hair. 'But...'

'I can't let you go this time; forgive me,' he groaned, even as he swiftly removed her gown and pushed it off the bed onto the floor. His robe followed. One strong arm slipped beneath her, pulling her over on top of him and as their legs tangled and her soft breasts yielded to the hard surface of his chest, he gripped the back of her head in one hand and brought her mouth down to meet his.

The fire within Juliet blazed out of control as she gave him back kiss for kiss and she could only moan softly as he swiftly pressed her back down onto the bed again. A tremor of delight shook her body as his hands caressed and kneaded her breasts and her own fingers eagerly traced the contours of the broad muscular shoulders above her.

'Your skin's like satin,' he whispered between bruising kisses. 'I want to touch every inch of it. But I don't want to take you, Juliet; I want you to give yourself to me. Can you?'

'Raul, I...'

'God, you have to now,' he muttered roughly before his mouth took hers again.

Drowning in sensual pleasure, aching for his lovemaking, Juliet was on the verge of total surrender when she heard the footsteps on the stairs. Then she remembered it was Wednesday and Rosita always came to tidy the house on Wednesdays. She tensed, instinctively pushing against Raul's chest. 'Please! Raul, you have to let me go,' she begged. 'Rosita's coming up the stairs. She'll come in here!'

Raul didn't seem to hear. His hands curved into her waist, holding her against him as he whispered her name into her ear and it was only as the bedroom door was opened, that he finally pulled away slightly.

As he turned his head, Juliet opened her eyes, then, with a barely audible groan, hastily tugged the sheet closer up beneath her chin. She could have died of embarrassment. It was bad enough for Rosita to find her in bed with a man who didn't love her but Jemena Ruiz was standing in the doorway too, as usual, in the wrong place at the wrong time again. Yet, even Jemena's presence was insignificant compared to the fact that Alicia Valaquez was between the other two women! And her obsidian eyes were as hard and cold as chips of ice as she glared at Raul and Juliet.

No one moved; no one spoke for what seemed an eternity of time until, at last, Jemina broke the silence by saying viciously, 'Well, well, we seem to be intruding, do we not, Dona Alicia?'

'*Silencio!*' the senora commanded. And as Jemena quickly obeyed and shut her mouth, the older woman ignored Rosita's tearful murmurings, eased the overwrought housekeeper to one side, and stepped farther into the room. 'Since I had business in town, I offered to drive Rosita here to do her weekly maintenance cleaning. Jemena was at the *casa* looking for you so when I told her you were here, she followed in her car. We did not intend to intrude on this—this scene but I think perhaps it is good that we did.'

Juliet could believe neither her calm tone nor Raul's response to it. He simply inclined his head at the explanation, as if nothing out of the ordinary was occurring. Why didn't he tell his grandmother that nothing had actually happened? That had to be made clear and at last, Juliet felt compelled to say it herself.

Her denial made no impression on Dona Alicia who merely gestured impatiently. 'My eyes do not lie to me, *nina*. I see what I see.' Then turning to Raul, she uttered a few words in sharp clipped Spanish.

In Spanish also, his reply was equally brief and elicited confusing reactions.

With a strangled imprecation, Jemena swung out of the doorway to stamp down the hall, her spike heels hammering the tile floor violently. Even more astounding, Rosita was grinning as Raul's grandmother regally preceded her into the hall and the housekeeper winked at Juliet, then drew the door closed again.

'You have to convince her that nothing happened!' Juliet insisted urgently, gripping Raul's forearm in supplication. 'You saw how upset she was to find us—like this. You have to ease her mind about it!'

Raul propped himself more comfortably on one elbow, his dark gaze holding hers. 'Telling her nothing happened would be useless. As she said, she sees what she sees and no one will convince her she didn't.'

Juliet pressed her fingers against throbbing temples. 'What she must think of me!' she whispered bleakly. 'What did she say to you in Spanish? And what did you answer that made Jemena so angry?'

Raul's jaw tightened as he simply looked down at her for a long moment. 'Abuela asked me what our plans were. And I told her that you will be a Valaquez bride after all. My bride,

293

Juliet, as soon as a wedding can be arranged.' And his expression was totally unfathomable as Juliet's amber eyes widened in stunned disbelief.

CHAPTER 10

'You can't mean that!' she gasped softly, her face paling. 'I mean, you can't just tell me we're going to get married simply because your grandmother misunderstands what she saw! That doesn't make any sense! It's...'

Silencing her by pressing one finger against her lips, Raul gave her a slight mysterious smile and his expression was still beyond analysis. 'Maybe it does make sense,' he countered softly. 'Maybe it's inevitable. I think perhaps it was always your destiny to become a Valaquez bride.'

'But you can't just accept the situation as inevitable! You haven't even tried to tell your grandmother that we didn't—that nothing happened between us despite what she saw.'

Raul lifted one shoulder in a slight shrug. 'I know Abuela. She can be a very obstinate woman. Nothing I say to her is going to change her mind about what she saw. You may as well accept that fact, Juliet. I do.'

Juliet shook her head, her expression incredulous, conflicting emotions causing her heart to hammer erratically. If only he loved her, she would have been eager to marry him, but he didn't and she had too much pride to enter into a marriage that a regrettable misunderstanding was forcing upon him. And actually she was astounded that he was taking this entire situation so calmly. Usually he was so strong-willed and in total command of his own life but that slight shrug he had just given seemed to have conveyed a near fatalistic attitude, as if he meant to accept this marriage without protest. Still clutching the edge of the sheet up beneath her small chin, she searched his face almost frantically. Could she have misread his personality completely? Perhaps the modern image he projected was merely a thin veneer. Perhaps he was more old-fashioned than she had ever imagined. Too confused to speak, she could only gaze at his dark finely carved features until he gently brushed a tousled strand of russet hair back from her cheek. Then she trembled and there was something of a beseeching luminosity in her eyes as they sought the dark green depths of his.

'Are you really trying to tell me you're going to let yourself be forced into a marriage?' she whispered tremulously. 'Oh, Raul, I don't think I understand you at all.'

'You will,' he whispered back, his gaze roaming over the delicate features of her face, then downward to take in the rounded contours of her slender body outlined against the thin sheet. 'After we're married...'

'But we can't get married! Not like this!' The edge of her teeth pressed down into the softness of her lower lip and her expression conveyed some anguish. 'You don't want to sacrifice your freedom because of a misunderstanding. And I don't want...'

'*Basta*. Enough, Juliet,' he commanded roughly, catching her chin between one thumb and forefinger. 'You must accept the inevitable.'

'But I...'

'You seem to be forgetting something very important,' he murmured, lowering his dark head until his warm minty breath was caressing her temple. 'What Abuela believes happened would have happened if she hadn't walked into this room a moment ago. And since even you must know that it's inevitable that we will make love sooner or later, don't you think it would be wise for us to get married.'

'You couldn't marry me just for—just to—oh, you know what I mean.'

'I only know that I can't wait much longer to possess you. You are exquisite, Juliet, and I want you,' he answered huskily, hot passion flaring in his eyes.

As his warm mouth covered hers, she tried to fight the traitorous response of her body but the battle was futile. His hardening lips caught the tender lower curve of hers, tugging gently until her mouth opened slightly and the tip of his tongue sought the sweetness within. Her senses came alive and as he gently prised open the small fingers that clutched the sheet, she released it with a soft moan of submission. Fire danced over her skin as his hand slipped beneath the sheet to brush over her bare shoulders. His fingertips probed the delicate contours of her collarbone and the shadowed hollow at the base of her creamy throat. Then his lips followed the path of his fingers, his teeth nipping gently at her sensitised skin.

She gasped softly as his hands took possession of her breasts, cupping the rounded cushioned flesh, stroking her satin textured skin with seeking fingers. His mouth sought hers again, parting her lips with swift demand, conveying a nearly insatiable hunger that took her breath away. He was very expertly seducing her. She knew that, yet as he traced the throbbing peaks of her breasts, then rubbed his thumbs across them coaxingly until they hardened with desire beneath his questing touch, she couldn't suppress the quickening shaft of pleasure that made her dizzy with longing for him. A central throbbing emptiness deep within her became an intolerable aching and she arched against him, seeking fulfillment and finding delight in his hard smooth body as he pressed her down swiftly into the mattress. His bare skin, hot against hers, was an enticement she couldn't resist. Wrapping her arms around his waist, she feathered her hands over his strong broad back, tracing corded muscles with eager fingertips.

'*Te quiero,*' he breathed raggedly close to her ear, then captured the tender lobe between his teeth and nibbled gently until she could withstand the piercing sensations that rippled through her no longer and urged his mouth to hers again.

Even then, the seduction continued. His lips played with hers teasingly until her fingers tangled in the thick hair on his nape, pressing him down, urging a rougher taking of her mouth. His kisses deepened, became slow rousing quests that demanded total surrender and when she was all warm and yielding beneath him, his lips sought the taut roseate peaks of her round breasts and the brushing touch of his tongue heightened the empty aching inside her.

Her slender legs tangled with his but as she felt the hardening ridge of his body surge powerfully against her smooth thighs, one hand curved possessively over one slight hipbone, pressing her down into the mattress, denying her contact with his upsurging masculinity.

She made a soft beseeching sound and her eyes fluttered open to see the slight triumphant smile that curved his firmly carved mouth before it descended on hers again. With gentle aggression, his lips plundered her own and when her hands began to move feverishly over his back, one muscular arm slipped beneath her gently curving hips and arched her soft warmth upward to brush against him. And she had never wanted anything in her life as much as she suddenly wanted to belong completely to him.

Turning over onto his side, he brought her with him, holding her slender pliant body close against the hard lithe warmth of his. A gentle hand stroked her tousled hair back from her face as he whispered, 'And now you finally begin to see how it is, don't you, Juliet? You're beginning to want me almost as much as I want you. So it is inevitable—married or not, we will become lovers soon.'

'Not if I go away,' she whispered back tremulously, trying to ignore the shiver of awareness that still trickled along her spine as he lazily massaged her slim waist with his other hand. 'We couldn't become—lovers if I leave Granada.'

'But you will not leave,' he declared, his low tone taking on a hard edge as his grip tightened around her waist. Entwining his fingers in her hair, he tilted her face up slightly, forcing her to meet the stern light in his green eyes. 'Is that understood, Juliet? You won't run away from Granada again. I'm the prospective bridegroom this time, not Pablo, and it would be a very foolish mistake for you to try to run away from me.'

Still too bemused by the intense needs he had aroused in her, she had no desire to run away from him, though her common sense was screaming at her that she should try to get as far away as she could. Confusion raged in her and with a muffled sigh, she burrowed her face into his neck, barely aware that she was seeking comfort from the very person who was tormenting her. 'I can't let you make me marry you,' she muttered weakly. 'I just can't.'

His lips brushed her hair. 'Marriage to me won't be all that bad, Juliet,' he said softly. 'I promise you I'll try to make you happy.'

Only your love could make me happy, she cried out to him silently, unable to voice the words, fearing he would utter the lie and say that he did love her, simply to get her to agree to the marriage. Instead, she nuzzled her cheek closer to the smooth warmth of his skin but as she started to remind him that he could not stop her from running away from him, he pulled away, shaking his head.

'No more discussion, Juliet. We are getting married as soon as we can. In the meantime, you will be kept very busy by Abuela, I'm sure, making arrangements for the wedding.' A smile hovered at the corners of his mouth an instant before he brushed a light, teasingly evocative kiss against her lips. 'So I suggest you simply relax and enjoy the next few days. Why fight against the inevitable?'

Why indeed? she wondered, longing to surrender to his demands and take him any way she could get him. Then all her inner turmoil was temporarily forgotten and she had to bite back a soft gasp as Raul lowered his feet to the floor suddenly and got out of the bed. The sunlight filtering through the windows glowed over his bronzed skin while he looked around for the terry bathrobe he had discarded. Having never seen a naked man before, Juliet blushed hotly and squeezed her eyes shut, only to allow them to flutter open again when Raul glanced down at her and laughed softly. By then, the robe covered him and he was tying the belt loosely around his waist and when she inadvertently released her breath in a soft sigh of relief, he grinned unabashedly and shook his head.

'How shy you are, Juliet,' he said softly, teasingly. 'I do believe you're going to be a typical blushing bride.'

'I'm not going to be a bride at all, blushing or otherwise,' she argued weakly. 'Raul, I can't be. This is so crazy. I...'

'You will not run away, Juliet,' he interrupted tersely, thrusting his hands into the pockets of his robe and gazing down at her intently, his green eyes darkly enigmatic. 'I plan to keep a close watch over you from now until our wedding day so make up your mind to it—you won't run out on me the way you did Pablo last year. And I think you realise I won't allow you to.'

She did. Deep down inside, she knew he was not a man who made idle threats so if he said he would be watching her closely, she was certain he meant it. Suddenly the reality of the situation overwhelmed her and as Raul turned and strode from the room, she pressed her fist between her breasts, hoping to ease the ache caused by her pounding heartbeat. He meant it when he said they were going to be married very soon and in that moment in time, she wasn't even sure she wanted to try to defy him.

Raul was true to his word. He spent the next day at the *casa* where she was and even when he decided to drive into Granada, he insisted she go with him.

'But should I change clothes?' she asked him weakly out in the courtyard where he had found her playing gin rummy with her uncle. 'Where exactly are we going?'

'Just to the gallery,' he informed her, sweeping a long gaze over her neat denim sundress. 'And no, don't change clothes. You look fine as you are.'

'She always looks lovely,' Will spoke up dotingly, then grinned at the younger man. 'And I'm sure you've noticed that dreamy-eyed look she's had in her eyes since yesterday. You can take the credit for that, you know. I guess brides-to-be *do* have a radiant inner glow.'

Entrancing colour bloomed in Juliet's cheeks and though she knew Raul was watching her, she couldn't meet his gaze directly. If she had a radiant inner glow about her, she wished her uncle hadn't mentioned it. She certainly didn't want Raul to realise exactly how susceptible she was to him.

If he had come to that realisation, he was too gallant to let her know it. Catching one small hand in his, he simply said good-bye to Will and escorted her beneath the stone arch and along the flagstone path that led them to the driveway where the cream-coloured BMW was parked. After she was settled in the car, he came around to slip in beneath the steering wheel, then, without a word, he started the engine and drove away from the *casa*.

Out on the highway a few moments later, he glanced at her and said softly, 'You're very quiet, Juliet. Don't tell me you're still trying to fight the inevitable.'

'I feel so guilty,' she blurted out, clenching her hands together in her lap. 'You just don't understand that I felt like the most awful fraud this morning when you told Uncle Will we were getting married. He was so pleased but of course he doesn't know you're only marrying me to placate your grandmother.'

'Do you think he'd be any less pleased about our plans if he knew about yesterday morning?' Raul countered tonelessly. 'He's an old-fashioned man, Juliet, and if he had been with Abuela when she found us in your bedroom, he would have expected the same thing she did—marriage.'

'But I would have been able to explain to him that nothing happened,' Juliet murmured. 'And he would have believed me. He trusts me and you and if we had told him nothing happened, he wouldn't have expected you to marry me.'

Raul turned his head, his dark intelligent eyes narrowing, seemingly piercing the amber depths of hers. 'Why didn't you tell Will the truth then?' he asked, his voice low and melodious. 'If you had explained the entire situation to him, you might have gained an ally in your fight against marrying me. I think you're right. He would have believed you so why didn't you tell him the truth?' As he turned his attention back to the road again, there was a barely perceptible tightening of his jaw. 'I think it's very interesting that you didn't tell him and try to gain his support, don't you?'

Averting her gaze, Juliet shifted uncomfortably in her seat. 'I really didn't see—any point in upsetting him.'

'How disappointing,' Raul said lazily. 'And I was hoping you didn't ask him to help you cancel the wedding plans because you'd decided being married to me wouldn't be such a terrible ordeal after all.'

Her eyes darted up to meet his and though she detected a hint of a teasing gleam in the dark green depths, she realised his tone had been half serious. A revealing warmth coloured her cheeks an entrancing pink and she hastily turned to stare out her window. He was too perceptive by far and at the moment, she was too unnerved by the truth of what he had said to even attempt to deny it.

During the remainder of the drive to Granada, Raul turned their conversation to impersonal topics so Juliet had relaxed somewhat by the time they reached the gallery. Even Jemina Ruiz's disparaging attitude didn't upset her unduly. Elegantly chic in a scarlet silk blouse and expensively tailored natural linen skirt, the older woman smiled rather snidely as her cold brown eyes flicked over Juliet's plain denim sundress. Not bothering to speak, she simply acknowledged Juliet with a curt nod, then latched on to Raul's right arm and with a proprietorial air, hauled him into the office in the rear of the gallery.

Waiting there was Luis Diego, the talented young artist Raul had talked to at Janine Elcano's party. He didn't speak English so Raul introduced him to Juliet in Spanish. Catching the word *novia,* knowing it meant fiancée, Juliet experienced a curiously warming sense of belonging, which didn't diminish even as Jemina bristled almost visibly beside her. Besides, Luis Diego nodded and smiled at her with frank admiration, as if he understood perfectly why Raul planned to marry her. As he lifted one small hand and kissed it gallantly, Juliet smiled, partially because his clipped black moustache tickled her skin but mainly because he was such a charming young man.

After all the social pleasantries had been taken care of, conversation turned to Diego's paintings. Understanding no more than every other word of the rapid-fire Spanish the other three were speaking, Juliet decided to browse through the gallery. Yet, as soon as she stepped quietly out of the office, she was halted by Raul, who caught one of her hands in both his.

'We must start those Spanish lessons

soon,' he declared softly, his darkening gaze capturing hers. 'I don't want you to feel excluded from this discussion simply because Luis can't speak English.'

His seemingly genuine concern for her feelings touched her deeply and the love she felt for him intensified with astonishing fervour. A soft radiance illuminated her golden amber eyes as she shook her head, smiling slightly. 'I don't feel excluded, Raul, really.'

The slow answering smile he gave curved his sensuously carved mouth, then he released her hand almost reluctantly and left her to go back to Luis Diego.

The main room of the gallery was circular with a gleaming marble tiled floor and off-white walls that didn't distract attention from the paintings displayed on them. While Raul and Luis discussed the works they would exhibit in Luis's first private showing at the gallery in two weeks, Juliet wandered around, pausing now and then to more closely examine a painting or sculpture that caught her eye. It was as she was admiring the vibrant colours of a painting of three children playing in a garden that Jemina came out of the office to join her, her high-heeled shoes rapping sharply on the marble floor.

Ignoring Juliet's questioning glance, she immediately launched into a mile-a-minute monologue in Spanish, accompanying it with exaggerated hand gestures. She was speaking much more rapidly than she usually did, apparently in a deliberate attempt to make Juliet feel rather stupid. Recognising only an occasional word, Juliet lifted her hands, halting Jemina's tirade midstream, then smiled politely. 'If you would try to speak a bit more slowly and more clearly, I think I might be able to understand what you're saying.'

Jemina snorted indelicately and folded her arms across her chest. 'You Americans are all alike, are you not? You expect everyone everywhere to accommodate you. But I do not feel like accommodating you, Senorita McKay. You are in my country and if you are too lazy to try to understand the Spanish language, then that is your problem, not mine.'

'But I am trying to improve my

Spanish,' Juliet replied flatly, striving hard to control her rising impatience. 'That's why I asked you to speak more slowly but if you'd rather not go to the trouble, then that's fine with me. I'm sure I can find other people who'd be willing to be more co-operative and understanding.'

Jemina snorted again, her eyes glittering malevolently. 'You may gain the co-operation of shopkeepers and other such peasants, senorita, but do not expect Raul's friends and family to be so accommodating. You will be an outsider in their circles and they will resent you from the beginning for trapping Raul into marrying you. His bride should be Spanish and from a family as distinguished as his own. None of his friends or family is happy that he is being forced into a marriage with you—an American with red hair and pale skin.'

Recognising Jemina's jealous motivation in lashing out at her, Juliet gave a careless shrug. 'I didn't realise Raul's friends and family had authorised you to be their spokesperson, and maybe they haven't. I suspect you're only expressing your own personal opinion.'

Her calm only served to provoke Jemina further. *'Imbécil!'* she spat out disgustedly. 'You are too stupid to see that Raul is only marrying you because honour demands it. He will not be happy with you. He will only tolerate you and you will never be part of his life. His friends will never accept you and both he and his grandmother are probably sick at the thought of *you* providing a Valaquez heir. Valaquez men have always married Spanish girls and had fine dark Andalusian babies. But you with your red hair and white skin will not be able to give him such children, will you?'

Juliet almost winced, her own doubts about the coming marriage re-enforced by Jemina's stinging statements. Yet, refusing to satisfy the older woman's vindictive nature by appearing the least bit upset, she gave a careless toss of one hand and turned back to the painting she had been admiring. 'I think it's a bit early to even think about having children,' she said tonelessly. 'So I'll worry about presenting the Valaquez family with a red-haired heir later. In the meantime, I'll just hope most of Raul's friends will be more polie to me than you are, Senorita Ruiz.'

'Oh, they will be polite but that is all they will be,' Jemina whispered viciously. 'They will just never accept you as one of them so it would be very stupid of you expect them to.'

'I think you owe Juliet an apology, Jemina,' Raul suddenly said, his voice dangerously low as he startled both women by appearing from behind a large metal sculpture to their left. Two long strides brought him close to Juliet and as he draped a possessive arm across her shoulders, he surveyed Jemina critically. 'You've taken too much upon yourself. My friends don't need you to speak for them. Most of them seem quite eager to meet Juliet, so eager in fact that she and I will be spending this weekend near Almeria so we won't have to contend with a continual stream of visitors to the *casa*. A bride-to-be deserves peace and quiet just before her wedding. And this bride-to-be also deserves an apology from you, Jemina.'

With an outraged toss of her dark

head, Jemina uttered something undoubtedly uncomplimentary beneath her breath then marched back toward the office, the ramrod straightness of her back indicating an apology from her wouldn't be forthcoming any time soon.

After she had disappeared, Raul turned Juliet to him, slipping his long fingers through the silky thickness of her fiery hair. His jade green eyes captured and held her gaze. 'Jemina is not a very diplomatic person,' he said softly. 'And I'm sorry if she upset you.'

'It doesn't matter. She's never liked me and to tell the truth, I've never liked her either,' Juliet admitted, then scanned his lean face with searching intensity. 'Is that true—what you told Jemina? Are we really spending the weekend near Almeria?'

Brushing his thumbs caressingly over her slender neck, Raul nodded and smiled knowingly. 'It's true but you needn't sound so apprehensive. We'll be properly chaperoned, I assure you. A friend Manuel Olvera and his wife have invited us to spend the weekend with them. I think you will like them, Juliet,' he added, tapping the tip of her small nose playfully. 'And despite Jemina's ridiculous comments, I'm sure Manuel and his wife will like you.'

Though Juliet nodded, the smile she gave was rather wan and uncertain and she couldn't shake the vague unpleasant suspicion that Raul was only being so supportive because he thought he should be.

CHAPTER 11

The drive toward Almeria on Saturday morning was a scenic delight. Following the craggy shoreline, the road over-looked the sapphire sea, gilded gold in the sunlight. A Mediterranean balminess was in the air and Juliet inhaled appreciatively the fresh salt breeze as she gazed out her open car window. Flat-roofed and flower-bedecked white houses clustered in villages that clung precariously to the rocky sloping shore above pebbled beaches where an occasional fisherman repaired his nets on the sand beside his beached boat.

Juliet found the quaint seaside atmosphere enchanting. Though she had seen Spain's famed Sun Coast before, when she, Holly and Benny had been in Malaga several weeks ago, she had never followed the Mediterranean this far east before. Here there was a blessed sparsity of the monolithic high-rise hotels, shopping complexes and parking lots that blemished the more popular resort towns along the coast. These peaceful little villages, however, still looked much like they had for centuries and their timelessness was part of their charm. Watching the sun-sparkled sea, Juliet settled herself more comfortably in the passenger seat and sighed contentedly.

The soft sound drew Raul's attention. 'What exactly did that sigh mean?'

Turning to look at him, she gave him a rather shy half smile and shrugged slightly. 'It didn't mean anything really. I was just thinking how nice it is that these villages haven't changed a lot in hundreds of years.'

'Ah, a romantic,' he said softly. 'I suspected you were but I never realised you yearned for the simpler life of the past.'

'I have no desire to return to the past, thank you. But I do think the past is worth preserving. It's sort of living history.'

Raul's dark brows lifted in mock surprise. 'Many people would be astonished to hear you say that. Americans in general have the reputation for putting progress ahead of everything else, even their own heritage.'

'We do as well at preserving our heritage as any other people, I'm sure,' Juliet replied heatedly, in no mood for such a remark though his tone had been undeniably teasing. She glared at him indignantly. 'You Europeans tend to forget that we Americans have only been on the continent for about three hundred and fifty years so of course we don't have a bunch of Dark Age castles to brag about. But we do have entire small Colonial towns preserved exactly as they used to be. So our heritage is important to us and I happen to think we've done a pretty good job of protecting it in our two hundred years of being a nation.'

Raul's expression sobered. His darkening eyes held hers as he reached out to stroke the back of his hand against her cheek. 'I was only teasing you, Juliet. I have no anti-American sentiments, I assure you.'

'I know that and I'm sorry I snapped at you,' she muttered, her defensive anger subsiding as quickly as it had arisen. Knowing she had only overreacted to his comment because of the snide remarks Jemina had made about Americans two days ago, Juliet now felt rather ridiculous. With a sheepish smile and an uncertain fluttering of her hand, she touched his knee with light fingertips. 'I am sorry. I guess I'm just in a prickly mood.'

'Why?' he inquired solemnly, covering her hand with his, pressing her small fingers against his hard muscular thigh. Turning his attention from the road for a brief instant, he gazed at her intently. 'You've been very quiet the past few days. You're not dreading this visit with the Olveras, are you?'

'No, of course not,' she murmured but averted her eyes because she was lying to him. She did dread the upcoming visit. Having never met the Olveras, she had no idea what to expect from them. Would they like her as Raul had said or would they consider her an outsider, as Jemina had so rudely told her all his friends would?

'I really think you'll like Manuel and his wife,' Raul reiterated, almost as if he were reading her mind. 'Pilar is about your age, maybe a couple of years older, so the two of you should have something in common.'

'You think so?' Juliet asked doubtingly, then breathed a wistful sigh as he nodded. 'Well, maybe you're right but I wonder. I mean, she is Spanish and I'm American and...'

'And young women are basically the same everywhere,' Raul interrupted gently, entwining her fingers with his. 'Now, I want you to stop worrying. I get the impression that perhaps you're still upset by what Jemina said to you the other day and you promised me you wouldn't be. So I expect you to keep that promise this weekend by forgetting everything she told you.'

'I'll try,' Juliet murmured but swept a rather anxious gaze over his sunbrowned face. 'But she could have been right in what she said, Raul. Even though she was unbearably rude, that doesn't mean she wasn't speaking the truth.'

'The truth has little to do with what Jemina says,' he retorted, his hardening jawline denoting some impatience. 'She wanted to upset you and obviously she did a good job of it.' Glancing down at Juliet, he gave her a stern no-nonsense look. 'Maybe you should tell me everything she said to you. I only arrived in time to hear the last part of it.'

'Oh, it was just mostly more of the same thing you heard,' Juliet lied weakly, unwilling to tell him about Jemina's sneering remarks concerning red-haired Valaquez heirs. She forced a cheery smile. 'Oh, why don't we just forget this entire discussion. It isn't important.'

'Oh, yes, Juliet, it is,' he contradicted gently, an enigmatic light flaring in his dark green eyes, before he turned his attention back to the road again. 'And we will resume this discussion later, but right now we're almost at the Olveras.'

As he released her to place both hands on the steering wheel as he turned the car onto a narrower secondary road, Juliet removed her own hand from his knee, feeling oddly bereft as she lost that physical contact with him. And that feeling of loss intensified as they suddenly rounded a curve in the road and came in sight of a gracious hacienda-style house with a lushly green sweeping front lawn. Tensing, Juliet clasped her hands tightly together in her lap, knowing she would soon discover whether or not she did have anything at all in common with Pilar Olvera.

She didn't have to wait long to meet her hostess for the weekend. While Raul was parking the BMW on the circular drive before the house, a petite young woman with olive skin, almond eyes and vibrant black hair stepped out onto the flagstone walk leading from the shaded veranda. Despite the vertical stripes of her crisp linen tent-dress, she was unable to conceal the burgeoning evidence of an eight-month pregnancy. She tried to smile at Raul and Juliet but her attention was diverted momentarily by the handsome three year old boy who was apparently in no mood to hold her hand. He tugged valiantly, trying to free himself from her restraint and when his small dark face began to pucker, she smiled indulgently and released him. Bending down slightly, she adjusted the straps of his sunsuit, spoke softly to him, then watched him as he toddled quickly toward the driveway.

By the time the child and the young woman approached the car, Raul had already gotten out and come around to open the door on Juliet's side. He barely had time to release her hand after she stepped onto the pebbled drive before the young woman placed her hands on his shoulders and kissed his cheek.

She took a backward step then and surveyed him affectionately. 'Raul, it is good to see you again,' she said in practically flawless English. 'I've missed you the past several weeks. You usually come to visit us more often than you have recently.' A knowing sparkle danced in her black eyes as she glanced at Juliet. 'But I suspect I know the reason for your long absence. If this is your Juliet, then I don't blame you for ignoring your old friends.'

'Yes, this is my Juliet,' Raul said, smiling at both young women. 'And Juliet, this is Pilar Olvera.'

Unnecessarily stroking back her thick lustrous hair which was confined in a fat bun on her nape, Pilar nodded at Juliet while smiling with genuine friendliness. 'It's such a pleasure to meet you. Since last week, when I heard Raul was engaged, I've been dying with curiosity. I thought Raul was a confirmed bachelor so I knew you must be something special since he had asked you to marry him.'

Glancing at Raul out of the corner of her eye, Juliet smiled. 'Well, I must admit our engagement came as something of a surprise to me too.'

'Really? Ooh, how exciting,' Pilar enthused, clasping her hands together and smiling dreamily. 'It sounds as if he just swept you off your feet.'

'Something like that, yes,' Raul answered wryly, slipping his arm around Juliet's waist and drawing her close to his side. 'I didn't want to give Juliet the chance to get away from me so what else could I do besides sweep her off her feet?'

Gazing up into his dark jade eyes, Juliet could almost imagine he was speaking the truth. Unwilling to give up that self-delusion, she allowed her head to rest against his shoulder and somewhat tentatively slid her own arm around his waist.

Shaking her head, Pilar gave them both a cheeky, suggestive smile. 'You know, I'm surprised the two of you didn't plan to spend this weekend alone together somewhere, instead of coming to visit Manuel and me. And Fredrico, of course,' she added, laughing down at her small son as he gazed up expectantly at Raul. 'He's been waiting all morning for you to arrive and toss him up into the air as you always do. But I must warn you— he's heavier now than he was the last time you did it, so be prepared.'

'I think I can handle you still, can't I, young man?' Raul said, grinning as the boy giggled delightedly as he was swooped up and tossed high in the air.

Watching as the ritual was performed twice more, Juliet realised she had never before seen Raul with a child and the picture they presented was intriguing to say the least. The truly affectionate rapport between him and Fredrico was evident even before the game ended and the boy wrapped his arms around Raul's neck, as if he meant to stay close to him for quite some time. And when Raul brushed a kiss against the child's plump cheek, she drew in a soft bemused breath, trying to imagine how it would be to see him with his own son. Lost in such thoughts, she preceded Raul as they followed Pilar across the flower draped veranda and into the cool recesses of the house.

After Fredrico was persuaded to leave Raul and go play with his tricycle, the three adults sat down in the casual living room, filled with rattan furniture and enlivened by fat poppy red cushions. Before they could begin a conversation, however, they were joined by Manuel Olvera, a dark handsome man in his late thirties who was not quite as tall as Raul and stockily built. As he entered the living room from the sun-dappled patio beyond sliding glass doors, his wife gave him a warm loving smile and patted the cushion beside her on the sofa.

With a welcoming smile for Juliet and Raul, he went to Pilar immediately, brushing a lingering kiss across her lips and patting her rounded abdomen affectionately before sitting down with her and draping his arm across her shoulders.

Juliet watched this display of affection with a stab of envy then berated herself mentally for feeling jealous of Pilar simply because her husband so obviously loved her. Refusing to spend the entire weekend silently bemoaning the fact that Raul didn't love her that way, she managed to smile sincerely as he introduced her to Manuel.

His black Spanish eyes conveyed frank approval as he looked her over from head to toe and he gave his wife an unabashed grin when she playfully prodded his ribs with her elbow. 'Come now, *querida,* don't be upset,' he teased. 'You can't blame me for staring at Juliet. Now that I have seen her, I know why Raul has decided marriage is preferable to the wild swinging life of a bachelor.'

'And you are an authority on the wild swinging life, aren't you?' Pilar retorted, wrinkling her nose at him, then smiling at Juliet. 'Believe it or not but Manuel was a notorious womaniser before he married me. And, even now, he has an eye for beautiful ladies.'

'As long as I only look and never touch, you have nothing to complain about,' her husband countered, patting her abdomen again with a wicked grin. 'Besides, you certainly can't accuse me of not paying enough attention to you. It must be obvious to the whole world that I find you too irresistible, so you shouldn't resent the fact that I think Juliet is very attractive.'

'I resent the fact that she's all curvy and slender while I look like a blimp,' Pilar replied, grimacing comically. 'So if you must stare at her admiringly, do so when I'm not present, if you please.'

'*Madre di Dios,*' Manuel sighed theatrically, raising his eyes heavenward. 'Deliver me from pregnant women.'

'Enough of this nonsense,' his wife proclaimed, nudging him in the ribs again. 'Raul and Juliet might take our bickering seriously and decide they shouldn't get married after all and I wouldn't want to be responsible for them calling off the wedding. Dona Alicia would probably never speak to me again.' With a toss of one hand, she smiled at Juliet. 'Pay no attention to us, please. We're really happily married.'

As Juliet nodded, amusement at their light-hearted banter glimmering in her eyes, Raul took her hand and idly began to play with her fingertips. If the very natural gesture was meant to convince the Olveras that he and Juliet were the typical, much in love, engaged couple, it did the trick.

Giving them the approving smile of a true romantic Pilar snuggled closer to Manuel and laid one hand on his thigh. 'Now, forgive me for being a busybody but I must ask this question, Raul,' she began. 'Why is it that we have never met Juliet before now? Have you just met her yourself? Is this one of those wild tempestuous romances that all women dream about?'

Raul laughed softly, looking down at Juliet. 'I think she could safely call our relationship tempestuous, don't you, *mi pequena.*'

'Even that might be an understatement,' Juliet retorted, attempting humour as a defence against the effect of his softly spoken endearment had had on her senses. With a great amount of effort, she managed to refrain from trembling slightly with each stroking brush of his fingers against the sensitive tips of her own. Yet, as he suddenly lowered his head and lightly kissed her, she couldn't prevent her lips from parting slightly beneath the firm warm pressure of his. When he drew away again and his dark mysterious gaze held hers, she was beyond wondering if he was acting this way only for the Olveras' benefit.

Drawing their attention by an exaggerated cough, Manuel eyed Juliet speculatively. 'McKay, McKay,' he murmured thoughtfully, then snapped his fingers. 'Of course, I thought I recalled your name, Juliet, but...' he frowned. 'Didn't I hear it in connection with Pablo? You're not the same young woman he was engaged to last year?'

'Pablo was never engaged to Juliet, except in his own mind,' Raul answered for her. 'You both know how persistent my younger brother can be when he decides he must have something or someone. He was so absolutely certain he could convince Juliet to marry him that he began to tell everyone she was going to. It didn't quite work out the way he planned as you can see.'

'And how does he feel about the way it did work out?' Pilar asked, a tiny frown knitting her brow. 'If he was so determined to marry you, Juliet, doesn't he resent the fact that you're going to marry his brother instead?'

'He wasn't exactly overjoyed to hear the news,' Juliet admitted, a flicker of concerned regret darkening her delicate features. 'But Pablo really never loved me and I'm sure he realises that now.'

'Besides, Margarita Alvarez is doing all she can to comfort him these days,' Raul added wryly. 'And Pablo seems quite content to let her ease his hurt pride.'

'Ah, Margarita,' Pilar murmured, smiling as she nodded. 'She's a lovely girl.'

'She certainly is. Pablo could have done much worse in choosing someone to comfort him. I must admit I've been watching Margarita blossom into womanhood with great interest,' Manuel said provocatively, then laughed down at his wife as she poked him in the ribs again.

Before they could begin another teasing spat, however, Fredrico careened into the living room from the patio at such a breakneck speed that his red and silver tricycle topped over and he set up a loud indignant howl of protest. As Juliet instinctively followed Pilar who went to comfort him, Raul and Manuel took the opportunity to get the luggage from Raul's car and take it up to the bedrooms.

The remainder of the day passed pleasantly. By the time evening came and Fredrico was settled in his bed for the night, the two couples shared a quiet dinner, then sat out on the patio beneath the stars to talk until past midnight. When Manuel noticed Pilar surreptitiously massaging the small of her back, he exhibited a natural concern for her weariness and suggested they all go to bed.

Up in a spacious, rattan-furnished bedroom a half hour later, Juliet finished a relaxing bath in the sunken marble tub in the adjoining bathroom. Slipping a pale green batiste nightgown over her head, she padded across the plush apricot carpeting to the bed, only to find that the covers had already been turned back, presumably by Pillar's house-keeper, Juanita. Though the day had been long and Juliet hadn't slept during the traditional siesta, she discovered she wasn't really all that sleepy now either. After brushing her thick russet hair briskly before the dressing table mirror, she bypassed the bed and wandered out on the balcony.

A warm salt scented breeze caressed her bare arms and legs and stirred the closed bougainvillaea blossoms on the vines that entwined the wrought iron railings. Hugging her arms against her breasts, she gazed out over the sweeping front lawn at the distant glimmer of the sea beyond. The light of a three-quarter lemon-coloured moon sparkled on the surface of the water and Juliet could almost imagine she heard the waves crashing against the craggy shore. Though it was a beautifully peaceful night, she couldn't really feel at peace. Despite the pleasant day she had spent with Raul and the Olveras, uncertainty still nagged at her persistently. Perhaps it was the very fact that Manuel and Pilar had such a wonderful marriage that made her feel uneasy and still, much to her dismay, somewhat envious. At that moment, she would have given anything, anything at all, to have known that her marriage to Raul might someday be half as good.

Gazing pensively at the dreaming sea, she breathed a sigh that became a soft startled gasp as large hands suddenly slipped around her waist. It was only as she was drawn back against Raul's lean familiar body that she realised that all the upper bedrooms of the house opened onto this long balcony. The stab of fear his unexpected touch had caused abated and she relaxed back against him, enveloped in the warmth that emanated from his lithe body.

'Can't you sleep, Juliet?' he whispered, his breath stirring tendrils of her hair. 'Is something bothering you?'

'N-not really,' she whispered back, unwilling to tell him that at that moment she was only aware of the overwhelming need evoked in her merely by his nearness. 'I—just didn't feel sleepy yet so I came out for a breath of air.'

'Hmm, and you're sure nothing's wrong?' he persisted gently, enfolding her in his strong arms and pulling her even closer to him. 'I hope you're not still fretting about what Jemina said the other day. Surely you see now that my friends are happy to accept you as my fiancée? Manuel and Pilar have, haven't they?'

'They've made me feel very welcome here and I like them both a lot,' Juliet admitted. 'But...' she twisted around slightly and tilted her head back to look up at him, a slightly knowing smile curving her soft lips. 'You really didn't have to ask them to speak English all the time just for my benefit.'

Raul shook his head in denial and heaved a soft exasperated sigh. 'I didn't ask them to speak English. No doubt they are doing it to make you feel more comfortable but, Juliet, it's no hardship for them. Manuel went to school in England for several years and after he married Pilar, they lived in London for nearly three more. So English comes almost as naturally to them as Spanish. But even if it didn't, why should you object if they spoke it only to make you feel at ease? What could possibly be wrong in that?'

'Nothing would be wrong. In fact, it would be very kind of them. But I just don't want anyone making allowances for me because I'm not Spanish. If you were engaged to a Spanish girl...'

'But I'm not. I'm engaged to you and you are an American,' Raul interrupted sternly. 'My friends understand that you don't speak Spanish fluently yet and if they don't mind making allowances for that, why should you mind if they do? I don't understand why you are letting something so unimportant upset you, Juliet.'

'Because I'm an outsider!' she blurted out, her voice catching revealingly.

'Can't you see that, Raul? I don't fit in with your friends. Oh, I'm sure they'll be very nice to me and try to make me feel comfortable but I'm still not one of them.'

'Nor do I want you to be.' Turning her around to face him, Raul cupped her face in both his hands. 'Juliet, friends are important, I can't deny that. But I don't let mine rule my life for me. After we're married, if some of them want to treat you as an outsider simply because you're American, then that's their loss, not yours or mine, and I don't intend to worry about them. And I don't want you to either. You will fit in with my true friends, simply because I choose to marry you.'

'You didn't really choose to though, did you, Raul?' she whispered tremulously. 'If your grandmother hadn't...'

'Be quiet,' he commanded softly, halting her words with a kiss as gentle as a breeze. 'Abuela isn't forcing me to marry you. She couldn't if I didn't want to.'

'You want me physically,' Juliet muttered bleakly. 'But Raul, that isn't...'

'I want you, Juliet, and you want me,' he reiterated huskily, passion blazing in his eyes. He clasped the back of her head in one lean hand, tangling his long fingers in her hair, holding her fast. His mouth descended to play teasingly, evocatively with her lips and between tantalising kisses, he whispered, 'You do want me too, don't you, Juliet?'

As the tip of his tongue touched first one corner of her mouth, then the other, she trembled and whispered back breath-lessly, 'Yes, oh, yes, Raul, I do want you. You know that but...'

'Hush, Juliet, or I'll take you to my room and keep you there all night with me,' he threatened, his voice deep and convincingly uneven as his hands ex-plored the enticing curves of her body, conveying a dangerous urgency. 'You must know that's what I want to do. *Dios,* I need you! And if making love to you is the only way I can stop you from arguing, then...'

He didn't finish his warning in words nor did he need to. As he widened his stance and hauled her firmly against him, she was made overwhelmingly aware of his obvious desire to possess her. Apprehension was suddenly overcome with delight as his hardening lips tugged her mouth open. She pressed against him entwining her arms around his neck as his hands burned her skin through the thin fabric of her her gown. Slipping her fingers beneath the open collar of his shirt, she traced the strong contours of his neck and shoulders, delighting in the feel of his skin, tautly smooth over his collarbone. Then, somehow, his shirt was unbuttoned and her hands were brushing over his hair-roughened chest, exploring his warm strength, her fingertips stroking over the flat hardness of his stomach.

Her tentative yet evocative touch sent a shudder over him. With a soft groan, he tightened his arms around her slenderness, lifting her up against him until the tips of her toes barely brushed the cool tiles. Her cushioned breasts yielded to the muscular firmness of his chest and as he pushed aside the cord straps of her gown, his lips brushed downward from her shoulder to seek the satiny outcurving of heated flesh. As his breath caressed the scented hollow between her breasts, Juliet moaned softly. Her head fell back against his forearm around her shoulders as he pressed burning, searching kisses over her creamy throat and the fragile line of her jaw. Then his mouth covered hers again, possessively hard and seeming to demand complete surrender.

And she was eager to surrender. The aching emptiness within her intensified with the electric touch of his hands and the taking power of his mouth. Yet as her lithe young body became bonelessly acquiescent, moulding with warm fluidity against his, he abruptly dragged her arms from around his neck and put her from him. The glittering passion in his eyes impaled the dreamy softness of her own and his breathing was uneven as he shook his head. 'Not yet, *querida,*' he murmured huskily, stilling her hands as they brushed over his bare chest. 'I want you but we'll be married in less than a week and I think you would really rather wait until then.' Smiling then, he put one arm around her waist, guiding her back into her bedroom. 'Come along. I'll prove to you what self-discipline I have.

I'll tuck you into bed, then go to my own room.'

As he proceeded to pull the covers farther down, then lifted her gently into his arms to lay her on the bed, Juliet couldn't drag her bemused gaze away from him. When he covered her with the sheet, she put her hands over his and pressed them down on her shoulders. 'Raul, I want...'

Leaning down, he silenced her with a slow rousing kiss but as her parted lips clung eagerly to his, he straightened again to give her a lazy smile. 'Temptress,' he whispered, his heavy lidded eyes travelling over the length of her body outlined against the thin sheet. 'You don't make it at all easy for me to show you how disciplined I can be.' When she started to speak again, he shook his head. 'Good night, *querida.*'

Then he was gone and it was several minutes after she had heard his footfalls recede on the balcony tiles that she realised he had once again thwarted her weak argument against marrying him.

Late the next morning, Juliet and Pilar sat on the shaded, flower scented veranda, watching Raul and Manuel play kickball with Fredrico on the lawn. Seeing once again how gentle and affectionate Raul was with the child, Juliet gazed at him longingly, then breathed a soft involuntary sigh.

Turning to stare at her, Pilar sat up straighter. 'Are you not happy, Juliet?' she asked softly. 'Forgive me for mentioning it but I have noticed a sadness in your eyes sometimes. It has worried me.'

After taking a small sip of iced lime juice, Juliet smiled faintly and shook her head. 'I don't want you to think you have anything to worry about. I'm fine, really.'

'But also a little sad?'

'Maybe.'

'But why, Juliet?' Pilar exclaimed softly, gesturing with a slender hand toward Raul. 'You are about to marry a fine man. So why should you feel sad about anything?'

'Maybe if he wasn't such a fine man, I wouldn't be sad,' Juliet replied cryptically, smiling weakly at Pilar's confused expression. 'What I mean is: if Raul wasn't so wonderful, then it wouldn't matter to me that he doesn't love me.'

'You don't think he loves you? I don't understand. If he doesn't love you, then why are you getting married next week?'

On impulse, Juliet told her the truth. When she had finished, she shrugged resignedly. 'So Raul's marrying me simply because his grandmother over-reacted to what she saw in my bedroom that morning. Not a very good reason to get married, is it?'

'It's better than the reason Manuel and I had,' Pilar stated flatly. 'At least you and Raul know there's an intense physical attraction between you. Manuel and I didn't know each other well enough to know that. Our marriage was something of a family arrangement.'

'An arranged marriage?' Juliet exclaimed, her eyes widening in disbelief. 'You must be joking! The two of you seem so happy together! I know you must love each other.'

'We do—now,' Pilar said, smiling reminiscently. 'But at first we were practically strangers and believe me, I was a very nervous bride.'

'Then why did you marry him? I just can't see you consenting to an arranged marriage.'

Pilar's black eyes sparkled merrily. 'Well, if I hadn't liked him just a little, I would have refused, of course. You see, our families had business ties. So when my father asked me simply to meet Manuel and get to know him, I agreed. To make a long story short, I was intrigued with Manuel from the beginning but we had no chance to get acquainted because my great aunt Theresa appointed herself my *duenna* and never left us alone together for a minute. I guess we really got married on pure instinct since Manuel wasn't even allowed to kiss me good night until *after* we were officially betrothed. And one kiss a day from a man doesn't tell you much about him.'

Juliet was still shaking her head disbelievingly. 'I never would have imagined your marriage was arranged.'

'Well, it was,' Pilar declared, touching Juliet's arm supportively. 'So now you know why your marriage to Raul has a better chance of succeeding than mine did.'

'Maybe, but I'm not so sure of that,' Juliet murmured doubtingly. 'I mean, both you and Manuel are Spanish. Maybe you and he can relate to each other in a way Raul and I never can since I'm American.'

'I don't believe that will make any difference,' Pilar argued gently. 'You and Raul seem made for each other to me. So just be patient. Love will come.' As Juliet glanced away, chewing pensively on her lower lip, Pilar gave a sudden knowing smile. 'So, it's as I suspected— you love him already.'

Seeing no point in lying, Juliet nodded. 'Unfortunately, the feeling isn't mutual. Raul isn't in love with me.'

'That doesn't mean he never will be. Be patient, Juliet, and show him you love him,' Pilar advised softly. 'He's fond of you, I can see that. Give him time and I know he'll begin to love you.'

'I'm sure you really believe that,' Juliet murmured, a smile trembling on her lips. 'Now, if only I could make myself believe it too...'

Later that Sunday afternoon, Pilar hugged Juliet briefly as they said good-bye beside Raul's car. 'I am sorry we won't be able to attend the wedding but my doctor doesn't want me travelling far in these last weeks.'

Nodding understandingly, Juliet lifted Fredrico up into her arms to give him a farewell kiss. His warm little body snuggled close to her, wrapping his arms around her neck, reluctant to give up his new friend until at last Manuel persuaded him to release her.

After both she and Raul expressed their thanks for the peaceful weekend, they got into his BMW but before they could say a last good-bye and drive away, Pilar stepped closer to Juliet's open window, grinning as she looked in. 'I have only one bit of marital advice to give you,' she quipped, laying one hand on her burgeoning abdomen. 'Never, ever be eight months pregnant in the summer, Juliet, unless you want to feel the way I do right now—like a hot air balloon.'

'I'll try to remember that,' Juliet answered, laughing and waving back over her shoulder as Raul slowly drove away from the gracious hacienda-style house. He didn't speak until he had turned onto the coastal highway a few minutes later. Then, resting his right arm across the back of Juliet's seat, he brushed his fingertips along her shoulder, giving her a slow lazy smile when she looked at him. 'Pilar's advice reminded me that we've never really discussed having children. So, would you like to have children some day, Juliet?'

Nodding, she swallowed with difficulty, the mere thought of having his child making her breath catch. 'Yes, I think I'd like to have children. W— would you?'

'Of course,' he said, his voice appealingly low. 'I like children.'

She was unable to meet his darkening gaze as he glanced from the road to her again. 'I know you like them but— maybe you're forgetting that we might have a baby with red hair and light skin.'

'So? We also might have a baby with dark hair and dark skin. Will it bother you if our children look like me?'

'No! Of course not but...'

'Then why should it bother me if they look like you? After all, they will be your children too,' he said, smiling endearingly so she could only nod in agreement, unable to argue that irrefutable fact.

CHAPTER 12

Six days later, on the eve of their wedding, Juliet hesitated outside Raul's bedroom door. Coming to see him was an act of desperation, a last resort, one that she wished wholeheartedly she could avoid. Yet, she had little choice. All her efforts to convince Dona Alicia that tomorrow's forced wedding was unnecessary had met with the argument that, even if Juliet was still an innocent, Jemina Ruiz was a notorious gossip. She would tell everyone what she had witnessed and Juliet's reputation would be ruined and Raul's honour besmirched if they didn't marry now. And Juliet found it was pointless to even think of talking to Uncle Will; in his ignorance of the real reason for the wedding, he was ecstatic. Under any other circumstances, Juliet would have been ecstatic too; she loved Raul and she ached to be his wife, but not like this. Feeling he had been forced to marry her for the sake of propriety and the family honour, he would resent her, perhaps even hate her. He would be miserable and she would be devastated. So something had to be done tonight. She had to convince him to refuse to marry her tomorrow; it was the only sensible answer. She was terrified that if he only married her because he felt it was the gentlemanly thing to do, both their lives would be ruined. As if she couldn't see her own life crumbling to dust before her very eyes already...

Drawing a deep tremulous breath, she gathered all her courage and made herself knock lightly on the dark carved door to Raul's room. There was no immediate response, but knowing he was home tonight and must be in there, she knocked again. A few seconds later, the door was pulled open and surprise flickered in Raul's eyes when he found her standing on the threshold, clenching her hands together in front of her.

'Juliet,' he said sleepily, rubbing his hand across his brown hair-roughened chest. 'It's late.'

'I know. I'm sorry but I had to wake you,' she murmured the apology, trying to ignore the fact that he was clad only in navy pyjama pants that hung low on his lean hips. It wasn't that easy to ignore his appearance however, and though she had worn a thick robe to come see him, she involuntarily tugged it more snugly around her. Then her hand fluttered out in an uncertain gesture. 'We have to talk, Raul. Could—could I come in?'

Although he seemed reluctant to let her, he finally nodded and indicated she should precede him inside. Never having been inside the masculine suite before, she glanced curiously around the sitting room, impressed by the warm comfortable atmosphere. Her gaze lingered on the royal blue winged armchair and the round table beside it on which sat a lamp and several books, one of which was open. It was fairly obvious that Raul spent some of his leisure time here and before she could allow herself to wonder what his bedroom was like, she turned to him, chewing her lower lip nervously. He was watching her intently and when he made no suggestion that she should sit down, she took one hesitant step toward him.

'Raul, we have to call this off,' she declared rather imploringly. 'I've been wanting to talk to you for days but you—you've always stopped me. Still, I know you can't be happy about this situation so that's why I came. This is all so crazy. We can't get married simply because your grandmother found us—in bed together and jumped to the wrong conclusion. You have to tell her you simply won't marry me.'

As he lit a cigarette, inhaled deeply, then exhaled the smoke, his eyes never left her and there was a somewhat brooding expression in them. 'The plans are all made, Juliet,' he said, his voice low and melodious. 'We can't call them off now. Your uncle and my grandmother are very excited about the wedding tomorrow and it will take place, exactly on schedule.'

'But you don't want to marry me. I know you don't,' she murmured, uncertain whether she was relieved or disappointed that he hadn't jumped at the chance of escape she had offered. Thoroughly confused by her own ambiguous feelings, she bent her head and sighed. 'And I don't want to get married this way. What chance will we have to be happy? Raul, we have to tell them we can't go through with it.'

'Oh, I think not,' he answered calmly. 'Accept it, Juliet. We are getting married tomorrow.' As if bored by the entire conversation, he walked to her, cupped her elbow in one hand, and guided her toward the door. Then when she suddenly found herself in the hall, he added, 'I suggest you go to bed and try to get some sleep. Tomorrow will be a busy day and you'll need to be well-rested. Good night.'

'But Raul, we...' As he closed the door firmly on her attempted protest, she could hardly believe it. He was taking this so calmly, without even trying to resist a loveless marriage that would cost him his freedom. Was he that much an Old World Spaniard? Were the old traditions so inbred in him that a strong sense of propriety overshadowed his own personal desires?

Feeling quite numb by now and cold, Juliet shivered as she made her way back to her own room. Too tired to really think coherently, she took Raul's advice and went to bed but sleep was a long time coming.

The wedding was held in a tiny white chapel in the small village near the *casa* and the actual ceremony was so brief that she felt she hardly had time to catch her breath before it was over and she and Raul were married. Since only relatives and close friends had been invited, she found it fairly simple to smile and get by with letting the entire event pass over her as if it were a dream. The wedding supper that followed at the *grande sala* at the *casa* was a different matter altogether.

She felt like such a fraud. There seemed to be hoards of people to be received, all of whom naturally assumed she and Raul were the typical bride and groom and their compliments and congratulations couldn't be ignored. The first few expressed felicitations made her feel like a terrible fake but, beside her in the receiving line in his black Oxford coat, matching trousers and white waistcoat over a white shirt, Raul seemed so at ease that she began to relax somewhat herself. At least she looked like the typical bride, she tried to remind herself. The slight blush in her cheeks was attractively highlighted by the long yet simply elegant ivory silk gown she wore and by the heirloom lace *mantilla* that framed her small face, which had been worn by Valaquez brides for several succeeding generations.

At last the repast began and after the traditional toasts to the bride and groom, Juliet tried to show some interest in the various courses of the delicious supper but everything seemed to have the taste and texture of sawdust in her dry mouth. Everyone else was having such a joyous time but, while she accepted the marriage as an accomplished fact, now she had come to the breathtaking realisation that this was her wedding night. A very different sort of nervousness mushroomed and she found herself often staring at Raul, worrying about how gentle a lover he would be, considering the fact that he believed her to be sexually experienced. Such thoughts played havoc with her emotions so she was eternally grateful for Holly and Benny's arrival after the supper was over because seeing them temporarily took her mind off the hours to come.

They arrived late because Holly had only been released from the hospital that afternoon. With them, they brought the baby, all dolled up in a tiny pink dress and matching booties, looking much less like a gnome than she did when she cried. Having never held her, Juliet couldn't resist taking her in her arms, despite Holly's warning that her wedding gown might get drooled on.

Supporting the tiny dark-haired head in the crook of her arm, Juliet rocked the baby gently, then smiled up at Holly. 'She really is lovely. Have you decided what to name her yet? You can't go on calling her ''the baby'' forever.'

'Oh, she has a name,' Benny answered with a secretive smile. 'We toyed around with the idea of naming her after my mother or Holly's but then we decided she should be named after you. So, she's Juliet.'

'Really?' Juliet exclaimed softly, smiling with pleasure. 'I'm very honoured.'

'It was a nice thing to do,' Raul agreed, stepping up beside Juliet. Draping his arm possessively across her shoulders, he smiled down at her, then glanced at the baby she held. In an incredibly tender gesture, he touched one finger against the child's plump pink cheek. Then he smiled up at Benny and Holly. 'Juliet is very appropriate. I'm sure she'll grow up to be as lovely as my beautiful bride.'

Juliet tried to fight the happiness his words elicited. He was just being nice. 'Wouldn't you two like some wedding cake?' she offered, effectively diverting attention from herself. 'And some champagne?'

'Wish we could stay a while but we can't,' Benny replied regretfully. 'It's about time to feed the baby and Holly's tired. She needs a good night's sleep before we catch that flight at eight in the morning.'

'Flight? What flight?' Juliet exclaimed

softly. 'Where are you going?'

'Back to the States,' Holly explained, then smiled gratefully at Raul. 'And we have you to thank for it all, Senor Valaquez. It was so kind of you to tell your friend about Benny. I know he's going to love teaching at the music conservatory.'

'What conservatory? What friend? What's going on?' Juliet questioned bewilderedly. 'Benny, you didn't tell me you had any prospects for a job in the States.'

'And I didn't have until the day before yesterday. Then, a Dominic Harrison called me from upstate New York. He had an opening for a teacher with knowledge of folk music and was even willing to send us plane fare to go there and discuss a contract. It's a terrific opportunity but of course, even though we haven't talked to you for the past two days, we thought you knew all about it. After all, your husband brought it all about by recommending me to his friend, Mr Harrison.' He held his hand out to Raul. 'We do appreciate your doing that, Senor Valaquez.'

'Raul, please,' he said graciously, then smiled down at Juliet rather sheepishly. 'I meant to tell you but with all the wedding preparations going on, I suppose it just slipped my mind.'

Juliet nodded automatically, as if she accepted his explanation but actually, the entire situation boggled her mind. Raul was completely beyond her understanding. He had never liked Benny, yet he had done something this nice for him. Why?

There was no chance to search for an answer to that question because Benny and Holly repeated that they really had to be going. Raul left them to say their farewells privately and after Benny hugged Juliet briefly, he took the baby from his wife.

As Holly kissed Juliet's cheek, she whispered tearfully. 'We're really going to miss you. But now that you're a wealthy Valaquez, you can fly to New York any time and visit us. And be sure to bring Raul with you. He's so nice. I can't imagine why you've ever felt intimidated by him.'

'Can't you?' Juliet retorted with a

nervous little laugh. 'Well, believe me, he can be intimidating. In fact, I'm shaking in my ivory satin slippers at this very moment.'

'Ah, yes, the wedding night jitters,' Holly said wryly as she retrieved the baby from Benny's arms. 'But I'm afraid even good friends can't help you with that, so we may as well leave. Besides, I suspect you'll discover you were jittery for no good reason at all.'

Praying silently that Holly was right, Juliet waved good-bye to her and Benny after they had promised to write as soon as they reached New York. Raul rejoined her as they began bidding good-night to the other guests and soon everyone was gone except Uncle Will and Dona Alicia. After kissing her uncle and watching him being wheeled away toward the wing of the house by his nurse, Juliet smiled at Dona Alicia, who was planning to spend the night with a friend.

'Welcome to our family, *nina,*' Raul's grandmother murmured as she embraced the bride gently. Then a small frown marred her brow. 'You are too tense. I recommend a glass or two of champagne before you go upstairs.' Having issued that advice and received a blush in answer, she went to kiss Raul good-bye and stood talking quietly to him for several minutes.

Then she was gone. Everyone was gone. The servants had disappeared and finding herself alone with Raul, Juliet swallowed convulsively. Her heart skipped several beats as he came to her, reaching out to brush pleasantly rough-textured fingertips across her cheek.

'You're tired,' he said softly, his gaze warm as it drifted lazily over her. 'Why don't you go upstairs and I'll be along in a moment or so.'

She nodded and went. A minute later, she walked nervously into Raul's vast bedroom. Rosita was there to undo all the tiny silk-covered buttons that marched down the back of her wedding dress and for once she had nothing to say though she did smile knowingly as she left Juliet alone to slip into a white satin nightgown and matching peignoir.

In the adjoining bathroom, Juliet brushed her hair more thoroughly than was necessary, then examined her re-

reflection critically. Did she look as nervous as she felt? She couldn't tell and since thinking about it made her more nervous still, she left the bathroom.

Raul was waiting in the bedroom, removing the gold cufflinks from his shirt, but he looked up at her immediately as she walked from the bathroom. His eyes narrowed.

'You could still get out of this, you know,' she blurted out foolishly. 'We can have the marriage annulled.'

Dropping the cufflinks carelessly onto the dresser-top, he shook his head. 'An annulment won't be possible after tonight, Juliet,' he answered quietly but firmly, then gave a slight smile. 'Don't look so surprised. You knew this marriage would be a real one in every way.' After removing his white bow tie, he inclined his head toward the bedside table. 'As you see, I had champagne brought up. Would you care for a glass?'

She nodded jerkily. After what he had just said, she felt like downing the entire bottle in an attempt to ease her tension. And when he beckoned her to him with an evocative smile, she felt rooted to the spot where she stood. Unable to maintain that disturbing eye contact with him, she glanced up at the heavy wooden beams that crisscrossed the ceiling, then down at the floor and finally her gaze involuntarily drifted to the wide high bed with its heavy carved head- and footboards and its wine-coloured coverlet and ivory satin top sheet already pulled back invitingly, probably by Rosita. Juliet swallowed repeatedly and since she couldn't and didn't move toward Raul when he beckoned, he came to her, taking her hand to lead her to the bedside table.

A moment later, as he handed her a glass of the effervescent wine, her fingers gripped the fragile stem tightly, nearly snapping it in two when he touched the rim of his glass against hers but, oddly enough, made no toast. She hastily took a sip, then rubbed the tip of her nose that the bubbles had tickled and tried to ignore an indulgent smile that set her pulses pounding.

'It was very nice of you to tell your friend in New York about Benny,' she spoke up suddenly, unable to look at

Raul. 'I mean, I was sort of surprised to hear you'd done that for him. You've never liked Benny so why did you want to help him?'

'What else could I do?' Raul murmured mysteriously, taking her glass and putting it with his on the table. Catching her wrist, he sat down on the brown, velvet-covered easy chair facing the bed and with slow deliberation drew her down onto his lap. Hard warm hands spanned her trim waist, his fingers tracing small circles over the smooth satin of her gown. Half turning her so that she had to look at him, he lifted one corner of his mouth in a rather sheepish smile. 'I had to get rid of Benny somehow, didn't I? Helping him find a job in the States seemed the best way to ease him out of your life so I had to do it. And you know why, Juliet. You know I'm jealous as hell of him.'

'Jealous?' she whispered, finding it nearly impossible to breathe. 'You're jealous of Benny? But why?'

'You know exactly why,' he whispered back. His hands came up to cup her warm full-cushioned breasts, his thumbs stroking over the rounded peaks until they surged taut against satin. 'I couldn't stand him being so close to you. You're too fond of him and I wanted him out of the way. Now he is and we're alone and...' he lowered his head to press his lips into the hollow beneath one ear. *'Juliet,'* he groaned softly. *'Te quiero.'*

Though she trembled as he gently nibbled the small lobe of her ear, she couldn't respond uninhibitedly. Pulling back slightly, she shook her head. 'I—I know you want me, Raul but I need more. I need...'

'Foolish *nina,'* he chided gently, scattering burning kisses across her cheek toward her mouth. 'I see I'll have to give you those Spanish lessons. *Te quiero* not only means I want you. It also means I love you and I do. God, how I love you!'

'Raul?' was all she was allowed to murmur incredulously before his mouth brushed over hers, then parted her soft lips hungrily, taking total possession. As he gathered her closer, cradling her against the unyielding broadness of his chest, Juliet's fingers fluttered up to stroke his hard cheek and she felt his jaw

tighten as he reluctantly released her mouth. Piercing jade green eyes probed her bemused gaze as he commanded huskily, 'Say it, Juliet. I need to hear you say it, please.'

'Oh, Raul, I love you too, so much,' she obeyed tremulously, then was lost in the triumph that flared in the dark depths of his eyes. Hardly able to believe any of this was really happening, she searched his dark face for some sign of duplicity and when she found none, she pressed against him. 'I didn't think you could ever love me. How...When?'

He laughed softly as his fingers gently explored her face. 'I think maybe I've loved you since last summer but wouldn't admit it to myself. You're really too young for me, *mi amada,* but when I touch you, I can't seem to remember that. And when you mentioned going back to school in the States, I knew I couldn't let you leave. I took you to meet Manuel and Pilar so you'd see that even an arranged marriage can be happy. And we'll be happy, Juliet. You'd better believe that because I'll never let you go now. Where you're concerned, I'm irrationally possessive.'

Tears of sheer joy shimmered in her eyes. 'Oh, Raul, why didn't you put me out of my misery and tell me all this last night?'

'Because you never would have left my room if I'd told you then,' he murmured wickedly. 'I didn't dare let myself tell you or touch you. If I had, I would have kept you with me all night.'

Bending her head slightly, she glanced up rather shyly at him through the thick fringe of her lashes. 'Would it have been so bad if I had stayed with you?'

'It would have been fantastic,' he whispered, then added teasingly, 'but very improper.'

'And you believe in always doing what's proper?' she had to challenge. 'Isn't that why you married me?'

'Don't kid yourself, *pequena,*' he retorted wryly. 'Propriety had nothing to do with it. I wanted to marry you or I would have gotten out of your bed that day at Will's when you warned me Rosita was coming. But I wanted her to find us. Then I knew I could probably make you marry me.'

'As if you had to make me. All you needed to do was ask,' she whispered, undoing the buttons of his pleated-front shirt. Her hands slipped inside gliding tentatively over his firmly contoured, muscular chest and as he crushed her to him and found her mouth with hard seeking lips, she shivered with delight in her ability to arouse him. As he trailed kisses along the slender column of her neck, she added breathlessly, 'I was in love with you last year too. If only *you*, instead of Pablo, had asked me to marry you then...'

'All these wasted months,' he said unevenly, tracing the outline of her softly shaped mouth. 'I think it's time we began making up for what we've missed. Don't you, Juliet?'

'Oh, yes, it's past time,' she breathed. And touching the fascinating indentations carved in his lean cheeks, she gasped softly as he caught one fingertip gently between his teeth. His narrowed gaze captured and held hers even as she lifted her face to receive a tenderly brushing kiss, then searing passion blazed between them. His fingers slipped through her hair; his hand cupping her cheek held her fast as the kiss deepened in awesome swift intensity that made her cling to him. His lips were irresistibly warm and hard; his breath filled her throat as his tongue tasted the sweetness within her mouth. He stroked her back, strong long fingers feathering along her spine down to the tantalising arch between slim waist and the irresistible outward curving of firmly rounded hips. His hand gently squeezed. Then, with an exclamation muffled in the scented thickness of her hair, he pushed the satin peignoir from her shoulders, then lowered the narrow corded straps. His lips traced the path of his caressing fingers down over the curve of one breast to linger with moist pulling warmth on the throbbing tumescent peak.

A hot longing ache quickened deep within Juliet until she was alive with sensation and the feel of smooth warm skin, roughened only by fine dark hair, beneath her fingers urged her to tentatively explore his body too. Her trembling hand slipped around to brush down his lean hard sides, then moved around to his back. And almost of their own volition, her fingertips slid beneath the waistband of his trousers.

He groaned softly. Firm lips, no longer capable of gentleness, plundered the parted softness of hers. Yet the hand that alternately played over first one swollen breast, then the other, conveyed incredible tenderness. A shuddering sigh escaped her. Her head fell back against the muscular arm that supported her shoulders and as Raul nibbled the silken skin of her creamy neck, he removed both peignoir and gown completely. The cold air of the room bathed her bare skin and she shook violently, though not from cold, as Raul lifted his head to gaze down at the slight, curvaceous body he would soon possess completely. His eyes devoured her, sweeping hungrily over skin so smooth it shimmered opalescently like fine satin in the soft glow of lamplight. His hand trailed over the rounded swell of breasts to the incurve of waist, then spread possessively across her abdomen and despite her sharply drawn breath, his fingers traced downward to close around one upper thigh, the heel of his hand brushing lightly against an exquisite inviting warmth.

'Beautiful,' he whispered hoarsely, his gaze seeking her face, the undeniable intent in his eyes impaling the softly shy luminosity of hers. 'Juliet, *amada*, I can't wait any longer.'

With breathtaking ease, he stood with her in his arms, strode the few feet to the wide bed, and put her down gently on the cool satin sheet. As a very natural fear of the unknown was reborn in her, she pulled the covers up and held them tightly beneath her chin. Recalling the glimpses of nearly uncontrollable passion she had seen in him other times, she felt her heart begin to thud so violently she was sure he must hear it. But if he did, it didn't deter him and as he undressed quickly, she was unable to look away from him. His own skin gleamed like bronze in the soft light and despite the slight apprehension she felt, she longed to touch him.

Yet, an agonising shyness swept over her as he started to pull back the sheet that covered her. 'The lamp,' she whispered tremulously. 'Y-you left it on.'

He simply smiled. Reaching down, he gently pried open the small fingers that gripped the sheet, drew it back, and came down onto the bed beside her. Turning onto his side, he drew her to him, close against his naked strength and as she compulsively burrowed her hot face into the hollow of his shoulder and her lips grazed his skin, his hands on her hips arched her against him. The evidence of his intolerable desire for her surged rigidly against the sensitised skin of her abdomen, both fascinating her and frightening her. She made a soft sound that was almost a whimper.

'Please don't hurt me,' she said almost inaudibly against his throat. 'I...You're wrong about Benny and me. We never— I've never...'

'God, don't you think I know that by now?' he muttered roughly, holding her slightly away from him to gaze lovingly into her eyes. 'Juliet, I was stupid for a while but I'm not completely insensitive. I realised what an innocent you are that day in your room at Will's house.' He shook his head admonishingly. 'I'll never deliberately hurt you; you must know that. I love you. Let me show you how much.'

'I want you to,' she confessed, a smile trembling on her lips. 'I'm sorry I'm so silly.'

'Inocente nina,' he whispered huskily. Pressing the side of his thumb against her chin, he tugged her mouth open slightly and lowered his dark head. His tongue probed the tender veined flesh of her inner lower lip, then his mouth covered hers, insistently but with a gentleness that stilled all her remaining fears. Bestowing intimate caresses on her bare body, he swept her up in a world of sensual delight that she had never known existed and she became pliant and utterly yielding as the masculine heaviness of his long body impelled her down against the softness of the mattress.

'You're exquisite,' he said softly, holding her bemused gaze as his hard knee parted her legs. 'Don't go all tense on me,' he instructed coaxingly. 'Try to stay relaxed.' And as his hands slid beneath her hips to arch her against him, his mouth covered hers, capturing her first soft surprised gasp as their bodies merged. He took her slowly, tenderly, until at last when she was his completely, he was still, raising his head to smile down at her. 'Finally, you're really mine; you belong to me.'

'I always did,' she uttered weakly, her entire being throbbing with quickening desire at his filling invasion of her innocence. Her parted lips sought his eagerly as he wound her hair around one hand. She abandoned herself to the ever-increasing pleasure he created inside her with each slow rousing stroke of his hard body.

He was infinitely patient, holding tight rein on his own desires in his quest to heighten hers to feverish intensity. He conquered all her inhibitions and swept her along on a tide of delight so devastating that she cried out softly as piercing ecstasy rippled in hot waves inside her. 'Raul, oh, I love you,' she gasped, her fingers pressing into the muscular contours of his broad back as she strained against him. The rippling waves receded, weakening and warming her with a fulfillment that far surpassed any of the virginal expectations she had ever had about lovemaking. The emotional rapture of finally being his equaled the keen physical satisfaction he had given her. She pressed her lips against his brown neck, inhaling the fresh lime scent of him as he sought his own satisfaction with a compelling urgency that made her arch against him and find even more joy in the giving.

Much later, Juliet smiled up at Raul with drowsy, contented eyes as he sat down on the edge of the bed beside her. Her hand stroked over the terry fabric of the sleeve of his navy robe, then she sat up against the pillow, the rumpled sheet draped across her bare breasts. As Raul took a sip of champagne from the glass they were sharing, his eyes glimmered teasingly at her over the rim. 'Just as I suspected,' he murmured lovingly. 'There's a passion in you that matches that fiery hair and those beautiful tigress eyes.'

'A passion for you,' she whispered, playing with the lean brown fingers spread possessively across her flat abdomen. 'Only for you, Raul.'

Nodding, he leaned down to press a

lingering kiss against soft slightly parted lips then sat up straight again to smile at her. 'You have an ally. Did you know? Tonight, Abuela very discreetly reminded me that you were a very sensitive inexperienced girl and that I should take great care not to frighten you tonight.' His gaze narrowed, roaming over her intently. 'I didn't frighten you, did I, Juliet? Being a Valaquez bride isn't quite as bad as you thought it would be, is it?'

'It's fantastic,' she confessed, blushing only slightly when he laughed. 'Of course I don't think I would have enjoyed it at all if I had become Pablo's bride, which is what I thought you wanted me to be last year. If I'd known you felt anything for me, I never would have left with Benny.'

'Benny,' Raul muttered, shaking his head and smiling rather sheepishly. 'If he knew how I longed to murder him when I thought the two of you...Well, suffice it to say I can be a very jealous man. As far as I'm concerned, Pablo had better not even talk to you ever again if I'm not with you.'

'You don't really mean that?' Juliet

exclaimed softly. 'Do you?'

'No, not really,' Raul conceded. 'But maybe I can say that because Pablo only had eyes for Margarita at the wedding supper this evening. Hopefully, he realises you belong to me now and that I'll be a very possessive husband.'

'Good. I like your possessiveness,' she answered huskily, leaning forward to drape her slender arms around his shoulders. 'Just don't lose interest in me. That I couldn't stand.'

'You have nothing to worry about.' As the sheet that had covered her fell down around her waist, baring her breasts, his eyes darkened. He put the champagne glass on the bedside table and, whispering her name, reached out to trace small circles around the tender roseate peaks. As she lifted her face, inviting his kiss, he gathered her to him and lowered her to the bed again. *'Te quiero,* Juliet,' he said softly, teasing her lips.

'And I love you, Raul; I always will,' she whispered back. And she surrendered with a contented murmur of pleasure as he proceeded to demonstrate again exactly what being a Valaquez bride meant.